PRAISE FOR *ACCOMPLICE TO ME*

Accomplice to Memory is a stunning achievement, an exquisitely rendered map to the mysterious territory of history, memory, and the imagination. In her quest to know her self and her family, Q.M. Zhang re-draws the boundaries of memoir, and the result is a moving and genre-bending story that is as universal as it is deeply personal.

— Ruth Ozeki
   author of *A Tale for the Time Being*

In comic book parlance, the blank space between illustrated panels is called "the gutter." It's in the gutter where the real story comes to light, where time past and time future meet, and where readers turn fragmented images into coherent narratives. In *Accomplice to Memory*, Q.M. Zhang constructs her own "gutter" out of an assemblage of aesthetic forms—moving between photography and memoir, history and poetry, and essay and fiction—to artfully excavate the truths behind Zhang's father's escape from China and his subsequent life in the US. History is filled with the voiceless and nameless, those who have disappeared into obscurity. *Accomplice to Memory* works to revive the lost, to memorialize the author's father and the many thousands who fled the wars that roiled China during the 20th Century.

— Paisley Rekdal
   author of *Intimate: An American Family Photo Album*

Q.M. Zhang has written one of the great fathers of recent literature, a father too large and restless for a single room. Thus, we have a whole house of him, built of memoir, fiction, documentary, and image. I can think of no other written father so capacious, so indelibly himself. This is dazzling, compassionate work, a book I'll return to again and again.

— Paul Lisicky
   author of *The Narrow Door: A Memoir of Friendship*

ACCOMPLICE
to MEMORY

ACCOMPLICE to MEMORY

Q.M. ZHANG

KAYA PRESS
LOS ANGELES

Accomplice to Memory
Published by Kaya Press (Muae Publishing, Inc.)
www.kaya.com

Cover and book design by: spoon+fork
Cover Photo by Robert Capa (full credit listed in Image Credits)

Manufactured in the Republic of Korea

Distributed by D.A.P./Distributed Art Publishers
155 Avenue of the Americas, 2nd Floor
New York, NY 10013

800.338.BOOK
www.artbook.com

ISBN 9781885030528
Library of Congress Control Number: 2016957089

This publication is made possible by support from the USC Dana and David Dornsife College of Arts, Letters, and Sciences; the USC Department of American Studies and Ethnicity; and the USC Asian American Studies Program. Special thanks to the Choi Chang Soo Foundation for their support of this work. Additional funding was provided by the generous contributions of: Amna Akbar, Jade Chang, Lisa Chen & Andy Hsiao, Floyd & Sheri Cheung, Prince Kahmolvat Gomolvilas, Jean Ho, Huy Hong, Helen Heran Kim, Juliana S. Koo, Pritsana Kootint-Hadiatmodjo, Ed Lin, Viet Nguyen, Chez Bryan Ong, Whakyung & Hong Yung Lee, Amarnath Ravva, Duncan Williams, Mikoto Yoshida, Anita Wu & James Spicer, and others. Kaya Press is also supported, in part, by: the National Endowment for the Arts; the Los Angeles County Board of Supervisors through the Los Angeles County Arts Commission; the Community of Literary Magazines and Presses; and the City of Los Angeles Department of Cultural Affairs.

For ZLM,
Real and Imagined

You in your insistence on ferreting out facts are like the man
who dropped his sword in the water and thought to find it again
by making a mark on the side of his boat.

— Cao Xueqin, *The Story of the Stone*

These are only hints and guesses,
Hints followed by guesses; and the rest
Is prayer, observance, discipline, thought and action.

— T.S. Eliot, *Four Quartets*

TABLE OF CONTENTS

NOTE ON CHINESE LANGUAGE

The question of how to transliterate Chinese sounds and characters is not an arbitrary or neutral one. Historically, this question has turned on how to represent the Chinese language for a Western audience—aptly referred to as romanization. Since the Jesuit incursions into China in the 16th century, Western powers have invented competing systems of romanization for their own economic and political purposes. The Wade-Giles system, named after two 19th century British sinologists, lasted for nearly a hundred years of unequal trade, treaties, and alliances between China and the West. Many of the names of Chinese places and persons that are familiar in the West derive from this earlier system. In 1958, the government of the People's Republic of China launched a new system, pinyin, for the purpose of promoting literacy among the masses. Today, even as pinyin has achieved global currency, these pre- and post-revolutionary names still coexist uneasily—Peking vs. Beijing, Chungking vs. Chongqing, Sun Yat-sen vs. Sun Zhongshan, Chiang Kai-shek vs. Jiang Jieshi—each carrying the faint traces of history and power that coined them.

As I moved across time and place in the writing of this book, I too have made choices about how to represent the Chinese language. Having studied Chinese in China during the '80s, I was schooled in the revolutionary pinyin system. Thus I have chosen to use pinyin in the sections of the book where daughter and father converse in the present about the past. Although my father and I spoke in English, he often used Chinese to refer to places, people, books, and food with which we were both familiar—our shared language. I use pinyin to represent this conversation, knowing that it was never my father's Chinese, since he learned to translate himself for an American audience vis-à-vis earlier forms of romanization. Indeed, when conversing with his fellow Americans, my father took pleasure in using Westernized place names such as Nanking and Canton, which I have never felt comfortable using. I have chosen, however, to use these and other pre-revolutionary names and spellings in the italicized sections of the book, since most of these stories take place in the 1930s and '40s when this nomenclature was popular. I hope that this simultaneous use of pre- and post- revolutionary systems of romanization will evoke for the reader a feeling for the different time periods and points of view of the stories being told.

To assist readers, I have created a list of corresponding spellings for various proper nouns and place names used throughout the book (all other Chinese terms that appear in the text—e.g., the game of "majiang," garments such as "qipao," and common sayings such as "weiji"—will use standard pinyin spellings):

Pinyin Spellings	Pre-Revolutionary Spellings
Chongqing	Chungking
Dai Li/General Dai	Tai Li/General Tai
Guangzhou	Canton
Guomindang	Kuomintang/KMT
Hankou	Hankow
Nanjing	Nanking
Sichuan	Szechuan
Suzhou	Suchou

Please note that the pre-revolutionary spellings I have chosen here and throughout the book are a mix of Wade-Giles and other popular spellings of the time—French and British as well as American. Readers familiar with the Wade-Giles system will note that I have dropped the apostrophes that are used to distinguish between aspirated and non-aspirated sounds, as was common practice. Similarly, tone marks have not been included for pinyin spellings.

As with all systems, there are exceptions:

1. Pinyin is used in the italicized sections of the chapter "What Happened on the Train," since the story is told from the point of view of the Baby, who was born and grew up in revolutionary China.

2. "Hong Kong" is used consistently throughout the book as the romanization of the Cantonese pronunciation of the city.

Finally, where Chinese characters are used, I have chosen the simplified version in which I was schooled and which, like pinyin, was introduced after the founding of the PRC.

PROLOGUE: BORNE OUT OF CHINA

When Wang Kun was lifted out of the masses and onto the train that spring day in Shanghai in 1950, carried aloft by a surge in the throngs of people desperate like himself to catch the last train out of China, he had a moment's panic that he'd left something behind. He was always leaving something behind, usually nothing more than a well-worn hat or a favorite fountain pen, but such oversights tormented him. He prided himself on being a man who looked ahead, who sensed the train coming down the track long before its whistle could be heard and was poised to jump aboard. He hated nothing more than having to dwell on the past. Yet his momentary lapses in attentiveness were always forcing him to backtrack: Where had he come from? How did he get here? What did he leave behind?

Now he searched behind himself for a clue to his unease. Outside the train, he could see down the entire platform: a swath of bodies heaving and surging and threatening to pull him in. There was no going back now. He gripped his small leather suitcase and made a mental list of its contents: one suit made in the capital just weeks before its fall to the Communists, a Chinese-English dictionary, a dog-eared copy of The Four Quartets, *his university diploma, and an address* book. This was all he had allowed himself to carry.

He had carefully planned for his departure. He'd given away all his books (with the exception of the unforsakeable Eliot) to his classmates in the foreign language department at the university. He'd burned every scrap of paper that might be linked to his public relations job at the U.S. embassy running a film library for the Americans. For the last two years, he and his crew had driven a jeep, loaded high with projector and films, deep into the Chinese countryside, where the not-yet-proletariat peasants waited eagerly to taste this foreign fruit. He had projected the films onto whitewashed walls in village centers as people squatted, mesmerized by the flickering 8-mm reels of American squadrons dropping their loads and cheering when the bombs found their Japanese targets.

He'd moved in American circles, getting to know many of the old China hands at the embassy, learning to speak their language, drink their wine, laugh at their jokes. He'd watched them pack up as the Communists marched south, promising that they would help him if he could only get to Hong Kong. During the last frenzied days of the Republic, he'd used his consular connections to get a copy of his college transcript and a passport, which he neatly quartered and mailed in four separate envelopes to a friend in Hong Kong. His last act before leaving had been to present to his mother the gold he'd bought with the money he had saved working for the Americans.

Chinese gold is pure and heavy, Wang Kun mused as the train pulled out of the station, a rich yellow gold that hangs heavily around the neck and pulls at the earlobe. He remembered the old woman at the gold shop laughing at his excessive purchases—"You'll surely drown if you fall into the water *wearing all that gold!"*

Of course that was why he felt so light now—no books, no passport, no gold.

As the train began to pick up speed, Wang Kun relaxed into its momentum, letting it pull him backward and then forward. He felt pleasantly weightless standing there on the moving train, pressed up against other hopeful, swaying bodies being slowly borne out of China.

This is the story my father tells me, when I finally think to ask, about how he left China. Of course this is not how my father tells it. At 86, he can hardly recall what he carried in his luggage or in his mind on that day when he left China for good, the border sealing up behind him. When I press for details, he waves his hands at me impatiently. For him, it's the destination that matters.

So I have to embellish the story for myself. The quartered passport is his, but the tailored suit, the dog-eared Eliot, the heavy, yellow gold—these details are all mine. Even his name is mine. Embellishments rather than fictions, fashioned from what hangs in his closet, what lies on his shelf, what sits uneasily on his chest. I need to dress up the man in order to see him more clearly.

And because he mentions the means of his departure with such indifference, I become fixated on the train.

"How did you get from Shanghai to Hong Kong?"

"I go to Shanghai, I take the train."

"You just got on the train?"

"Yes, just get on the train."

"You didn't have to hide?"

"The Communists, first thing they do is link the railroads, because they chase after all these Guomindang."

"So you just got on the train in Shanghai and rode all the way to Hong Kong?"

"Just get on the train, I don't think you even need tickets. All kinds of people, moving..."

"It was that easy?"

"It's not that difficult."

"You didn't have to... escape?"

"I just walk over the border, there's no checks, the Hong Kong police don't care. But they close it after a few months, that's it. There's a window there, just a little window there..."

Just a little window there.

That little window lodges in my mind and I strain to peer through it.

Could one so easily leave behind a country, a family, a childhood?

Knowing my father's penchant for planning ahead and his tendency to obsess over misplaced car keys and other elusive household items (the sugar bowl, his slippers, the television remote), I cannot imagine him taking leave so lightly. My father is not a man who takes anything lightly. Selling his house nearly killed him. I think: If there was a lightness to his leaving, it must have been a strange lightness, at once pleasurable and disquieting, infused with as much regret as relief. As if he had left something of great weight behind him.

The lightness of loss.

The backward glance and the forward pull at the same time.

This is what I think I see as I peer through that little window.

I come on the weekends with my notebook and recorder to the two-bedroom condo in Western Massachusetts where my parents have recently moved to be near me. When they sold their raised ranch in upstate New York, my mother walked away without a backwards glance while my father went into mourning. He pines for the loss of his beloved home, which he had built brand-new and lived in for twenty-five years, in the town that made him into an American and made me feel less of one. When I left for college, I left for good, but my father was content to remain there, a big yellow fish in a little pond of red, white, and blue. Now this once gregarious man rarely leaves the house and refuses all company except for mine.

He's shaved and dressed and waiting for me when I arrive: long sleeves, wool sweater, corduroy pants, no matter the season. I tell him I've seen crocuses, try to lure him outside. He sits in his recliner in the living room, surrounded by the spoils of his many returns to China: wool carpets, cloisonné vases, ink paintings and calligraphies, a black lacquer dining-room table with matching chairs and cabinet, an enormous redwood laughing Buddha, ceramic statues of dancing ladies and tricolored horses and wizened old men with oblong heads. All these ornate furnishings make the tiny condo feel crowded and unworthy, yet my father still manages to look the part of the emperor—that abominable stereotype he's so happy to perform in the company of white Americans. I refuse to play his games, but as my father grows older, I find it harder to resist him.

He looks pretty good for his age, still boyishly handsome when he smiles and formidable when he doesn't. He still commands attention and respect when he walks into a room, even leaning on a cane. Even through cataracts and myopia, his eyes look sharp, and his sight is set on some distant prospect that only he can see.

"You must always have a goal," he tells me now as he has told me at regular intervals throughout my life.

"I brought you tang yuan," I reply.

My father never cared much for cake and cookies, but he craves Chinese desserts. I stop at the Asian grocery weekly to buy him some sweet treats: red bean buns or eight treasure porridge. Today I have brought his favorite and mine: sticky rice balls filled with black sesame paste. I tell him I will make him tang yuan and his favorite tea, Lipton decaffeinated, to warm him up. He stands up and says he has to go to the bathroom. I can see that he is unsteady, but am uncertain whether to help him. He turns and shuffles out of the room without his cane. Neither of us is comfortable yet with these impending role reversals.

We sit together at the dining room table eating from blue and white porcelain bowls. I watch as my father scoops up a ball of sticky rice with a little broth in his spoon. When he bites into it, the black paste oozes down his chin. I hand him a napkin and turn on my recorder. We will talk now.

My questions have stirred something in him, the tastes and smells and sounds of a childhood. Sweet bean paste and hot sticky rice. Tang poems memorized as a boy. He tells me the one about the emperor and his concubine. The one about the two lovers saying good-bye at the kingdom's border. I tell him I will buy rice paper and brushes and ink for him to write the poems down. He asks me to look up characters he has forgotten how to write. I become official calligrapher's assistant, cook, and scribe, helping my father to exhume his past. Tastes that lay buried. Desires gone underground.

The irony of this is not lost on me. That after all these years, I should be the one to return and sit in attendance at my father's side. I, his fiercest critic—the only one who could ever win an argument with him. I, who spent my childhood renouncing all things Chinese—including my father. That I should have to work as hard at being Chinese as I had worked at denying it.

When did I first look and begin to see my father?
On that first trip to China, the summer before my senior year of college, the beginning of my family's abrupt turn

toward the East, I looked and thought I saw him step off the train and become a son. I didn't know what I was seeing. I didn't see where he was looking. He'd asked me to go along with him "just in case." I didn't think to ask, in case of what? The drama of my own arrival eclipsed any questions I might have asked about my father's departure 33 years earlier.

Before that summer, China had lain dormant in our lives except for the tiny black-and-white photographs of an unsmiling old woman that arrived in the mail via a mysterious Mrs. Han in Hong Kong. I watched as my father slit the thin, blue envelope with a knife and the photos slid out onto the table. The photos were accompanied by a single sheet of diaphanous paper on which all usable space had been filled with characters so minute my father had to use a magnifying glass to read them. Your grandmother, he'd said, and left it at that.

Growing up at a time when Americans referred to China as Red, I interpreted my father's stony silence as evidence that his departure must have been an escape. I imagined him stealing across borders that always appeared to me as bodies of water, cleanly dividing one country from another. Or slipping into a muddy river under the cover of darkness and floating downstream until he saw the bright lights of a city. I'd seen him float like that in the swimming pool, face down, corpse-like, coming up only after long intervals for air. This must be how he evaded capture, I thought, though as a child I had no idea who or what he might have been fleeing from. In another version, I pictured him as one of the "boat people"—a phrase that washed so easily over all Asians then—crammed into a vessel with hundreds of other brown bodies, adrift on the Pacific.

The problem was, these quixotic images did not fit my father. Never did.

He was never a rebel or a risk taker, but rather a careful man who always made sure he knew exactly where he was going before he set out. He was the kind of man whose only gamble was with life insurance, which he lost by stubbornly outliving the terms of the policy. He was not a floater or a drifter, but moved steadily forward the same way he swam. He knew only one stroke, the front crawl, which he executed slowly, deliberately, and only in water in which he could stand.

I never saw my father swim in water that was over his head.

And he was certainly no FOB, Fresh Off the Boat, even if he liked to play the part.

He was a child of competing revolutions—Out with the Old! In with the New! Out with the New!—none of which ever competed for his heart. From the moment it began to beat, his heart had but one desire: to go to the Beautiful Country. Meiguo. America. In the Beautiful Country, so they say, anything is possible—and my father was nothing if not a man filled with the certain knowledge of his own possibility.

What does escape look like?

Does it look like this?

Or this?

Or this?

It's the first of April, one of those prematurely warm spring days when one is easily fooled into thinking that summer has come to stay. My father has ventured out to my house this time, and we sit on the deck drinking tea. He sips his noisily and spits the loose leaves back into his cup. He looks around and comments on the size of my house and yard. You've done well, he says, and I feel my face burn with pride and resentment at his measured approval. But I'm glad to see him looking and acting like his old self.

When I turn on the recorder, I notice how my father sits up taller in his chair. How each time I ask a question, he crosses and uncrosses his legs, clasping his hands around first one knee then the other in the manner of an overconfident schoolboy. In the white New England light, the skin on his hands and face shines translucent and tight, as if it can barely contain the man, as if he is about to molt.

"So going back to your question, why this idea, why America, why I have this inner urge to go to America?" Like the good journalist he'd once been, my father returns to my question.

"Yeah, but there are really two questions here," I interject, "not just why did you come to America, but why did you leave your country?"

He is obliging. "As far as leaving China... I know I want to study here. Knowledge is the thing. I think all old Chinese are like this, you want to make something out of yourself. To advance yourself, you must seek an education. Leaving China was not in the back of my mind. It was to find a way to come here, to study, that's what it was."

"Yeah, right, study hard and you'll get ahead."

"And I never look back," he continues, ignoring my sarcasm. "You remember those years when the call of China was for people to go back, to rebuild the country? I wasn't fooled, I know what they are," he smiles wryly. "Somehow I'm suspicious of all these movements."

He recounts the story of two professors of literature, sisters from a powerful family—the Kennedys of China, he calls them. He studied under them in university and later met up with one of the professors in Hong Kong. "I remember the first thing when I walk into her office, she says to me, 'Why you leave China? We are going back to reconstruct the country. That's where we belong! You have education and you worked hard, you should stay and help build the new China. You shouldn't leave. Go back!' Oh my goodness, she give me a lecture!" he says with a howl.

"Yeah, what kind of Chinese are you?" I laugh sharply. "So how did you feel when she said that? Did you have second thoughts?"

"No," he answers without hesitation. "I have ideas about the life I like to live. Somehow, I see America, the streets paved with gold..."

"That's what everybody thinks!"

"Imagine if I listen to her? She went back and was later appointed full professor at Beijing University. Then during the Cultural Revolution, they purge her and she jumps. She commit suicide, her sister commit suicide, some of my classmates commit suicide. You see all these people caught in this turmoil. I was lucky to keep my life and utilize the opportunities I have and come here. You see luck with me all this time."

The sun beats down strong and bright, and I feel little beads of sweat forming on my nose. But my father doesn't sweat. He leans back in his chair and waits for my next question, clearly pleased with himself.

"Yeah, you certainly knew a lot of people," I can't help but point out. "The woman who helped you get the job at the U.S. embassy. The official who helped you get your passport. The Americans who helped you come here to study."

"I have a lot of connections," he says proudly.

"And you never felt... ambivalent about leaving?"

"I never doubt there's a future here. It's a selfish kind of feeling," he admits.

"But at the time when you left, you didn't feel... it wasn't... a choice?"

"No, there's no if and but. There's no choice. Whatever way you can, get out."

I have not set out to wrest the past from him.

I don't imagine there is anything to wrest.

I'm just the prodigal daughter returning home after seven years in the land my father was borne out of. Come home to write the family history. I'm a woman at the halfway point in life, when the backward glance has begun to exert greater force than the forward pull. Where did you come from? How did you get here? What did you leave behind? Questions the second generation finally thinks to ask of the first.

I'm not looking for romance in my father's story.

I'm not expecting grand revelations.

I have not set out to wrest the past from him.

I don't imagine there is anything to wrest.

He tells me the same stories over and over. The one about

the Kennedys of China. That little window.

One day he adds something new. Did I know he was a boy scout? That he crossed the Pacific on a presidential line steamship—he can't recall the date but still remembers the name of the ship, the Ulysses S. Grant—to attend the world's first-ever boy scout jamboree in Washington DC?

This new detail ever-so-slightly jogs my mind. I cannot imagine my father in a scout uniform pledging his allegiance to God or Country. I didn't even know there were boy scouts in China. What do Chinese boy scouts pledge their allegiance to?

But it's his Pacific crossing, placing him in the U.S. more than a decade earlier than his original story, that unsettles me. Why had he not mentioned this before? A whole month at sea! Were the waters rough? Was he seasick? Did he ever stand at the stern of the ship and watch the furrow widening behind him? Why do such details as the manner in which one moves from place to place matter so little to him and so much to me?

I just take the boat.
I just get on the train.
I just walk over the border.

His matter-of-factness is irritating. And his perpetual positivism. As if cause and effect were a single, straight, unbroken line between two points that could be easily traced. I was there, now I am here. Carried along by history. Always arriving at something better.

His words do not line up with my experience. Never did. The Laughing Chinaman with a violent temper. The little girl with the hands of an old woman. Both of us running through the house at night searching for an exit.

"I'm tired," my father says, "come back tomorrow."

The next day, my father tells me a story I've never heard before. A story he never told anyone this side of the Pacific. A story he must have spent his whole life in America trying to forget.

I have forgotten my recorder and notebook. I sit there bare-fisted, trying to make sense of his words.

The story begins the same way. The quartered passport. The last train to Hong Kong.

But then: We had a plan. I would go first, she would follow. I waited as long as I could.

The confusion lies at the level of grammar. *We* had a plan. *She* would follow. The personal pronouns dislodging me from my place across the table from him. Setting loose meanings that had held us all in place for so long.

Released, I float above the table, a feeling of abandon that is not entirely unpleasurable. The hint, half guessed. The gift, half understood.

"Why didn't you tell us?" I scream down at him.

"I just skip that over. There is nothing to be gained, everything to lose. I don't want to open a box of worms," he says, his incorrect use of the English idiom heightening his foreignness. This man, my father.

"Heroes don't make history, history makes heroes," he tells me. "I thought you of all people should understand this."

The next day I come back with my recorder and notebook.

We sit in the basement with the door closed. My father speaks in furtive whispers, warning me to keep my voice down. My mother's footsteps ricochet through the house. She calls down to us to ask whether we would like a drink. I reply no, we're fine, and at my father's request go to make sure the door is securely closed.

I press "record" and we begin again.

Tomorrow I will come again with my steamed buns and sticky rice, my history books and maps and photographs, my carefully constructed timelines.

I am not the filial daughter I appear to be.

I am simply after the truth.

Later, after his fall, as history begins to unwind backwards through that little window, I will try to separate historical fact from hospital hallucination. A good story from a true one.

I will sit beside my father's hospital bed, transcribing his every incredible word.

I will fill in his holes.

I will get on the boat with him.

I will follow him upriver.

I will squeeze with him into the tightest of spots in order to know for myself just how he got out.

THE FALL

"I want you to tell me the most daring thing you've ever done!"

These are my father's first words upon waking from his fall down the carpeted steps of his American Dream.

The dream may have been downsized in recent years, but the steps remain carpeted. Thank goodness, or he might not have woken up at all. My father's insistence on having something soft underfoot sometimes went to extremes, as when he piled thick Chinese carpets on top of the wall-to-wall that already blanketed the condo. When the rugs wouldn't lay flat, he asked me to tape them down with duct tape. I worried this would cause him to trip, but the piled carpets had in fact cushioned his falls on several occasions.

My father was always falling, thanks to a medical condition that caused his blood pressure to drop precariously low when he stood up and to rise dangerously high when he lay down. Especially after eating, he would stand up and drop to the floor. After several superfluous trips to the emergency room, my mother and I knew enough to let him lie there until his pressure started to rise and he regained consciousness.

"Are you trying to kill me?" he would accuse us upon waking on the floor.

As his body became frailer, my father's temper grew more fierce. It was all he had left of his former self, and he could still wield it, causing my mother and me to tread lightly when it came to his personal care. I repeatedly warned him to limit his trips up and down the stairs and never to do so alone. This was, I knew, an impossible request.

My father wandered the condo, looking for what he was certain he had lost in the move, still following an internal blueprint of that other house that he had built from scratch to his exact specifications.

He had chosen the raised ranch for its quintessentially modern design: the open floor plan, the wood-paneled family room, the walkout basement, the built-in garage. He had laid out every inch of space according to his liking, from the placement of each piece of solid maple on the carpets, to the ornamental fans and scrolls that hung from the walls, to the planting of every tree in the yard: elegant mountain ash in front, trailing forsythia and lilac along the driveway, stately pine in the back. His office was on the second floor across from his bedroom, a corner room with two windows and an expansive view of his property. He spent hours in there with the door closed, accounting for every bill received, every check written, every letter exchanged, sorting each into an elaborate filing system.

Now he kept only what he could carry—a wallet full of obsolete credit cards, the checkbook he could no longer use, an expired passport—in a single suede attaché case that traveled with him from room to room around the cramped condo. The sagging files had been relegated to the unfinished basement, where he braved the stairwell daily to go down and sit among his remains.

After my father opened that box of worms to me, I would find him down there in the basement digging around. It was there he asked me to keep his secret for him. When I refused, he reluctantly agreed to tell my mother, but only if I were present. Help me, he pleaded. We strategized together about what he should say.

On the day of his confession, we took my mother out to lunch, then came back to the condo to talk. Don't get excited, he started, I have something to tell you. I was surprised by my mother's reaction, the absence of shock or anger or tears. My mother had only one practical question: Is she still alive? After that, the matter seemed to drop into a well between them, never to be raised again.

After that, the daily demands of my father's aging body precluded any discussion of his past indiscretions, as I accompanied him on weekly doctor's visits and inquired about the results of this lab test or the side effects of that medication. The slow but unstoppable degeneration of eyes, skin, teeth, bowels, and bladder became a never-ending topic of conversation between my father, my mother, and myself as we veered from one fall to the next.

When my mother called that winter morning poised between New Years, the American and the Chinese, I came running. I found my father lying on the stone foyer at the foot of the stairs, eyes opened but unfocused.

"What happened?"

"What do you think?" My mother was moving frantically about the house stuffing objects into a plastic bag: a blood pressure kit, a book of crossword puzzles, a ream of paper cups, a banana.

I knelt beside my father and lifted his head, feeling with my fingers the wet lump that had already formed there.

"Dad, are you in any pain?"

His eyes focused momentarily on me with a look of surprise.

It was not hard to imagine what had happened. My father in the bathroom reading his *Time Magazine* on the toilet, shouting down to my mother to bring his glasses, a roll of toilet paper, a washcloth. How many trips up and down before she stopped listening?

Probably he yelled again when he was ready, then grew impatient. I could picture him standing at the top of the stairs in his bathrobe, shaking his head as he listened to the hum of the microwave below heating his instant oatmeal. He would go down the stairs one slippered foot at a time, even though I had repeatedly demonstrated how to stop on each step with both feet for balance. Now I felt a raking sensation in the sole of my right foot as I imagined him slipping off the rim of the smooth, worn stair, his head striking the sharp edge where the carpet had worn thin.

When the paramedics arrived, I insisted on riding in the back of the ambulance with my father. On the way, I explained to him what was happening, and where we were going. He remained wide-eyed yet indifferent to the drama unfolding around him.

At the hospital, a CT scan was performed and the emergency room doctor declared perfunctorily that my father had a "bleed on the brain" and needed to be transported right away to a bigger hospital.

"What does that mean?"

The doctor must have heard the panic in my voice, because that's when he slowed down and explained how little space there is between the skull and the brain, how they might need to drill if the blood did not dissipate on its own.

That's when I understood that this was not just another fall.

On the next ambulance ride, I continued to narrate for my father. I noticed that his face had changed, his eyes grown puffy and his mouth gone slack.

At the second hospital, the staff let me accompany my father into the emergency room, where I held his hand and tried not to get in the way. Under the bright surgical lights, I noticed how much my hand resembled his, lined and leathery, the result of a skin disorder I had inherited from him.

"I'm here, Dad," I told him. His eyes were now closed.

A doctor came in and gave my father a brief exam before admitting him to intensive care.

"I'm sorry," a nurse said gently, "you'll have to leave now."
I squeezed my father's hand once, then let him slip into
the sea.

*The ship pitched and rolled on the black waves. In his upper
bunk, Wang Kun swallowed the rising bile and tried to breathe.
The air inside the cabin was sweet with the stench of vomit. All
around him he heard the groaning and retching of the other boys
as they spilled their guts into the metal buckets provided them.*

Only he refused to give it up.

*At the age of 17, he had already learned to hold himself so
that no one could see what rose and fell within him.*

*He was not so much hiding something as preparing himself
inwardly for whatever might come his way. Danger or opportunity. In Chinese, both possibilities were contained in one
word, "weiji," meaning "crisis."*

Be prepared. The mantra of a Chinese boy scout.

*He whispered the word to himself over and over now as the
ship pitched again. He tried to breathe in opportunity, "ji...,"
and breathe out danger, "wei...," but this proved impossible,
opportunity getting stuck on the roof of his mouth.*

So he reversed his breathing, telling himself that this was the way it worked anyway: You had to be willing to take in danger in order to create opportunity.

Soon Wang Kun was breathing slowly and deeply, the ship rocking him to sleep with the promise of Opportunity Born of Crisis.

The ship was the USS Grant. Formerly the Konig Wilhelm II. A 9,410 gross ton passenger liner built in Germany in 1907 and seized by the Americans when they entered the war. Though the Germans had sabotaged the ship's machinery, the Americans made her seaworthy again, and she spent several years as the Madawaska, transporting American soldiers to and from battle in Europe before changing names again and making the trans-Pacific voyage on which Wang Kun was her seaworthy passenger.

Wang Kun knew nothing of the ship's past, but he knew that he was making history. He and twelve other Chinese boy scouts were on their way to a gathering of the Free World's greatest youth movement. A ten-day jamboree of boys from all over the world dedicated to the modern ideals of Industriousness, Cheerfulness, Cleanliness, Thrift—and above all service to one's country.

The future face of China.

Wang Kun, the boy scout, understood this.

In his application to the jamboree, he had proven his patriotism with an essay on the loss of Manchuria to the Japanese, including a precisely worded statement on the need for cooperation between the Nationalists and the Communists.

Impending Crisis.

Be Prepared.

Wang Kun was what his classmates called "shuai," especially in uniform. His hair always oiled and neatly parted on one side, his shirt tucked smartly into his belted trousers, his sleeves rolled up to display slender forearms and finely chiseled hands. He had high, sharp cheekbones and a tall nose that was the envy of the other boys. How they all longed for such a nose! Though short in stature, he carried himself with a combination of self assurance and good humor that made it impossible for anyone to look down upon him. If he had his doubts or sorrows or fears, he did not show them. His eyes were always smiling, his exquisite black eyebrows perpetually arched in anticipation.

Looking in the mirror, Wang Kun couldn't help but admire himself.

He was indeed shuai. Clean. Cheerful. Industrious.

The forward-looking face of a backward nation.

Wang Kun sat up in his bunk. The motion of the ship had changed. The sea was strangely still except for a churning sensation that seemed to emanate from somewhere below his navel. He climbed down the ladder and made his way through the narrow passage and out onto the deck. Gone were the unbounded views of the Pacific that had burned themselves into his imagination over the last six weeks, exhilarating and terrifying in their limitlessness. In their place, in his face, hot black walls of steel rose vertically on either side of the ship. Heavy mooring cables steadied the vessel as it was slowly borne upward, rising with the water that poured into the lock from below. Wang Kun knew at once where he stood. A deep narrow cut in the isthmus between North and South. A short-cut between oceans. A man, a plan, a canal: Panama! (He often bragged to his classmates that he knew the English language backwards and forwards. This was by far his favorite palindrome for the way it held its meaning both ways). As the USS Grant and its cargo of thirteen Chinese scouts rose 50 feet above the Pacific Ocean, Wang Kun laughed out loud—the laughter of a boy with a plan.

When the ship finally cleared the walls of the lock, Wang Kun was surprised to come face to face with those who had come to watch the spectacle of these massive foreign warships being squeezed through the canal's waterways. Some of the faces were pale white. They wore dark sunglasses and walked with long, easy strides, their hands thrust casually into their pockets. The look of those comfortably in charge.

On the shoulders of one man was a small boy waving what Wang Kun recognized as an American flag. He had never seen such beautiful golden hair on a child. He took off his scarf and waved it at the boy. The boy waved his flag back excited-

ly, then did something Wang Kun had never seen before. He brought both hands to his face and pulled with his forefingers at the corners of his eyes, round eyes becoming narrow slits. Wang Kun hesitated, unsure what to make of this gesture. It unsettled him, pricking a hole in the euphoria of the moment.

Then the cables released, and the ship plowed forward again. Wang Kun touched his fingers to his eyes and waved goodbye. He watched the boy alternate between waving his flag and pulling at his eyes until he was lost in the crowd.

The ship exited the lock and entered one of the many artificial lakes that had been created to catch the spillover. Along the banks of the lake, Wang Kun saw the twisted branches of mahogany trees that had once been a forest reaching up out of the water. The branches were washed clean and their bone-white limbs beckoned to him. He thought of the golden-haired boy. He remembered riding on his own father's shoulders and watching the soldiers march north to fight the warlords. He remembered his father's strong, brown arms lifting him high above the crowd, the feeling of tremendous well-being that this gave him. He remembered the elegant curve of his father's ear. Then the new magistrate had come to town and his father had disappeared, the door to their house sealed up and covered by angry black characters on screaming red banners...

He did not follow these thoughts further. He had learned how to shut down a thought midstream, how to stop the frivolous flow of associations that could lead him where he did not want to go.

At the mouth of the lake, he saw a sign informing him that they had just crossed the Continental Divide. He let out a long slow breath, "ji..." All waters flowed east to the Atlantic now.

Fare forward, he whispered to himself.

I conjure all this from one grainy, black-and-white newspaper clipping.

When I finally find the clipping, after combing through the archives of the *New York Times*, it's the first evidence I have of my father's stories. I bring it to the hospital, eager to show it to him when he wakes up. How thrilled he will be to see himself sitting there on the steps of City Hall looking sharp in his boy scout uniform, a Chinese violin tucked between his legs. He is surrounded by other scouts wielding flags, drums, a sword. The caption reads "An Oriental Accomplishment not in Western Boy Scout's Curricula." The accompanying story describes how these thirteen "sons of the orient" had entertained New Yorkers by playing a "plaintive tune" on their native instruments. But I can see nothing mournful on the faces of these forward-looking boys.

According to the article, the jamboree was cancelled at the last minute due to a polio epidemic, so the Chinese scouts were hosted by the city of New York with visits to Radio City and Coney Island, where they rode the Shoot-the-Chutes and took in the freak shows on the Boardwalk. After their tour, one of the boys was heard to remark that of course he had read all about New York in his geography book. I'm sure this upstart must have been my father.

I search for other evidence. On a Navy website, I find a photograph of the USS Grant together with a log of its previous lives and journeys. Though the ship had in fact made several excursions through the canal, the delegation of Chinese scouts heading for the never-to-be jamboree in Washington DC disembarked in California and then took a train across the country. But I invoke my authorial privilege and ship my father by way of Panama. He'd always wanted to see the canal, that audacious feat of American engineering that had taken so many lives.

I take a virtual tour of the locks, sensing danger where I know my father would have seen only opportunity. His glowing admiration, his unabashed emulation of the Americans, has always confused me. The pulling of eyes. The jokes at his expense. Don't be so sensitive, he'd tell me. Learn to play the game!

I find an on-line memoir written by an American marine who, as a boy, had been stationed with his family in Panama. The words of one who is comfortably in charge. And I read everything I can find about the Chinese boy scouts.

The boy scouts lead me in directions I never expected to go. Into secret organizations with portentous names such as the Society for Vigorous Practice, the Three People's Principles Youth Corps, the Bureau of Investigation and Statistics. Professionally dry-cleaned names. Forward-looking names. Names that a boy might use to fashion a future for himself.

A future that always leads to the Americans.

POSTCARDS FROM THE MOON

He's been talking nonsense in his sleep, ripping out his IV and kicking off the sheets and playing with his penis.

"Don't be a bad boy," the nurse flirts with him as she ties down his hands.

If he were awake, I think, watch out, he would flirt right back.

When he does wake, he accuses the nurses of molesting him.

You don't know him! I want to scream.

I am terrified by the anonymity of the hospital. Every day a different doctor or nurse. They assume my father can't speak English, and that I am there to translate. They ask for his history, and I am confused. Which version should I give them?

As a child, I watched my father play the Laughing Chinaman to American audiences. He knew all the jokes about Chinamen, their inscrutable nature and their pidgin English, and always beat his fellow Americans to the punchline—"Why don't the Chinese have phones? Because there are so many Wings and Wongs they're afraid they'll wing the wong number!" Always positioning himself as the butt

of the joke. Upon request, he would recite Confucian prov-
erbs to red-faced white men downing their drinks at cocktail
parties. When all the men in town grew beards in honor of
the bicentennial, and all my father could manage were three
long, wispy tails sprouting from his chin, he just laughed
and pressed his palms together in a low bow. And when the
town held its annual Ethnic Fest, he would don a silk smoking jacket, set up a booth, and wield his calligraphy brush
with great flourish, smiling broadly as he offered sage advice
in bold, black strokes on strips of auspicious red paper.

"Your father's a real character," people would tell me.

He was well-known and well-liked, one of only a hand-
ful of Chinese living in the town (the others being either
university professors or restaurant owners who spoke little
English). He was often asked to appear at public events such
as the opening ceremony of the baseball season, his foreignness heightening the pleasure and excitement of the
occasion. The local press regularly ran stories and photographs of him. In one photo, he stands grinning on second
base wearing a silk cap with a long black braid and holding
a sign on which one large Chinese character has been written: "tou," meaning "to steal."

I hated these photographs with their ridiculous captions. This laughing buddha in a smoking jacket was not the man I knew as my father. A man with impossibly high expectations of himself and his children. Who worried constantly about money and the future. Who woke up shouting in the night. A man who trusted no one but desperately wanted the respect of others. A charming man with a frightening temper.

I could not hold these dissonant images of my father together. I could not reconcile the Chinaman who had captivated the town with the proud, angry man I thought I knew so well. I did not know what to do with my father's anger. How to hide it. Where to keep it. Much less to ask where it came from.

Growing up, I knew neither affluence nor ambition. The small town on the winding river where my father had planted his dream had not inspired the same of me. A middling town, neither poor nor prosperous, made up of strip malls and family businesses that had long ago realized whatever meager aspirations they had started with. There was no sense of urgency—no revolution, no danger, and little opportunity. If there was crisis, it was the kind that crept by unnoticed—a factory closing here, an empty office building there, cracks in the sidewalk.

No red flags.

Into this town I was born, a child of the sixties. I wore bell-bottom pants and flower-power shirts and a velvet choker with a wooden peace symbol, but was oblivious to the sixteen-year war that coincided with my childhood. When I try to recall that childhood, my memories are always of place rather than person or event. A kind of topographical memory that knows exactly where to step over a crack and when to turn a corner. I remember the steep slope of the ceiling in my attic bedroom. I remember the thin, shady strip of soil between the driveway and the house where the bleeding hearts grew.

For the first decade of my life, I lived in a brown bungalow on a tree-lined street with cement-slab sidewalks that rose and fell with the contours of the earth, breaking open where the roots of trees refused to lie down. The houses stood close together with their backyards bordering those on the street behind, separated by a low, chain-link fence. Our backyard had a swing set, monkey bars, and sand box, all painstakingly erected by my father. The yard afforded little privacy, and whenever my brother and I played out back, the old man who lived in the house directly behind would come to the fence, lean on his cane, and mutely watch us. The only sound he'd made was a sharp grunt each time one of us jumped off the swing. We learned to perform for these measured grunts of approval. The higher the jump, the stronger the grunt. We would pump our legs and hearts so hard that the base of the swing set would uproot then drop back into the earth with a hollow thump each time we reached the peak of our arc.

The elementary school was only a few blocks away, and by the time the I was old enough to walk to school by myself, I had memorized each rift and rise in the sidewalk so that I could step without looking, daring myself to keep my eyes closed until I turned the corner. In the winter, I walked on the tops of snow banks. I imagined myself crossing a mountain range, negotiating narrow paths, and traversing steep ravines between home and school. Below, a swollen river raged. "One-false-step, cer-tain-death, one-false-step, cer-tain-death," I chanted to myself. I tried to ignore the golden-haired boys riding their banana-seat bikes up and down the street, changing gears and popping wheelies and letting out long, slow whistles. These same boys once lay in wait in my third-grade classroom in order to catch the girls as they came back from recess, two grabbing for the arms and one lifting up the skirt. Having resisted my mother's attempts to get me to wear a dress, I was spared this humiliation but remained wary.

Once the boys got off their bikes and followed me, sing-songing that ugly rhyme about the Chinaman on the fence who tried to make a dollar out of ninety-five cents.

"He missed, he missed, he missed like..."

"Like this?" I spun around, my fist connecting with the boy's freckled nose and letting loose a bloody tide.

After that, they kept their distance.

In those days, China was an absence inside the brown bungalow.

There were no scrolls hanging from the walls or lanterns from the ceilings, no oversized fans adorning the mantel or thick carpets under foot. These all came later. After a family vacation to Taiwan, our homecoming captured in the local newspaper: my mother draped in silk, a lantern suspended from my father's hand, my brother and I holding up the flag of the Republic. After Normalization, when the door between China and the U.S. finally swung open and my father stepped smartly through. Each subsequent return to the homeland required the bearing of treasures both ways—televisions and refrigerators flying East, paintings and carpets winging West. Over the years, while our Chinese relatives' demand for the latest technology grew and eventually surpassed my family's ability to keep up with it, my father steadfastly acquired pieces of China that he had boxed and shipped to our upstate address. By then we had moved into the brand-new raised ranch, which soon came to resemble a museum of which my father was the devoted curator. When his mother died, he had her boxed and shipped too, her ashes interred in a carved wooden urn that assumed the central spot on the mantel under her life-sized portrait, mouth grim but with a spark in her eyes, forbidden cigarette caught between gnarled fingers, turning museum into mausoleum.

But before Normalization, China was hard to find.

Where to look?

In the refrigerator. Those links of sausage bought from the one Asian grocer in town who made a weekly trek to New York City with my father's list in hand. The freezer would be overflowing with obscure lumps that he would release by steaming them open, buns bursting with sweet bean paste, salty duck eggs oozing their golden yolks, the fatty insides of sausages turning translucent and giving off a pungent scent of rice wine and fermented beans that lingered into the morning.

He cooked late at night after the rest of the family had eaten. We rarely took meals together, each eating whenever he or she felt hungry. My mother disliked cooking and was a firm believer in the simplicity and practicality of prepared foods: cereal, peanut butter, canned soup. My father could not tolerate these strange, foreign foodstuffs and simply waited until everyone had gone to bed to satisfy his hunger. I would sometimes join him in these late-night repasts, my main motive being the sausages that were sweet and salty at the same time. Even asleep, I could sniff out those fragrant links and would join my father at the kitchen table.

"I cooked extra links."

"Thanks, Dad."

"Did you finish your homework?"

"Yes, Dad," I would lie.

Our chopsticks voraciously scraping our bowls as the rest of the family slept.

The smell and taste of those sausages are still a delicious contraband, evoking those clandestine meals with my father, when I would devour delicacies I'd never admit to in the light of day.

Afraid to leave the hospital, I spend the night on a sofa chair that pulls out into a bed in the lobby of the neuro unit for traumatic brain injuries. The unit is shaped like an ellipse, with a nurse's station in the middle of the floor from which all the rooms can be seen and monitored at once. A bow-tied neurologist comes daily to test my father's reflexes, using an array of shiny instruments he pulls out of a black leather satchel. The patients who are mobile circle the station in their johnnies, mumbling profanities and dragging their IVs on wheels behind them. Some stop at the lobby to watch the television that runs round the clock. I feel exposed sleeping there under the fluorescent lights and the incessant beeping and buzzing of all those monitors. Unable to fall asleep, I play a familiar game with myself, closing my eyes and revisiting the houses and rooms, doors and windows, of my childhood.

My bedroom is at the front of the bungalow directly above my parents' room. To get there, I have to pass through a ground floor bedroom, climb a steep flight of stairs, then proceed through my brother's room—really no more than a vestibule with a bed—and down a long, narrow hallway bordered on either side by mirrored doors that open into the attic crawlspace, making me feel as if I live at a great distance from the rest of the family. The hallway grows to frightening lengths at night, the mirrors catching my silvery image from both sides as I dash past. But by day, I revel in my attic perch. From my bedroom window, I can look out over the porch roof onto the street below, where the neighbor kids ride their bikes and play hopscotch and foursquare. I can watch without being watched. Through a network of air ducts and registers that run through the old house, the noise of my family drifts into my room—the clatter of dishes on tables, the shattering of dishes on walls, my father's unpredictable temper, my mother's growing hysteria.

My family was always on the verge of such explosions, never knowing when or why they would occur. My father's rage was our dirty little secret, contained inside the bungalow, spreading through the cracks and registers between rooms, slowly infecting us all—my mother, my brother, and me—until we each became a carrier of our peculiar strain of muted rage.

On the ground floor, just off the living room, are the double French doors that lead into my father's study. The doors have brass handles and are covered from top to bottom with square glass panes, just opaque enough to make it difficult to see anything but light and shadows. When the doors are closed, I can't be sure whether my father is inside. I inch closer, trying to make out his presence behind the glass. I press the plastic faces of my dolls against the cloudy panes and put their tiny ears to the crack between the doors where an inviting draft blows. When I am certain of his absence, I turn the handle of one door until it cracks open just enough to see inside before stealthily slipping through.

The room is cool and dark and smells of ink and film and newspapers. Books and photographs line the walls and shelves. The photographs are all black and white formal shots of people sitting stiffly or standing in rows, dressed in suits or gowns. I easily find my father, always in the back or at the end of a row, leaning in, his boyish face beaming.

Along one wall are his camera cases, three of them, which I open in turn: the Polaroid Land Camera, the Canon Rangefinder, and the mighty Speed Graphic, which I can barely lift with one hand. A typewriter sits on the desk along with a bottle of ink and an inkwell, a clutch of fountain pens, and a tray stacked with crisp, white paper. I hold up one sheet to the shaft of light between the doors so I can see the watermark.

It's here that I find the book, wedged on a shelf between a Chinese dictionary and an anthology of English literature. The initials catch my eye: T.S. This is what my mother sometimes calls my father in those rare moments when there is something more than a fight brewing between them. The book has a broken binding, and the pages fall out when I open it. As I hastily pick them up and try to put them back in order, I notice that some pages have been scored with fine blue ink.

Time past and time future

What might have been and what has been

Neither flesh nor fleshless

Neither from nor towards

In my beginning is my end

And the way up is the way down, the way forward is the way back

And what you do not know is the only thing you know

The nonsensical words remind me of Alice in Wonderland and Dr. Seuss, everything in opposites and reversals. Nothing like my father. Yet the handwriting in the margins is unmistakably his, a cross between cursive and print, each letter meticulously scripted to stand on its own without touching another.

The lines stick in my head, delicious absurdities that I whisper to myself in bed at night. "And what you own is what you do not own. And where you are is where you are not."

And then, without meaning to, I memorize a few more lines each time I sneak through those double doors. I never dare take the book from the study, though sometimes I steal a page or two. By the seventh grade, I have learned the first quartet. By the time I enter high school, I know the whole book by heart and recite my favorite, "The Dry Salvages," for my tenth-grade public speaking class.

"I do not know much about gods, but I think that the river is a strong brown god."

I think I saw them once on a family vacation, that knuckle of rocks off the coast known as the Dry Salvages because they are never completely covered by the sea. I remember watching the gulls landing and taking off, imagining myself standing on those rocks, sure-footed and dry in the midst of all that roiling water, beacon swinging with the swell of the earth. Like the time before I could swim, when my father carried me into the sea, the waves pounding us from all sides, the undertow sucking at his feet. And me, high and dry and unafraid in his arms.

I cannot explain the poem, but it feels like the first solid truth my hungry mouth has spoken. I feel the weight and lift of each word and know when to inflect meaning in all the right places, earning bored looks from my classmates and high praise from my teacher.

In the hospital, I dream of escape.

In one dream, a train approaches. I stand at the intersection of the tracks—no, not tracks, cables, intersecting cables suspended in air. I stand petrified in my nightgown and bare feet, toes curled around the point where the cables come together, making an X. An enormous star hangs beneath me like a safety net. But I do not feel safe. I hear the train approaching, feel the cables tremble and burn, but cannot tell from which direction it is coming. The roar of the engine is all around me. Its hot breath billows up under my nightgown. I see the star looming up at me, getting bigger, or closer, I can't tell which. It terrorizes me, this star, even more than the oncoming train. I run, the cable becoming wide and solid under my feet, down the long hallway, past the mirrored doors, down the stairs, running, screaming, into my father's arms.

In another dream, I am lying in my bed in the bungalow. The light on the ceiling opens and becomes a portal into space. A ladder descends, and I climb up through the light into a galaxy of stars, my bare feet and hands feeling their way through the dizzying darkness. I climb rung by rung all the way up to the moon, where my feet land with a soft thud on the dusty surface. I look down at my footprints and it begins to rain postcards that twirl like leaves to the earth. The postcards are raining down into my room now, collecting in piles on my bed. I cannot make out the pictures on the front of the cards nor what, if anything, has been written on the back, but I know they are all from me.

These are my dreams, visiting me over and over again until they belong to me as much as any other memory of childhood. The door in the light in the ceiling as familiar as the cracks in the sidewalk, the heat of the star-train as oppressive as the hot air that rose through the register in my bedroom floor, carrying with it the sounds of the house below, the daily coming together and breaking apart of my parents.

This is what they will find when they open my bedroom door in the morning. An empty bed. A ladder to heaven. Postcards from the moon.

DARING

"I want you to tell me the most daring thing you've ever done!"

My father's words jolt me awake.

"Dad, how do you feel?"

"Tell me the most daring thing you've ever done!" The pitch of his voice rises as it always does when he grows agitated. Spittle flies from his mouth.

"Dad, you're in the hospital, you fell down the stairs." I try to appeal to his stubborn rationality, the terra firma on which our relationship has always stood.

"I want you to be daring, to do the most daring thing in your life!"

The bait. In the past, I would have taken it.

"OK, I'll try to be daring," I say in a voice that does not sound like my own.

"Were you in the Blitz?" he continues conversationally.

"What Blitz?"

"They're bombing Chongqing!" His eyes flick furtively around the room, and he motions me to come closer. "Are there any Japanese here?" he whispers.

Hope sinks. "No, Dad, there are no Japanese here."

"Who are the other passengers on this boat?"

"Where are we, Dad?"

"The Pacific Ocean."

"Where are we going?"

"Nowhere."

"Where have we come from?"

He looks directly at me. "What are you doing here?"

"Dad, I've been here all week. Mom's here, too, she's gone to get something to eat."

"You and your mother shouldn't be here, it's too dangerous. They're bombing Chongqing. You shouldn't see..."

Then a veil seems to lift. I have never seen such a look in my father's eyes. Completely unguarded. Humorless. Exposed.

"What is it, Dad, what do you see?"

But he is already slipping away. The naked moment gone. I have to put my ear to his mouth to catch the soft syllables that fall one by one from his lips.

"The-most-daring-story-I-will-never-tell-"

December 13, 1937.

Wang Kun stepped lightly up the ship's ramp. He did not hesitate to board, but neither could he sink his full weight into the soles of his feet. This ship, he knew, would take him in a direction he did not want to go. Upriver rather than down. Deeper into the interior of a country at war. He felt the ramp shudder beneath him.

It had been two years since his return from the Beautiful Country to a hero's welcome, and the glory of that moment had remained with him. How he had marched down the gangway, still looking shuai in his scout uniform in spite of the salt and sweat that had become a second layer of skin af-

ter weeks at sea. How he had marched back onto Chinese soil under the banner of "Loyalty." He knew that most of the crowd could not read the English letters on his banner, and this only added to his pride. "Lo-yal-ty!" he shouted to them, showing off his American pronunciation. The other boys followed suit, their intonation less exact than his: "Ho-nes-ty!" "Cour-te-sy!" "Re-spon-si-bil-i-ty!"

For the first time, Wang Kun noticed the sizeable military presence in the crowd. He was not impressed. He knew these conscripts for what they were: those without the means or the smarts to buy themselves out of the draft. Peasants, cleaned up and force-fed a thin gruel of self-discipline. Slaves. He would never be one of them.

The procession came to a halt in front of a reviewing stand, the 12-point star of the Republic flying from each corner. A large red banner hanging across the front of the stand declared "One Country, One Doctrine, One Leader, One Enemy." At the front of the stand he spotted his old scoutmaster seated next to a man in an undecorated uniform whose sharp eyes and fastidiously trimmed mustache he recognized at once. The blood rushed to his face: The Generalissimo had personally come to welcome him home!

The Generalissimo stood and began to speak in the cold, shrill voice Wang Kun had heard so many times on the radio. Now that voice was speaking to him, praising his worldliness and calling him the new life of the country. Now the Generalissimo was pointing his finger and asking Wang Kun to read the word on his banner.

"Loyalty!" the Generalissimo screeched.

Wang Kun swooned.

For a brief moment, Wang Kun felt a terrible desire to

give himself over to this man, to become a part of something greater than himself. Then the speech was over, and the crowd burst into applause. The moment passed. Wang Kun felt himself shrink back to his own very small, very wary, very practical self.

Wang Kun had returned to a country at war, and in the weeks and months that followed his glorious return, his practical self had been overwhelmed by invitations to speak and offers to join and to lead. By autumn of the following year, the Japanese had taken Shanghai, and there was a growing sense of urgency at his school. How soon before their own small town would fall?

When the principal announced that the school would hold an early graduation and then close, Wang Kun knew it was time to make his move. He was invited to a secret meeting of the Three People's Principles Youth Corps and offered passage upriver to the Generalissimo's new headquarters. The price for passage: his English, put in the service of the Nationalist cause. The Nationalists were retreating inland, but for Wang Kun, this would be a way forward.

A way forward, he reminded himself now as he stepped aboard the little steamship. The deck was soon filled to standing-room-only with young men, some in civilian attire, others in uniform like him, jostling for a view at the rail. He found a hole and squeezed into it. He was relieved to be free of the crowds on shore fighting for passage, desperate to put distance between themselves and the encroaching Japanese. He tried not to think of the mother he had left behind, comforting himself with her parting words: What would the Japanese want with an old woman with such useless feet?

The river was muddy, the color of the milk coffee he'd learned to drink in America. Above him, two blackened stacks spewed smoke into December morning air that was already thick with fog and something else he couldn't identify blowing from upriver. A ragged American flag whipped in the wind.

"Hey, Little Beauty!" A hand clapped him on the head. He ducked and turned toward the familiar voice.

"Old Man!" Wang Kun greeted his friend. "You said we'd be traveling on a real American steamer, not this junk!" He tried to sound reproachful but could only muster a momentary frown, for the sight of Luomin instantly lightened his mood.

He'd first met Luomin at the Youth Corps meeting, held late one night in a classroom at his school. Luomin was sitting at the teacher's desk dressed in a long silk robe, the embodiment of New Life. Though only a few years older than Wang Kun, his hair was already greying, and he wore thick, round spectacles that made him look professorial. He spoke earnestly of the war raging around them and the need for youth such as themselves to respond. He warned not only of the Japanese threat, but of those traitors hiding in the hills who had the nerve to kidnap the Generalissimo in his pajamas!

"Who will join me in restoring dignity to this country?" Luomin had asked. He took off his glasses, holding them between manicured fingers that bore not a trace of tobacco stain, and looked intently around the room. The other boys bowed their heads and sat on their hands. Only Wang Kun dared to meet

his gaze.

"Don't worry," Wang Kun spoke up, "the Americans will support the Generalissimo. They will send their planes to fight the Japanese."

Luomin looked with amusement at the small, self-possessed boy sitting in the front row and asked his name. When Wang Kun replied, Luomin laughed, "Oh, the boy scout, I've heard about you. Let me tell you, the Generalissimo does not need the Americans, though he welcomes their support. What he needs is you, your boldness and your will to build a new China!"

Wang Kun was not fooled by such rhetoric. He knew when he was being made an offer he could not refuse.

It's in rehab that my father first speaks of Luomin.

A colleague, he calls him at first.

Then, a friend.

My best friend.

My brother.

Luomin materializes in bursts and fits of memory over days and weeks in the hospital.

He's on the boat from Nanjing, then he isn't.

He resurfaces at the training camp in Hankou.

He's on the riverbank in Chongqing when the bombs begin to fall.

Can you describe him?

He is tall.

Anything else?

He is good at calligraphy.

He recruited me.

He saved me.

He was ashamed to go home.

I pour through the history books, searching for some clue to this man who would become my father's benefactor. What kind of man was he? A soldier or a politician? Was he more concerned with manners or morals? Why did the path of revolution lead him to the right rather than the left? And how far to the right did he go? I ask of Luomin all the questions I cannot ask of my father.

I find a book of photographs taken by mostly Western observers in China during the war and study the images of the Guomindang: the shape of their faces, the length of their fingernails. When I finally drape Luomin's body in long blue silk, it is a relief.

"Will we meet any little Japanese upriver?" Wang Kun asked, as the steamer churned and strained to push off from the mooring. He tried to keep his question light-hearted, but in truth he was afraid. Though he'd never seen a Japanese person before, he'd heard stories about them.

Luomin hesitated before replying. "Don't worry," he said finally, "the Japanese would not dare to bomb a ship bearing an American flag."

Wang Kun was not reassured, but he did not question further.

The little steamer was plowing upriver now at a steady clip. Though it was nearly noon, the sun had not yet burned off the morning miasma that seemed to lie even more thickly over this section of the river. It was disquieting to move so swiftly through such dense fog.

"How does the pilot know there are no boats coming toward us?" Wang Kun wondered aloud.

"No one in his right mind would be going in that direction."

Luomin's earlier nonchalance was gone. He stood motionless at the bow of the ship squinting into the vapors. His face and hair were beaded with water. Most of the other boys had gone to their cabins to wait out the weather. Wang Kun was cold and would have liked to go inside, too, but did not want his friend to think him weak.

"What are you looking for?" Wang Kun asked, wiping his dripping nose.

"We should be passing Nanking soon," came the barely audible reply.

The ship slowed as it made a sharp turn northward, following the bend in the river. The grinding of engines brought a few of the boys out of their cabins. They made a game of *slipping and sliding on the wet deck. One swift glance from Luomin put an end to this brief interlude of frivolity. Wang Kun was amazed by the authority that his friend commanded and basked at his side.*

The river and the ship veered south now.

The pilot cut the engines.

Wang Kun looked to Luomin for some sign of what this might mean, but his friend remained expressionless.

Then the indeterminate smell that had hung in the air all morning hit Wang Kun full in the face, burning his eyes and forcing his hand to his mouth.

"Go inside!" Luomin commanded.

But Luomin himself did not move, and neither did anyone else. They were all transfixed by the scene materializing on the south bank of the river: half-human shapes and forms revealed then hidden again by thick plumes of smoke moving across the water.

As the city of Nanking burned in the distance, it seemed that everything imaginable was leaping, falling, hurtling into the turgid river: wooden tubs, railroad ties, door frames, intricately carved window shutters, anything that would keep a body afloat. And in between, screaming babies lashed to bits of driftwood, half-naked women, soldiers crying "jiu ming! jiu ming!" amidst the bloated heads and headless torsos of countless conscripts, their ragged buttocks bobbing indecently in the silty water. And, making their way upriver through this human detritus, the retreating KMT generals standing stiffly on their launches with their eyes tightly shut.

The other boys had turned away. Only Wang Kun remained standing next to Luomin. His gaze was torn between the stony faces of the generals and the grotesque expressions on the severed heads in the water. One appeared to be smiling at him. He felt disgust for those men who could close their eyes to this brutality—and ashamed of his own desire to look.

A woman clinging to a board off the port side of the ship caught his eye. Long black hair tangled wildly around a gash of a face. She was trying to swim toward their ship while balancing a small bundle on the board. She was calling to him and gesturing to the bundle. Suddenly the pilot started the engines again, and the ship began to turn away from the woman. Wang Kun was horrified to see the woman lift the bundle off the board and, with surprising strength, toss it toward the ship. It hit the stern with a dull thud followed by a wail, then slipped back into the water where it floated mutely.

The ship was steaming westward now. Wang Kun did not look back at the woman. He turned to Luomin for consolation, only to find his friend weeping softly into the broad palms of his hands.

Of course my father could not have saved the woman or her baby because he could not have witnessed any of this from a ship passing by as the Rape of Nanjing began. According to my timeline, he could not even have been there. He had to have started his journey upriver weeks before that, before the Japanese began minesweeping the river to the east of the capital, during that little window of time—a month at most—between the Fall of Shanghai and the Rape of Nanjing.

How did he always manage to stay one step ahead of the Japanese?

How does one remain one step ahead of history?

What kind of person is always ready for that little window when it opens?

HOSPITAL BOAT

In his hospital bed, my father is adrift in a stream of time.
Time is a river, an ocean, a sea on which he floats dispassionately from bygone port to bygone port. Shanghai. Nanjing. Hankou. Chongqing. He watches the waters run black and blue, turn red. Look, he points to a body drifting past. He speaks politely to the doctors and nurses, inquiring into their names and nationalities and what they are doing on this boat.

"Zuo chuanzi hui qu!"

Take the boat back, he shouts.

"Shenme chuan? Qu nar?"

What boat? To where? My pronunciation is perfect, but the Chinese words feel awkward, performative on my tongue.

By the time I was fluent enough to converse with my father in Chinese, after studying the language in college, our way of talking and relating had already become firmly grounded in the English vernacular. My advantage. Even when we traveled together in China, we spoke only English with each other. His advantage.

"Ba zhaoxiangji, shoushi hao!"

Pack up the cameras! he barks.

He's his old self again, all business, making preparations, staying one step ahead of the game. He tries to get out of bed and becomes aware of the restraints on his arms. "Eh? Zhe shi zenme hui shi?" He studies his predicament, looks shrewdly around the room, then asks sweetly, "Could you please take these off?"

"You have to leave them on, Dad. You've been pulling out your IV. You're going to hurt yourself."

He seems to know there is no use arguing. He struggles briefly to free himself, then collapses back onto the bed, closing his eyes. When he opens them again, he looks around and asks, "What are all these people doing here?"

"What people? Who do you see?"

He names members of our family, some in the U.S., some in China, pointing around the perimeter of the bed as he goes. He stops suddenly at the foot of the bed, his finger shaking in mid-air. "Eh? What is she doing here? And him? They shouldn't be here!"

"Who?"

He begins to do what looks like some sort of calculation, first on his fingers, then on the bed sheets. With a heavy sigh, he wipes the sheets clean with his hand. "It's too difficult to do the math," he says.

He looks ruefully at the mute crowd around his bed. "How did you people get into my life?"

He turns to my mother, who has just come back from the cafeteria with a carton of hot soup and a package of Saltines. "Do you trust me?" he asks her.

"I love you, so I trust you," she answers.

"That is your first mistake."

In the hospital, my mother divides her time between the cafeteria, the gift shop, and my father's room. She never returns to the room empty-handed—a slice of cheese pizza, a tub of ice cream, the latest issue of *Reader's Digest*, anti-bacterial hand lotion, a box of tissues, a macramé wall hanging that reads "God grant me the Serenity to accept the things I cannot change, the Courage to change the things I can, and the Wisdom to know the difference," which she hangs on the wall beside his bed. Her hands, like her eyes and her tongue, are always moving, warding off Hunger, Illness, Boredom, and any Danger that might prey on her family. A different kind of preparedness than my father's, born of a different kind of necessity.

Every time my father and I begin to converse, my mother disappears, returning later with a pack of gum or some throat lozenge that she will try to ply on me. I refuse all my mother's palliative efforts. I cannot see my mother, am not even looking in her direction, so intent am I on tracking the man in the boat. Whenever he begins to rant about bombs or blitzes, my mother breaks in with a cheery litany of whom she just saw or what she just ate.

"I got your favorite ice cream for you, isn't it good?" she asks hopefully.

The man in the boat just smiles and nods his head, spooning Cherry Garcia into his mouth as he leans over the rail, watching the furrow widening behind him.

Listen. This is how father and daughter talk to each other in the hospital.

"What would you do if I stepped off the boat, but it wasn't a real boat? I would be in Hong Kong, but it wouldn't be Hong Kong."

"Is that where you are now, Dad, in Hong Kong?"

"I'm not in this world anymore."

"Where are you?"

"My reality now is… do you know how expensive these telephone calls are?"

"Listen, this is interesting. Because of the technology, a person can be dead but still talk on the telephone."

"But you're not dead!"

"You shouldn't be sad because your father is gone."

"But you're not gone yet!"

"I'm already gone."

"But I can still feel you!"

"That's where the problem comes in."

"You try to make me think I'm in the reality world, but I'm not."

"Where are you?"

"I'm in a dream world."

"How did you get there?"

"You people manipulated this boat!"

"How do I get off this boat?"

"Is it a real boat?"

"You think it's real, but if you step off, it's not real anymore. You cannot manipulate it physically. Do you have permission to do it?"

"Dad, why does the hospital feel like a boat?

"They picked up people last night. You do not want to be here, under the control of the government."

"Which government?"

"It changes according to the time. New laws, new government, new dreams become reality. I was dreaming about this imaginary boat. I was stuck there, I couldn't get off."

"Dad, would you like to get off the boat and come with me back to the real world?"

"Yes, too bad I can't do it. The law won't allow it. They're running these people as if they are dead before they get on the boat. There's no way to get off the boat except dead."

When I first hear the absurdities spilling from my father's mouth, I mourn him, for just one night, sobbing under a hot shower. The next morning, I recover and buy a new notebook at the hospital gift shop and begin recording our conversations again.

Something has been loosed.

A partition has fallen between past and present, two great, irreconcilable nations, and now he moves freely across the divide.

"If you are writing this down," my father says, "it will seem real to you, but it's not. You are trying to extend your living space from the reality world into the dream world. But you are not T.S. Eliot. He can step into another world and pretend to be in that world. You can't do it. You don't have a visitor's permit!"

I feel a prickle of excitement.

He is not gone yet.

His words are like little tugboats, pulling me along upriver with him.

ROMANTIC HANKOU

I come to the hospital lugging books, photos, maps, videos, hoping to resurrect whatever traces of the past are left in my father. I drop names—the head of a department, a city gate—trying to determine whether the carefully wrought meanings I have arrived at line up with his experiences. Occasionally, a glimmer of recognition lights his face, but what seems clear one day turns cloudy the next. Each time I show him the photo of the bodies on the steps, he looks as if seeing it for the first time. Mostly he just shakes his head when presented with these historical artifacts.

Still, he seems to look forward to my visits. What I will bring him, where I will take him. He is curious about what I am writing and asks me to read my stories to him. He is mesmerized by my voice speaking his life backwards to him. He recognizes himself in my stories, but is confused by his proximity to history.

All this time, he tells me, he never thought to ask what he was being recruited for.

"Some of this is not in my favor," he says.

It was the wireless shortwave radio that first seduced him. An American-made AN/PRC-1 model tucked into a small leather suitcase that could be easily carried to the front and back (if one made it back). Compact and quick to travel, just like him. Intelligence on the go. The leather case had a rich, redolent scent, and the well-oiled brass latches released with just the right amount of pressure from his thumbs, sending a shudder of delight through him each time he opened them. Inside the case, soft leather straps held a set of headphones and a black and chrome machine with silver knobs that his fingers quickly learned to fine-tune in synchrony with the sound pulsing through the headset. He plugged himself in and sat perfectly still, thumb and forefinger making barely percep-tible turns of the dial, waiting and listening until the sounds took the form that his ear had been trained to hear. The long and the short waves beating like an arrhythmic heart.

/ Dah-dit-dit-dah-dah-dah / Dah-dit-dah-dah-dah-dah-dah-dit-dit-dah / Dit-dah-dit-dit-dah-dah-dah-dit-dit-dit-dah-dit / Dah-dah-dit? /
/ Do you love me? /

He played this game with her at the training camp whenev-
er they were lucky enough to be paired up. Though there were
a hundred students in his group, he'd noticed her immediate-
ly that first day when they lined up in front of the gymnasium
for morning exercises. Any trepidation he might have felt on
the boat was quickly supplanted by the thrill of finding him-
self on a university campus surrounded by buildings of such
grand geometry that he couldn't help but feel hopeful.

This was the backdrop against which he first saw her,
a tall girl with a peach-shaped face, clearly a Northerner,
standing with her heels together, hands on hips, back arched,
eyes closed, and nose upturned to the winter sun with a look
of beautiful contempt on her mouth. She wore her uniform
tightly belted around her waist and her cloth leggings so
closely wrapped around her calves that, from a distance, it
looked as if she were wearing stockings.

"We must beautify ourselves in order to beautify the coun-
try," she retorted when he teased her about her vanity. "And
what about you, pretty boy? Do you part and oil your hair

before going to bed?"

He had met his match in her.

During the days, they marched through the streets singing their youthful optimism to the throngs of refugees pouring into the city:

Revolutionary youth, quickly prepare,
Be wise, humane, and brave!
Grasp the pulse of this stage.
Stand before this great age.

Wang Kun didn't care much for the lyrics, but he liked the rousing German tune as it accompanied their goose-steps up and down the streets of Hankow. As the leader of their group, it was his job to keep them moving, and he made it a point to march alongside her row, calling out commands and showing

off his studied northern pronunciation.

Six months later, she would be sent to the front and he to Chungking, where he would spend many long nights caressing those radio dials, trying to find her out there. The radio would be his first modern lover, arousing him at night with secrets whispered in his ear.

/ Hankow has fallen /
/ Changsha has been burned to the ground /
/ The Japanese will begin bombing Chungking as soon as the winter fog lifts /
/ Be prepared /
/ Do you miss me? /

Romantic Hankou.

That's what one historian called the city, devoting an entire book to a year in its life: 1938. That was the year my father arrived in Hankou, still wearing his boy scout shorts. The same year that Hankou became a mecca for an international, left-leaning set of journalists and filmmakers, poets and novelists from all over Europe and the U.S. Hot off the tail of one war of resistance and into another. Looking for history. Looking for heroes. Looking to tell a love story about a last united stand against fascism. Even Hemingway was in Hankou, I am surprised to discover.

But by October of that year, the Japanese had taken the city, and the foreigners had fled, leaving behind a trail of mostly Chinese bodies as well as widows, orphans, and refugees.

They also left behind a trove of images, prose, and verse. The historian is trying to understand what the romance was all about. I am trying to understand what my father was doing there at the center of this world stage.

When I find the photographs taken by a Jewish refugee from Hungary with a Hollywood name, a door opens onto that stage. I walk through and into a parade of people: soldiers, boy scouts, politicians, children in long, padded gowns waving flags with the 12-point star or banners that declare "Never Die!"—all come to celebrate the first anniversary of the Anti-Japanese War. Then I'm in the inner sanctum of the war council, walls and tables papered with oversized maps, Nationalists and Communists sitting together with shaved heads and contemplative faces, monk-like in their mutual resolve. Then I'm back on the street as men hang out of windows or stand craning their necks to witness the air battle above the city, mouths agape as if watching a sporting event, the sun and leaves forming an illusory canopy above them.

The black-and-white images arouse my imagination, filling in holes in my father's stories.

How to march like a Chinese boy scout.

How to tell the difference between left and right.

What to do when the siren sounds.

How to balance on top of a moving train.

I search each image, certain that I will find my father there at the edge of the frame, leaning in with a grin on his face, hamming it up for the photographer. Knowing that these photographs were taken by foreign journalists on assignment in China only heightens their power over me. After all, that foreign gaze was the lens through which my father viewed the world—and himself.

Look, there he is on the street as the bombs begin to fall.

And there, caught in the crush of the crowd.

And there, waiting to board the train that will bear him safely into the interior.

When I show the photographs to my father, he immediately recognizes the Generalissimo and the First Lady but is nonplussed by the street scenes.

""Who took these pictures?" he asks suspiciously.

He is duly impressed when I tell him that some were published in *Life Magazine*. He asks for his glasses, though they do little to correct his cataract-clouded eyes, and holds each image up close to study it.

"When was I in Hankou?" he asks me.

He remembers marching every day, but cannot recall where he marched or lived or slept or ate.

He remembers the teacher sitting at the front of the classroom tapping out codes, the dit-dit-dah-dah-dah pulsing in his ear.

"They watch us to see if we are loyal."

"How could they tell if you were loyal?"

"Because I know Luomin."

He cannot recall a freak snowstorm in March, but re-members the hot summer night he was sworn in.

"We know at that moment we are joining the secret service."
"You knew? And you didn't mind?"
"It is considered an honor."
He lingers over the photograph of the women soldiers.

"There are only one or two women in my group," he says slowly, memory flooding his eyes. "I am the duizhang, the leader. I give the marching orders: 'yi, er, san, si!' I holler different words. She is marching in my group. I was madly in love with her. Finally she was sent to the front, back to her hometown. I still remember the night before she left. I go to her place. I can't think what to give her, so I unwrap the gold watch from my wrist, the watch I got when I was a boy scout in America, and I give it to her."

"Did you ever hear from her again?" I ask, though he has told me the story of the night he found her out there on the airwaves many times.

But today he is not so sure. Sometimes the signal was strong, sometimes weak, depending on the weather. Perhaps he had only dreamed it?

Upon his arrival at the training camp, Wang Kun was assigned to take classes in cryptology, photography, and driving, as well as a required course called "Elementary Knowledge for Special Services Work."

"What does that mean?" he asked Luomin.

"It means," Luomin chose his words carefully, "you will be trained in the latest technology for gathering and transmitting information. It means you will learn state-of-the-art communications technology."

And that was how the seduction began. With radios, cameras, and cars. His hands would not so much as touch an exploding pencil. Luomin would make sure of that.

"State of the art!"

I could hear the pride in my father's voice when he

showed me the camera. "This is what all the big press reporters carried with them, you know, those big shot *New York Times* guys. I was just small potato, but I had my own Speed Graphic."

In the middle of one of our early interviews, before his fall, he'd gotten up and gone rooting around in his study until he found it. The Speed Graphic. He opened the case with great care and lifted the camera out.

"This is how the professionals do it."

He demonstrated the proper way to hold the camera, gripping the handle with his left hand and popping the flash in my face.

"Gotcha!" he laughed as I blinked. "All famous photographs of this century were taken with Speed Graphic. Hindenburg. Iwo Jima. I even took a picture of President Eisenhower at his inauguration with this camera. Now that was a big assignment!"

I was always surprised by his stories of brushes with greatness. The way he talked, it seemed as if he'd had a close encounter with nearly all the world leaders of the 20th century. When I was in high school and nearly failing Social Studies, he'd saved me more than once by staying up late with me and turning a list of arbitrary dates and names to be memorized into gripping accounts of the Bataan Death March, the Suez Canal Crisis, the Gulf of Tonkin Incident. He could talk about McCarthyism and the Cuban Missile Crisis and Watergate as if he'd witnessed each first-hand.

Now, watching him sleep, his hands twisting the bed sheets, I wonder whether back then my father was trying to tell me something more than what I needed to know to pass a test.

Daming Temple sat on a bluff overlooking the river. Villag-
ers came daily to the temple to burn incense, lay fruit, suppli-
cate themselves before the statues of various deities, the fierce
and the compassionate as needed. The fruit piled up brown
and desiccated among the ashes on the altar tables. Ash was
everywhere. It kicked up under the feet of the recruits and
stuck in their throats, causing them to cough as they stepped
over the gate and filed silently into the Great Hall. Dark green
lanterns had been hung to light their way, casting a demon-
ic glow over the relief-carved faces of the 18 bodhisattvas
that lined the hall, benevolent witnesses to this midnight
ceremony. At the front altar, a portrait of the Generalissimo
was mounted in the place where the Shakyamuni Buddha
should have sat. Or maybe the Buddha was still there, and the
Generalissimo was sitting on its lap. In this light, Wang Kun's
eyes played tricks on him.

Standing in front of the altar were three men. Luomin was
nearly unrecognizable, wearing a mask of a face that Wang
Kun had never seen before. The training camp director was

there, looking oily and arrogant as always. And a man whom Wang Kun didn't recognize but would not forget after that night. This man was the shortest of the three, solidly built, with a neck like a horse. He had a wide nose with flaring nostrils, steely eyes set unnaturally far apart, and a grim determined mouth. When he opened it and began to speak, his mouth was full of gold. His voice was coarse and sugary. His words were all praise and welcome for them.

"You are the first class of recruits for the Bureau of Investigation and Statistics. This work is not for ordinary people. Each of you has been selected for your high cultural levels and your special talents. You will serve the Generalissimo and your country."

A cock appeared on the altar table, a beautiful brindle with flecks of orange in its feathers and a crown and waddle of brilliant red. It strutted across the table, jabbing its head this way and that as if trying to figure out who was responsible for its predicament. The man with the mouth of gold reached for the cock and stroked it, all the while making soothing little clucking sounds. The cock arched its back with obvious pleasure and allowed the man to wrap surprisingly delicate fingers around its lovely neck. Still clucking softly, the man raised a sword that had magically appeared in his left hand and severed the cock's head from its body in one smooth stroke. The cock's head fell on to the altar table, a look of

*astonishment frozen on its face. Blood spurted from the cock's
neck, still held tenderly in those feminine hands, and Luomin
was there to catch it in a hollowed-out gourd.*

*Luomin signaled for the inductees to form a line in front of
the altar. One by one they stepped forward to take the gourd
and drink the freshly spilled blood, which had been sweetened
with plum wine. "Don't breathe when you drink," she whispered as she returned from the table, lips glistening, cheeks
flushed. When it was Wang Kun's turn, he held his breath and
managed not to gag as the warm, viscous substance passed
down his throat. He returned the gourd to its master, seeing
the look of approval in the man's wide-set eyes. But it was
the man's neck that fascinated him, so thick and sinewy.
He couldn't help but wonder how hard it would be to pass a
blade through that neck. A wave of nausea suddenly over-
came him. Still holding his breath, he quickly returned to the
anonymity of the line.*

As the newly inducted members of the Bureau of Investigation and Statistics pledged their allegiance, Wang Kun tried to breathe deeply and forget the sweet and salty taste of the blood. He was confused by the feelings that this man and this ceremony had stirred in him. Pride. Revulsion. And something else. He felt as if a chain had been slipped over his head, a chain made entirely of silk knots so soft and so light that it would be easy to forget it was there. He must take care not to move too fast or too far in any one direction. He loosened his collar, fighting the urge to run.

Trying to get his bearings, he looked at her. She was glowing in the green light with a radiance that Wang Kun wished had been reserved for him.

He looked at Luomin. The mask had fallen slightly and Wang Kun was relieved to see his friend looking back at him with expectant eyes.

THE REVERSALS
YOU LIVE WITH

Lunar New Year's Eve.

I wheel my father through the hospital hallways, empty now except for the night-shift nurses and those few family members who do not dare leave. A small paper lantern hangs from the IV pole attached to his wheelchair. My brother walks in front of us, rolling a pellet drum between the palms of his hands, the steady beating of the wooden pellets on the membranes of the two-faced drum bouncing off the walls like popcorn. My mother follows, smiling and nodding and offering candy to those who turn to watch this impromptu parade. My father has a dazed look on his face, the corners of his mouth twisted upwards in a grin or a grimace, I can't tell which, as if he knows he's supposed to be happy but can't remember why.

Earlier that evening, he had poked suspiciously at the pork dumplings I'd made, seeming to recognize their shape but refusing to put them in his mouth.

"You made these?" he asked.

"Yes, Dad, for the Chinese New Year."

He nodded knowingly, but a minute later was asking again: "You made these?"

The book on head injuries I was reading advised that

when a person starts going in circles, it's best to redirect or ignore him. But it was impossible to do either with my father. No matter the nonsense he spoke, it was impossible to treat him as if his brain were injured. When he posed questions like this, I was a child all over again being asked to explain herself.

"You made these?"

Where was the emphasis of his question? Was he doubting my ability to cook Chinese food, commenting on my foreignness, as he always did with my mother? Or was he expressing his surprise over the fact that they were home-made dumplings rather than the store-bought variety that usually filled our freezer? Or was he worried that someone else had made them and, perhaps, had used bad ingredients or even poisoned them?

"Yes, Dad, I made them myself, with my own hands, in my own kitchen, and brought them directly to the hospital for you."

But he still refused to eat them. The association of the dumplings with the Lunar New Year, with lanterns and noisemakers to scare away evil spirits, with all the elaborate stories he used to spin for his American audiences and the equally elaborate parties and performances our family had given over the years—all these associations were broken for him now, I realized. The dumplings were free-floating in a soupy concoction in which Past, Present, and Future were indistinguishable. They were potentially dangerous, as likely to be made of human flesh as of pork.

"You made these?"

I go back to the condo looking for pieces of the past to

jog my father's memory. Going through his files in the basement, I find pages and pages of yellowed newspaper clippings, all about my father and our family. As if we had been some kind of celebrities in the town.

In one piece, my father is interviewed about his escape from China. In this version, he dressed up as a coolie in order to cross a bridge to get to Hong Kong, fooling the border guards who thought him just another laborer.

In another piece, a colleague at the newspaper recounts how my father fled China "one chop ahead of the executioner's axe" and wangled his way into America with his "high-pitched laugh," his "funny talk," and his "nose for news."

In yet another clipping, my father write about his naturalization ceremony, describing his feelings upon leaving the courthouse: "I felt lighter, the grass looked greener, even the sun appeared brighter. I felt like a lost child who had suddenly found his home." He contrasted his newfound freedom with "the less fortunate millions who suffer behind the Bamboo Curtain." "I have hopes and make my own plans for life," he wrote. "They are slaves at the mercy of the Red Master. They are cogs in a giant machine, assigned to labor until death."

The same familiar embellishments.

The same glaring omissions.

And then I find the photograph.

The caption reads: "Don't let them get deeper." The accompanying article is about the shortage of revenue for road maintenance in a town in Pennsylvania I've never heard of. There's no mention of my father. The clipping is from a publication bearing the innocuous name, *Country Expressions*. How did my father's head end up in a pothole on a country road in a small-town rag in Pennsylvania?

It takes me a full minute to see the obvious. Even though I know as well as anyone born and raised in the U.S. on a steady diet of Saturday morning cartoons: If you just dig deep enough, you'll eventually get to China.

Of course he'd probably cooked up that photo himself, most likely with the help of one of his sidekicks at the paper. He was always pulling these kinds of gags.

I never saw him play the Chinaman role so shamelessly as that Fourth of July when he was growing that awful bicentennial beard. I remember one night that summer when we'd gone out to eat, as we so often did, my father telling the waitresses in the restaurant that he was an emperor and demanding that they bow to him. One waitress got down on her hands and knees and touched her forehead to the floor. "Three times!" he commanded, stroking his beard, "and you'll get a bigger tip!" He introduced my mother as his Number One Concubine and my brother and I as his Number One Son and Number One Daughter. My mother had smiled dutifully and bowed her head, but my brother and I dropped our forks on the floor and slid under the table, refusing to come out until the waitress was gone.

At the local high school where my father taught journalism, there were more opportunities to play the game.

Even if I didn't want to, I had to play along. In one photo, I stand holding court between two robed students, my hands laced guardedly in front of me and my eyes fixed warily on the pale-skinned boy in the silk cap with the sardonic grin.

My father's familiar script hangs in the background of these photos, the same eight characters over and over, offering salutations for the new year again and again for the benefit of the town. For the benefit of the town. I can't remember a single Lunar New Year that was just for our family.

In those days, even as our family publicly performed the obligatory Chinese holidays, we privately celebrated Thanksgiving, Christmas, Easter, and the Fourth of July with all the trimmings and trappings. We would dress up and go to church on Christmas Eve and Easter morning, sing carols, and take communion, even though my father had declared himself a devout atheist. My mother cooked reluctantly on these occasions, roasting turkey and mashing potatoes despite the fact that my father dismissed such food as tasteless. Yet he could always be counted on to make a good show of carving the bird, and he talked as if he had been raised on gravy. "I'm a gravy man!" he would howl as he poured my mother's lumpy brown sauce over everything on his plate. Each Christmas, he would insist on cutting down a tree himself and was determined to string up more lights than any other house on the block. Inside, he would hang every Christmas card received until the living and dining rooms were joined together in an elaborate string maze. On Easter, there were live bunnies and chicks, and on the Fourth, he would don a chef's hat and flip burgers and dogs as if he'd been doing it his whole life.

I remember one Christmas Eve when my father took his holiday decorating to new heights. That year he'd conquered his fear of the ladder and had strung colored lights around the entire perimeter of the bungalow: every window and doorframe, the porch and roof, and even the mailbox. After the Christmas Eve church service, as we made our annual rounds of the neighborhood, my father was ecstatic to see that his lights were indeed the most impressive.

"Look," he picked me up and held me in the middle of the dark street, "see how big our house looks compared to the others. Our house looks like a palace!"

"I can see my room!" I cried with delight. "My room is at the top of the palace!"

When we came back inside, he put on a Santa hat and, humming "We Wish You a Merry Christmas" over and over in his slightly off-pitch register, hung the last of the cards received that day.

That night I lay awake in bed until my parents had finished carting out the gifts and wrapping them up and piling them under the tree. When the only sound that drifted up into my attic room was the whir of hot air blowing through the register, I stole downstairs to find my father sitting alone amidst his labyrinth of lights and cards. He was rocking back and forth in his armchair, though it was not a rocker. He was still wearing the Santa hat, and at first I thought he knew I was there. I waited for him to turn, laughing, and say, "Ho, ho, ho, you don't still believe, do you?" But he continued to rock silently. In the glow of the blinking lights, I saw that beneath the hat his face was contorted—in pain or rage? I couldn't tell. And this uncertainty kept me from going to him.

I thought I'd seen that face before, the time I'd been woken in the night, not by the scent of sausages, but by the squeals rising through the register from my parent's bedroom below. I had run downstairs and, without thinking, thrown myself in front of my mother's body. In the morning, I thought I'd dreamed it all.

But here was that face again. The colored lights were playing a game with that face, morphing blue-green pain into orange rage and back again. His mouth was clenched tightly shut in a grim line, and I thought I could hear his off-pitch humming following me as I crept back upstairs to my room at the top of the palace.

There are no newspaper clippings or photographs, but I remember Halloween in kindergarten as clearly as if there had been a visual record of it.

I am dressed as a clown for a school party. I wear a one-piece purple jumpsuit with a bright red sash and a ruffled collar and cuffs. My mother paints my face white with a wide, cherry-red smile. Looking in the mirror, I am startled to see my own anxious eyes peering out from behind the clown's garish face.

At the bus stop, my mother holds my hand tightly as if afraid I might bolt. As soon as I spot the yellow bus coming down the street, a familiar spidery feeling begins to creep up from the hollow of my stomach. I pin my lips together and steal a glance at my mother, whose face is already preparing to meet the bus.

"Mom," I groan.

"What's wrong?" My mother drops to one knee and her hand flies to my forehead.

"I think I'm gonna be sick."

"Oh no, not again." My mother's eyes flit frantically between the approaching bus and the little girl in the clown suit.

And then the bus is there.

I feel the blast of hot air as the door springs open and hear the bus driver call out jovially, "Bozo!"

I feel the press of my mother's hand at the small of my back. The faces at the windows. The buzzing in my ears.

I remember the vomit steaming on the sidewalk in the cold morning air. The bus driver's sympathetic murmurs. My mother's mortified smile. The mocking eyes at the back of the bus as it drove away without me.

When I check this memory against my mother's, she insists that I got on the bus that morning and went to school.

It could happen at any time in any place without any

provocation.

I might be sitting in class and glance up at the clock on the wall to see what time it was. Suddenly I would be acutely aware of the buzz of the fluorescent lights. The flow of air in and out of my lungs. Blood pumping through veins. Without moving my head, I could sense the entire room revolving around me as if through a 360-degree fish-eye lens—the rows of wooden desks, my classmates shifting in their seats, the world maps hanging precariously on the walls. Panic rising, I would try to calm myself by focusing on my hands, only to find that I did not recognize them. Pure unrelenting existence overwhelmed me at those moments. And the inexorable knowledge of my own certain death.

The only way to break the spell was to pinch myself hard or to cough loudly or to suddenly change position. Or, if no one was around, to shout a word, any word.

"Eraser!"

When I was in the company of others, I tried not to let on that anything out of the ordinary was happening. She has nervous energy, my teachers used to say about my sudden need to jump up and walk around the room. In primary school, they tried to be accommodating. By high school, I was doing detention.

I never spoke about these episodes with anyone. I didn't know whether such things happened to other people, and I didn't ask. I kept to myself the certain knowledge that, at any moment, the world could dissolve into light and sound, blood and breath. That one's hands could become strangers to oneself. That the truth of a hand or a clock or a person could be hiding behind its appearance, which was only a diversion. I knew all this intuitively, corporeally, yet still longed to be so diverted by something or someone that I might not even notice the next time the world dissolved around me.

INTO THE INTERIOR

In the rehab hospital, my father is leaking history.
He's just finished another round of testing.

What year is this? Who is the President of the United
States? What's 5 × 7? Kitten is to cat, as calf is to what?

The same ridiculous questions he was asked yesterday
by the same baby-face in a white lab coat with the same
humiliating results.

"Who does that guy think he is?" my father grumbles as I wheel him back to his room.

"Never mind him." I am eager to talk to my father about what he can remember. As the blood slowly dissipates from his brain, words tumble from his mouth. "Tell me about Chongqing," I ask.

"Oooh," he groans and rubs his chest, "why do you want to talk about that? Such a dirty, dirty city."

"What did you do there?"

"I work for the Chinese FBI," he blurts out. "There are two branches, military and civil, jun tong and min tong. I am min tong, the civil branch... no, jun tong... min tong, jun tong, which is it?"

He closes his eyes, muttering in Chinese to himself. Just when I think he has fallen asleep, his eyes snap open and he hisses, "Have you heard of Dai Li?" He looks around the room, then leans forward in the bed. "I operate secret radio stations," he whispers. "I am so good at it, I become part of the inner circle. Such a dirty, dirty job, but I survived." He falls back on the pillow and closes his eyes again.

As I am leaving the room, I hear him chuckle and say, "I don't think you can find another one like me, so American but still so Chinese." When I look back, he appears to be sleeping.

Chungking during the war was center stage of the China Theatre. All variety of drama—farce, tragedy, tragic farce, theatre of the cruel, theatre of the absurd—would be performed there by the World's Greatest Players.

By the Fall of 1938, they had all arrived. The Generalissimo with his gold-mouthed Spymaster and their invisible

Blue-Shirted Men who could do the neat trick of making someone disappear from a crowded street and turn up in pieces in a suitcase on a railroad platform miles away. The Communists masquerading as everyone else, shading into the city's notorious alleyways, folding into every office corner and teahouse recess. The Americans with their hard-headed generals and their many-headed politicians and their intelligence-gathering academics working the backstage. And all the rest who made their way westward through the Three Gorges' perilous straits: students, farmers, bankers, peddlers, whole schools and factories, families that had been broken down and moved upriver. All seeking sanctuary and opportunity on the hastily built set of Free China.

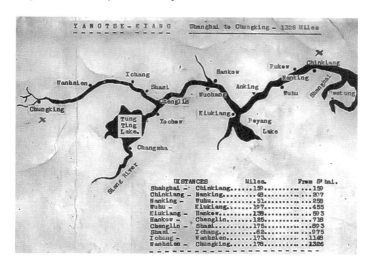

Wang Kun had arrived too. He had a bit part but, as always, was ready to improvise.

No matter how I pose the question, my father cannot tell me how he got from Hankou to Chongqing, oblivious to the fact that he was part of one of humankind's greatest mass migrations. When he awakens in his hospital bed, he is always already in Chongqing, his boy scout shorts exchanged for the cloth leggings of the Guomindang soldier.

So I have to imagine his arrival for myself: *the great walled city of Chungking rising up out of the mist to greet Wang Kun as he emerged from the smallest yet most violent of the Three Gorges. Never had he been so certain of his impending death. Death by water!* (My father would carry this fear with him to the end of his life). *Never had he felt so buoyant, so exhilarated by his own daring. The ecstasy of survival!* (He would carry this, too, as far as he could).

Ironically, an old novel in which the narrator is an ambitious American engineer traveling upriver in the 1920s in search of a dam site helps me to reconstruct my father's journey. The narrator's spare yet vivid descriptions of the wild river landscape ring true: the towering limestone cliffs and the gigantic granite rocks strewn carelessly in the waters, the furious currents and the frenzied rapids and the whirling, mesmerizing eddies that threaten to pull you in. I am pulled in and along by the narrator's animated account of the junk, its owner, his wife, the cook, and the indefatigable trackers who lean into their harnesses, towing the lot of them upriver along paths hand-cut into the face of cliffs with names like Ox-Liver Horse-Lungs and Wind-Box Gorge. I approve of the narrator's admission of his smallness in the face of this Sisyphean terrain, the way his American largesse is progressively diminished by his journey into the interior of China.

But it is the book's caricature of the Chinese, with their shiny heads and their wispy beards, their unhurried movements and their infuriating cheerfulness, that hits closest to home.

Waves of recognition assail me as I read the narrator's depiction of the head tracker:

> At the time I wanted to believe him, and mostly did, though I thought him full of guile; in my Occidental complacency, I then considered all Chinese liars anyhow. I guess I wanted to believe that he was a simple good man, but I was troubled by his obvious inner enjoyment of his account of himself; from time to time he had pursed his lips, so that his face had looked shrewd, as if he had been saying to himself, "I am the grandest liar in the world, and see how I have this stupid foreign boy on my tow-line!"

Reading this passage is like standing in a hall of mirrors. Who is laughing at whom? I see the snickering white faces. I see my father looking so pleased with himself. And I see myself, stupid foreign girl, refracted in the farcical light of this funhouse, trying to find my way out.

I run along the riverbank, tracking my father upstream through the steep, narrow gorges to the place where the rivers violently converge.

"Stay in the main stream!" he calls back. "Don't go against the current!"

He doesn't leave footprints. He doesn't always wait for me. Sometimes he forgets I'm there, rushing ahead, then backtracking, getting me so turned around that I don't know what direction he's taking me in.

I look for the rocky peninsula I know must be there but cannot see through the thick fog that has descended. I hear the grunts and calls of the trackers towing their skiffs through the churning waters. A relentless drumbeat accompanies their wretched song. And in the background, the drone of approaching planes.

My body tenses. I know this place. The fog that drips for six months of the year. The vulgar sound of mud sucking at feet. The sharp bite of sulfur on the tongue.

Hongzha Chongqing.

It was the third of May and there was a lunar eclipse— this much is indisputable. When the bombs started to fall, my father was likely in his post outside the city on Gele Mountain, where the Bureau had set up their telecommunications department and where, thanks to Luomin, he had been assigned along with forty others. The Fourth Department, he called it, and the books confirm this. Probably the most important department in the Bureau, in charge of monitoring all communications in and out of Chongqing.

They worked at night when the radio reception was better, so he was probably wide awake when he heard the planes. He must have known they were coming. Maybe he'd just received a warning message.

/ *The Japanese have taken off from Hankow* /
/ *The 8th Route Army is on the move* /
/ *There are Communist spies in the Fourth Department* /

"But I never know what I am receiving," my father insists. Just sounds. That his ear learned to detect and his hand to transcribe. Before turning it over to someone else to decode. He was just a small potato after all.

I imagine this small potato in his outpost on the steamy hillside. A skinny boy in a sleeveless white undershirt (the kind he wore until they were threadbare, the kind he is wearing at this very moment), earphones riding jauntily on his head, a fountain pen clenched in one hand and a sweat rag in the other, methodically transcribing each "dah" and "dit," watching the smoke rise over the city and waiting once again to make his move.

But I get stuck on this detail: What form did the sounds take on the page? Letters or numbers? English alphabet or Chinese character?

"San-wu-ba." He drops the number casually into our conversation.

Incredibly, on the website of a mathematician whose hobby is cryptography, I find and download the entire Chinese Telegraph Codebook. Each four-digit code corresponds to a Chinese character. Some of the codes are missing, but there are six that begin with that number.

> 3580: Iron
> 3581: Boil
> 3583: Hot
> 3584: Sparkling
> 3588: Break of day
> 3589: Flaming

A fire radical burns in each: 火

When I show my father the codebook, he just shrugs. "Not my job," he says.

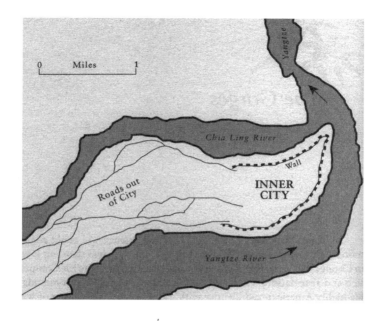

From the rocky ledge, Wang Kun could see the point where
the rivers came together, the city sticking out like a thirsty
tongue into the dirty brown waters. He took a swig from his
canteen and passed it to Luomin. They had hiked all afternoon for this view, Luomin finally giving in to Wang Kun's
plea to see what the city looked like from above. He needed
to see his surroundings from on high—to know the lay of the
land and which way the rivers and roads ran, where the walls
stood and the gates opened—before he could sleep at night.
Ever since their arrival in Chungking, he and Luomin had
been hiking the hills nearly every day, but the fog had hidden
the views from them. Now, after months of being socked in,

his eyes ached and his legs trembled as he took in the vistas. His legs always betrayed him. Though he would never admit it, he was afraid of heights even as he sought them out.

"The city looks almost beautiful from up here," he declared loudly in an effort to steady himself.

"Yeah, you can't see even one of the millions of rats that make their home in Chungking."

Wang Kun looked at his friend in alarm. At the training camp, Luomin had been known for his almost religious rants on hygiene and sanitation. Wang Kun and the other recruits had learned to keep their fingernails free of dirt not just for Luomin's sake, but because he had convinced them that personal hygiene was one of the pillars on which a new China would be built. Since their assignment to the Fourth Department, however, Wang Kun had observed a change in his friend, a finger of sarcasm that crept into Luomin's voice whenever he came to inspect their quarters or lecture them on what it meant to have a "thoroughly awakened conscience."

"It means having a sense of shame!" Luomin had barked at them that very morning as they lined up in front of their bunks.

Now Wang Kun probed his friend cautiously. "What about the campaign to catch rats, you know, two fen per dead rat? I heard the rat population has already been greatly reduced."

"And I heard the locals are now raising rats as a source of income!" Luomin came back. His laughter was genuine, and Wang Kun joined in, relieved that they could still joke about such things.

The late afternoon sun turned their faces a deeper shade of crimson. Feeling the heat, Luomin pulled off his shirt and Wang Kun followed suit. They stretched their smooth, hairless arms out at their sides, admiring their new color, the expansiveness of their limbs. On this rocky rise, they turned into boys running and leaping, then into birds soaring. Then back into men as they descended into the darkening valley.

"Among such as these I cannot hope for friends..." Wang Kun recited as they started back down the mountain, initiating one of their favorite word games.

Luomin was but a step behind him. "...and am pleased with anyone who is even remotely human."

When my father closes his eyes, this scene plays over and over across his inner lids:

He is with Luomin in downtown Chongqing. They have come into the city for some fun. The air-raid sirens have been silent for weeks and even Luomin is upbeat. He throws an arm across his friend's shoulders and they saunter down the crowded street. They nearly fall into an open sewer and jump back laughing, colliding with a woman in a calf-length gown and high heels, a package clutched under one arm and a small boy trailing reluctantly behind her.

Now the package has fallen into the sewer, the woman is fuming, the boy begins to cry.

Now Luomin is dropping to one knee, he is scooping up the package and wiping it on his trousers, he is making an offering.

Now the boy is curious, he is peering from behind the woman, she is trying not to smile as she pushes him forward to take the package.

Now the sirens are sounding, the boy is covering his ears, the package lies forgotten on the ground.

Now they are running for the city gate.

Now they are running for the tunnel.

The woman is calling to the boy.

The boy has fallen on the steps.

Someone is wailing like a siren.

Someone is flying up to the sun.

Someone is falling naked to the earth.

The smell of excrement.

The taste of sulphur.

The burning of flesh.

Who is crawling at his feet.

Who is reaching for her hand.

Her knee between his legs.

His arm across her chest.

They sprawl like lovers in perfect rest.

But these are not my father's eyelids, they are mine.

No matter how many times I've seen the photograph of the bodies on the steps, I look as if seeing it for the first time. The photo's impossibly random detail—the couple's embrace, the child's outstretched arm, the turn of the man's muscled calf, the arch of the baby's back—summons me, commands me to tell a story.

Never mind that this is not my father's story.

Never mind that I know these people did not die on the steps, frozen in a flash of fire. Nor did they fall from the sky, limbs unfurled, in postures of perfect repose. They perished only after long hours of trampling and clawing and suffocating in the Great Tunnel, locked inside the very shelter that had been built to protect them.

Someone had to lay those bodies there.

Someone had to carry those 992 bodies from the tunnel and lay them out one by one on the 18 steps leading down to the Heavenly Gate, perhaps positioning a limb or turning a head.

If, like me, you compare this photo with others taken that day, you will see the piles of bodies rise and fall. And if you study the photos carefully, as I have, you will notice how some bodies have been moved or turned or repositioned. Whether in an effort to make room for more, or to make it easier to identify a loved one, or out of sheer weariness of the task at hand. Or perhaps, just to get the perfect shot.

Yet, even knowing all this, I cannot shake the photo's power over me. In this single recurring image, the fates of my father and Luomin and the woman and the boy become one.

When my father mentions the wall, I simply fold it along with the photograph into the story.

Now the sirens are sounding.

Now he and Luomin are running for the river.

Now they are hiding behind the wall.

Now they watch from the wall as the bodies are pulled from the tunnel and laid to rest upon the steps.

I dream I am going through customs.

The man in uniform behind the desk is not your typical stony-faced airport security officer. This man is friendly, charming, interested in me. Why have you come? How long will you stay? Do you need a guide? He checks my papers, looking me up and down against my passport photo. Satisfied, he invites me in, welcomes me with an embrace. He takes me by the hand and walks me through the security gate without stopping, waving at the guards.

We walk together down a long hallway, mirrored doors on either side. At the end of the hallway is a curtain. He pulls the curtain aside, and I step through to a breathtaking view.

We are standing on a precipice looking down into a lush valley. He takes a handkerchief out of his pocket and shakes it out until it is as large as a blanket, then spreads it on the ground. We sit and watch the sky turn orange, then crimson. I turn to him and suddenly realize who he is.

"Luomin," I say, "you look just like my father when he was young."

"How do you know?" He laughs at me, not unkindly.

"I've seen the photograph."

"There is no photograph." He is serious now.

"There is," I insist, "I've seen it in my father's study."

"There is no photograph," he says again. "We did not have a camera."

"Then who took it?"

He does not answer.

I am confused. I remember a tiny black-and-white contact print of a man in a white collared shirt rowing a boat, but don't know now whether that was Luomin or my father or someone else.

Then he is gone, and I am descending the 18 steps. There are bodies everywhere, cell phones in hand and children in tow, all headed in the same direction. Around us, a carnival of new life blooms: hawkers hawking lychee and ice pops and brightly colored plastic toys, skyscrapers vying with mountains, legions of kites flying at the ends of strings so long it looks as if the city is tethered to the skies. A loud speaker with a resounding baritone promises longevity for this megalopolis risen from ash. As we pass under the Heavenly Gate, I hear the amplified picking of guitar strings and then the youthful warbling of a Canto-pop love song.

The stairs lead directly into the water, and I am tempted to keep going down into the churlish, muddy currents. I've heard that on some days you can witness the separation of the rivers, the blue-greens of the Jialing Jiang and the yellow-browns of the Chang Jiang pressing up against each other like two mighty solitudes. But on this day, the rivers are one, the color of weak milk coffee, lapping at my feet. I am not fooled. I know that the river is really a strong brown god. Standing on this tongue of land, I feel its draw and drag at the same time.

This is what I came for.

At the water's edge, people squat and scoop up handfuls to wash their arms or stand cooling their feet in it. Boats posing as restaurants beckon with their gaudy signage. An empty fishing net slung between bamboo poles flashes in the sun each time it breaks the water's surface.

On the bottom stair sits a skinny girl in overalls with birdlike limbs and a tangled mane of long, black hair. She is scratching herself. White flakes of skin float in the air around her. She concentrates on a patch of skin on her outer right calf, digging deeper and deeper into herself. Each time she pulls off a layer of skin, there is another little raised edge waiting to be peeled back. She can't resist that little raised edge. She digs until she bleeds, satisfied that she is getting closer to the truth.

THE TONGUE
IN THE WATER

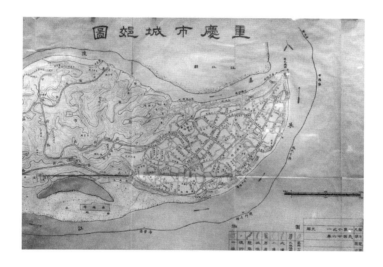

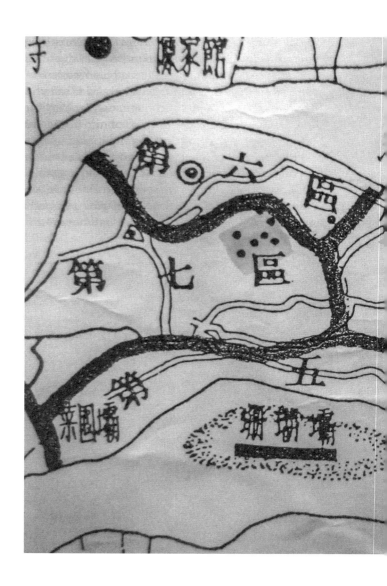

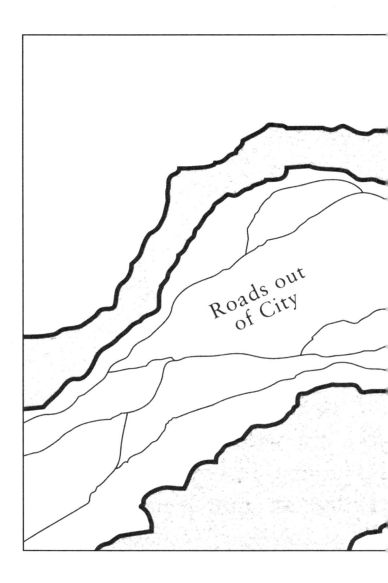

Roads out
of City

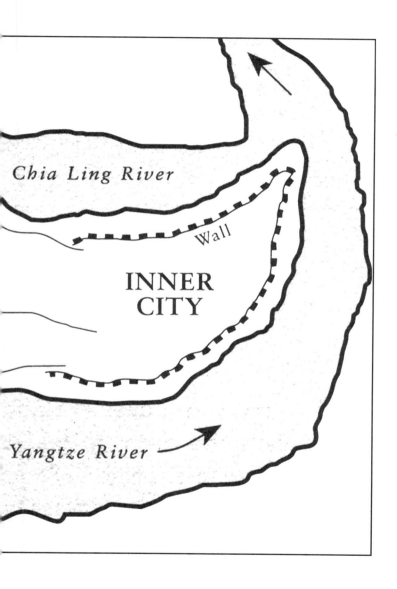

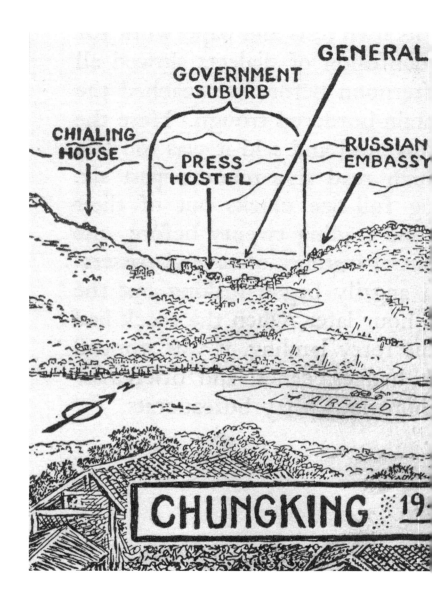

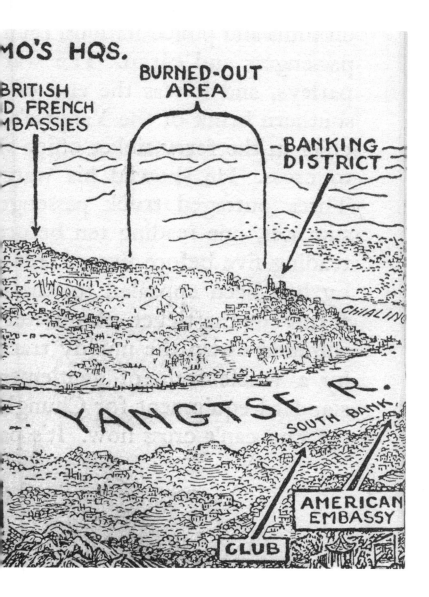

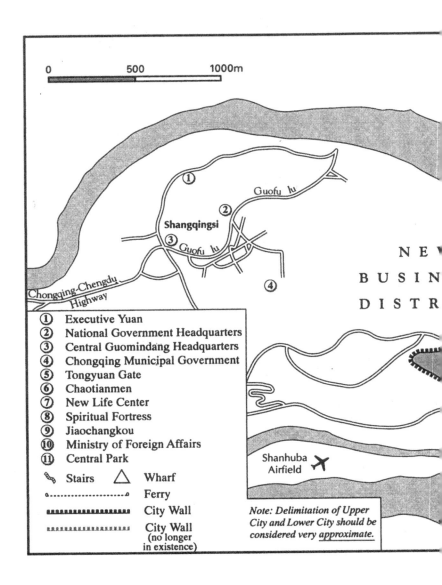

① Executive Yuan
② National Government Headquarters
③ Central Guomindang Headquarters
④ Chongqing Municipal Government
⑤ Tongyuan Gate
⑥ Chaotianmen
⑦ New Life Center
⑧ Spiritual Fortress
⑨ Jiaochangkou
⑩ Ministry of Foreign Affairs
⑪ Central Park

Stairs   △ Wharf
········· Ferry
▮▮▮▮▮▮ City Wall
▪▪▪▪▪▪ City Wall
      (no longer
      in existence)

Note: Delimitation of Upper City and Lower City should be considered very approximate.

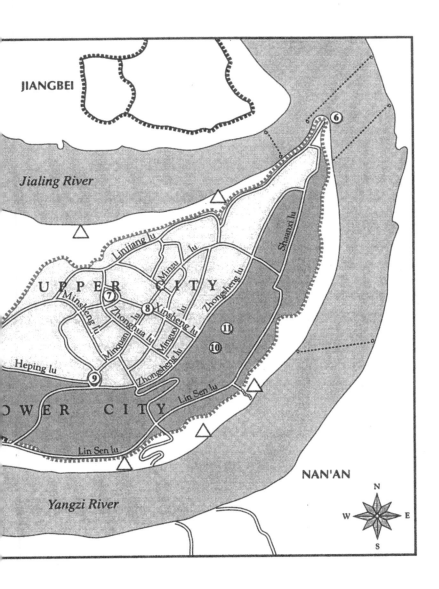

JIANGBEI

Jialing River

UPPER CITY

Linjiang lu

Minzu lu

Minsheng lu

Zhonghua lu

Yinsheng lu

Minquan lu

Minquan lu

Zhongsheng lu

Shaanxi lu

Heping lu

Zhongsheng lu

Lin Sen lu

OWER CITY

Lin Sen lu

NAN'AN

Yangzi River

N
W   E
S

THE MAVERICK

The way my father tells it, the way I try to write it, he was just an unwitting bystander. A passerby on his way to something better. Never saw a Japanese. Never knew a Communist. Never witnessed the civil and world wars that just happened to coincide with the first three decades of his life in China.

He only had eyes for the Americans.

Never sent to the front. Never touched an exploding pencil. Never was privy to the meaning of the radio messages he received or the violent ends to which they were put. And, except for that one day when he just happened to be in the city, he never saw the bloated bodies that piled up on the streets of Chongqing over three years of bombing.

Such a dirty, dirty city.

Such a dirty, dirty job.

How does a beautiful boy stay clean?

And, having gotten dirty, where does he go to get clean again?

In the winter of 1938, a lone American arrived in Chungk-ing. He was a famous cryptologist, Luomin told Wang Kun. During the first World War, he'd broken the Japanese diplo-

matic code, then pissed off the Americans by publishing the ciphers. He'd been invited to China by none other than General Tai himself. Here in Chungking, at the Bureau, he would teach a new training class called the Chinese Black Chamber.

It was Luomin's idea to assign Wang Kun to be the American's driver. Even though he knew that this position was beneath his friend and carried great risk. Wang Kun would be required to report on this man's every move: where he went, whom he talked to, what he said. Still, it was a singular opportunity to get close to an American. And it would keep Wang Kun from being sent to the front.

Three days a week, Wang Kun drove this large, effusive man from his chateau overlooking the Jialing River in the diplomatic section of the city to the Bureau headquarters just outside Tong Yuan Gate.

"Call me Harry," the American said, winking at Wang Kun.

On these drives, Harry would rant about truth serums and incendiary pencils, about how the American government didn't appreciate his special talents, about how much he missed his girlfriend, and, by the way, could Wang Kun help him to get laid? He winked and sweated and swigged from a slim glass bottle he carried in his briefcase.

"I'm a maverick," Harry said to Wang Kun. "Do you know what that is, boy?"

At first, Wang Kun thought Harry was confiding in him, but soon realized that he talked this way to everyone. Treating everyone as his personal confidante. Posing questions that he would then answer himself.

Wang Kun had never met anyone like Harry. He seemed to know no boundaries between private and public. He said whatever he liked whenever he liked without apparent con-

sequence. In Chungking, he was courted by everyone everywhere he went—most notably by the man with the gold in his mouth, whom Harry jokingly called "the Hatchet Man." Never to his face, of course, and always in English, winking at Wang Kun.

How does he do it? Wang Kun marveled.

I learn about this man whom I call Harry—who went to China under the cover of a pseudonym to work as a code-breaker for the Guomindang secret service—from the many books he wrote about his sensational life of espionage, including three memoirs and several fictions and screenplays. Harry's life, unlike my father's, seems to be an open book.

In his second memoir about his two-year stint in Chongqing, Harry lays bare his homesickness, his love of the bottle, and his contempt for his Chinese hosts. Whether servants or generals or students, the Chinese men in Harry's stories never fail to bow deeply and speak in ancient, unintelligible idioms, addressing him as "Honorable Advisor," all the while conspiring behind his back to filch his food, siphon his gas, leak his intelligence. Women—whether Chinese, Russian, or German—are portrayed as equally two-faced, though not as troublesome, appearing only as colorful accessories to Harry's intelligence work and often turning up dead at the end of a chapter.

My father makes no mention of this infamous American expatriate. When I drop his real name, my father shows not a glimmer of recognition, though they worked in the same department under the same general at the same time.

Lessons with Harry.

That's how Wang Kun came to refer to his thrice-weekly driving dates.

He had happily accepted the assignment and took each encounter as an opportunity to learn from and about this American. How to sip soup from a spoon without making a sound. How to insert his tongue between his teeth in order to pronounce words like "thirsty" and "thanks." Some of what he learned he shared with Luomin, such as when Harry told him he suspected there was a Chinese spy operating out of Chungking who was sending daily wireless messages to Hankow where the Japanese were based. Other details Wang Kun kept to himself, such as Harry's photographic memory, his preference for young girls, his fear of small, enclosed spaces.

Once, on the drive back to the chateau, Harry asked Wang

Kun to stop at the Chungking Hostel for a drink. Wang Kun knew that the hostel had a reputation for being a place where foreign men went to play poker and hook up with local women. He had always wanted to see it for himself, but had been turned away at the door the one time he had dared to venture there alone. Now, at Harry's side, Wang Kun swaggered past the doorman and felt the admiring glances of the women around the poker tables. The men all seemed to know one another, calling out, "Hey Harry, who's your China boy?" They pulled up a seat for Wang Kun and proceeded to educate him in the art of deception, conceding his relative advantage as a Chinese. They taught him how to play low ball and spit-in-the-ocean, when to call and when to bluff, and how to maintain a poker face no matter your hand. They plied him with foreign cigarettes and single-malt Scotch and ardent advice about the difference between Chinese and American pussy.

"Watch this," Harry instructed, "this is how I play Chinese poker." He sidled over to a woman in a long silk qipao standing at the bar and grabbed her buttock with his hand, winking over his shoulder at Wang Kun.

For the first time, Wang Kun felt like one of the boys.

This, too, was all part of lessons with Harry.

I try to imagine my father in Harry's world, where everyone appears as a caricature and no one is who they appear to be. I see the way Wang Kun studies Harry in the rearview mirror. The way his hungry eyes follow Harry as he wisecracks and wangles his way through some of the most powerful and dangerous circles in Chongqing.

I've seen that look in my father's eyes before, at the high school's annual New Year's Eve party, the room filled with

smoke and aftershave and once-respectable-schoolteach-
ers-turned-predators whose wanton winking and joking
frightened me as a girl. These men were hardly the power
brokers of wartime Chongqing, but I could feel their stature
grow in direct proportion to my father's diminishment.
More frightening were my father's attempts to partake in
the ribaldry, turning into a garish version of himself that I
did not recognize. As the evening wore on and my father's
face grew redder and the pitch of his laughter grew higher, I
grew more uncomfortable. I sensed rather than understood
that the jokes were at not only at his expense but also at
mine, that my father's entry into this circle of white men
required a female sacrifice, and I was furious at him for his
betrayal.

If given the chance, I think, Wang Kun would slip his thin,
hungry frame into Harry's deep, well-lined pockets.

Wang Kun was no fool when it came to Harry.

*After months of driving him to the bars and brothels of
Chungking, he knew more about this man than he cared to.
He knew that Harry might appear as a jovial, card-playing
drunkard, but he was dead serious about gathering intelligence and took advantage of every drink, every handshake
or embrace, every game of poker as an opportunity to do so.
He observed the way Harry interacted with his local counter-
parts and saw that beneath the endless jesting was a disdain
for all people and all things Chinese. And he understood that
his own Chinese face was, paradoxically, his one strong card.
If he played this card right—played the China Boy to the Honorable Advisor—he just might win a ticket to America.*

Wang Kun also knew that Harry would do anything to

carry out what he dubbed his "truth experiments." Harry had recently confided in Wang Kun that he'd brought samples of the truth serum sodium amytal with him to Chungking. The drug had been outlawed in the U.S., so Harry was determined to try it out in China. He just needed some naïve subjects to test it out on. Pop's, he proposed, would be the perfect site for such an experiment.

Pop's was a ramshackle, two-story compound on the river that offered a restaurant, a bar, and rooms for rent to a motley clientele that Harry referred to as the misfits and mongrels of Chungking. At Pop's, Wang Kun discovered a world he never knew existed. Pop himself was a wonder to behold, with his white handlebar mustache and perfectly pointed goatee. He was Danish but carried a German passport in China to protect himself, Harry explained. He'd lived in Chungking for 45 years and had previously been a maker of munitions, selling them to whomever happened to be in power. Now Pop's place offered a kind of sanctuary for people like himself: a German Jewish engineer with a Honduran passport; a Greek importer with his Chinese wife and their three Eurasian children; a Russian woman who had followed her Chinese diplomat husband back to his homeland, only to find herself divorced and without citizenship; a Chinese student recently returned from France and his ex-wife, who had studied in Russia, along with his mistress and her 16-year-old daughter, with whom Harry admitted to having taken some liberties. People whose faces and tongues and hearts didn't necessarily match up.

"Do you know what all these people have in common?" Harry asked Wang Kun in his usual rhetorical style. "Secrets, they've all got secrets to hide."

Wang Kun was glad Harry did not expect a response. He couldn't believe his ears, but kept his face impassive as Harry hatched his elaborate plan to administer sodium amytal to a few select subjects at Pop's. He nodded affirmatively as Harry explained that this would involve kidnapping and possibly restraining some subjects, but was certainly more humane than the kinds of torture typically used to extract intelligence. He understood that Harry expected him to go along with the plan, and maybe even help carry it out. And he sensed at once that this was the opportunity he'd been waiting for to prove himself to Harry.

If Wang Kun had any misgivings about the ethics of all this, he did not let on. If there was one thing he had learned from Harry, it was how to play the game.

In his third memoir, the real Harry wrote about the game of poker as a skill that applied not only to espionage, but to life itself—"including where and how one learns to win," as promised in the book's subtitle. Luck was irrelevant. Probability was everything.

My father was never a card-playing man himself, so it's unlikely that he would have appreciated these words of wisdom.

Reading the memoir, I am appalled by the lengths that the real Harry was willing to go to get the truth out of someone.

Until I remember that Harry—along with Wang Kun and Luomin and the misfits at Pop's and the mavericks at the Chungking Hostel—are all unwitting subjects in my own relentless experiments with truth.

May 3, 1939.

The planes with the red sun on their tails approached Chungking just as the last sliver of moon was swallowed up by the earth's shadow.

By the time Harry and Wang Kun arrived at Pop's, the planes were already upon them.

Pop said there was a cave at the foot of a nearby cliff, an old Buddhist grotto that now served as a bomb shelter. At the mention of the cave, Wang Kun noticed that Harry fell strangely silent.

They followed Pop down to the cave, the path dimly lit by scattered fires that had broken out on the hillsides. Wang Kun heard fragments of foreign languages—English, French, German—coming toward him as the embassies emptied out. They walked rather than ran. He heard the clinking of glass. An impeccably English voice said, "It looks like the Japs don't have very good aim."

Indeed the bombs appeared to be dropping mostly along the banks or into the river, where they erupted in a magnificent water show. Someone clapped. They all stopped to watch as the planes made a wide arc, then turned back eastward. A glass of wine was offered to Wang Kun and he took it.

"Cheers," a man said.

"Cheers," Wang Kun replied, savoring this word with the wine on his tongue. He felt giddy with relief. He made small talk with these foreigners, who were captivated by this pretty Chinese boy in a suit jacket and knee socks and who spoke English like an American.

What happened to Harry that night would remain a mystery to Wang Kun ever after. One minute he'd been following Harry's substantial figure as it bobbed and weaved down the path. The next time he looked, Harry was gone. Pop and the embassy staff formed search parties and set out looking for Harry, but gave up after several hours, concluding that he must have fallen asleep drunk somewhere and would turn up in the morning.

He did. Pop found Harry's pasty white body, not a mark of violence on it, washed up with other debris—the claw of a crab, a glass bottle—on the south bank of the Jialing River, a look of astonishment on his face.

The real Harry left Chongqing alive and well, albeit thirty pounds lighter after suffering repeated intestinal bugs and severe underappreciation by both the Chinese and the Americans. But I will not let him go so easily. Squatting on the bank of the river, I wash Harry's blood from my hands. I do not like Harry, the way he takes up so much space in the car and on the page and in Wang Kun's eyes. I will not give him any more space than absolutely necessary.

I will try to keep my father's hands clean.

But Harry is already an idea taken hold inside of Wang Kun. Or maybe the idea was always there but, before Harry, had no name.

Maverick.

I look up the word in the dictionary. The first definition my father would find affirming:

1. Someone who holds independent views and who refuses to conform to the accepted or orthodox thinking on a subject.

But the second definition would surely give him pause:

2. An unbranded animal, especially a calf that has become separated from its mother and herd; by convention, it can become the property of whoever finds it and brands it.

ENTWINEMENT

From his post on the hillside, Wang Kun considered the social landscape of the city below. There were, he decided, three groups of people that mattered for his future: the Americans, the Kuomintang, and the Communists, in order of importance.

Since Harry died, Wang Kun regrettably had no direct con-

tact with any Americans, though he often waved to them as they drove by in their jeeps. They would doff their helmets and shout "ting hao," which meant "very good" and didn't make any sense, but which made him laugh anyway. The Americans always made him laugh.

The Kuomintang, on the other hand, took themselves too seriously. In Wang Kun's mind, there were two kinds of Kuomintang: Big Potatoes and Small Potatoes. Big Potatoes grew to gigantic proportions on the rolling hills outside Tong Yuan Gate just beyond the business district in a maze of grand buildings and villas that together constituted Government Headquarters. Some potatoes were of course bigger than others and there was an elaborate potato pecking order. Small Potatoes like himself were usually sent to the farthest front or up into the mountains, where they were kept in the dark and thereby prevented from growing too large or sprouting too many eyes. Small Potatoes could, of course, become Big Potatoes if they happened to show qualities that the latter were trying to cultivate in each new crop: discipline, self-sacrifice, and a willingness to suffer and die for one's country. Luomin had risen through the potato ranks in this way. Wang Kun, former boy scout, knew that he could be as cheerfully disciplined and self-sacrificing as the next potato, but only if it brought him a step closer to the Americans.

As for the Communists, Wang Kun had never met one, at least not to his knowledge. The possibility that someone might turn out to be a Communist presented itself at every encounter, as Luomin repeatedly warned. This meant that the threat of being branded a Communist was also ever present. The other Small Potatoes in his department often jokingly used this threat against each other whenever someone spoke *in a particularly self-righteous way. But Wang Kun couldn't fathom the difference between the self-righteousness of the left and of the right.*

As for himself, if he were honest, Wang Kun had to admit that he had chosen the Kuomintang only because they had asked first.

General Dai had been watching the Fourth Department closely for some time, and, in the winter of 1942, he uncovered a Communist espionage ring composed of seven spies. The ringleader was described as a femme fatale who, over several years, had managed to transfer all the department files, including personnel charts, radio frequencies, and codebooks, to CCP headquarters. The seven were arrested, tortured (supposedly using the latest American equipment and techniques), and eventually executed in the infamous Happy Valley Prison.

"I don't recall any women working in the department," my father says.

He does remember, however, a man with a pockmarked face. "Nice guy, too bad about his face. We work all night, so during the day we have free time. Every day we climb mountains and explore villages. We really have fun. Once we even put on a play, and I am the female lead! Then one morning I wake up and the pock-face is gone. His desk clean, his bunk empty. Some others are gone, too. I never knew what happened to them."

"Did you ask?" I want to know.

"No, no one dares to speak of them."

This is the closest his stories have ever come to lining up with history.

When Wang Kun was introduced to Pocky, his first thought had been that he resembled a bitter melon. Smallpox had pitted his cheeks, forehead, and chin with ugly scars, and his left eyelid was so ravaged he could no longer close it properly around his eye, which had gone blind. In some places, the scars had joined together to form ridges and troughs that crisscrossed his face, giving his skin a warty texture that, when combined with the oblong shape of his head, was remarkably like the gourd with the pungent bite that Wang Kun had never learned to eat. Just looking at Pocky made Wang Kun's tongue recoil. He felt certain that Pocky must be equally bitter on the inside.

But Pocky defied Wang Kun's expectations. He greeted him affably with a smile that stretched his scars across his cheekbones. "My hundred pots of wine," he called them. Wang Kun was speechless.

On Pocky's first morning at the department, he'd been the earliest to rise and could be heard singing exuberantly from the outhouse in a rich tenor's voice. He continued to sing as he did his morning exercises, squatting and jumping with amazing agility for such a stout man. "Come on," he shouted to a bleary-eyed Wang Kun, "let's see if you can do this!" He squatted flatfooted on one leg with the other stretched straight out in front of him, toes pointed upward, then, with a sprightly hop, switched his legs. He did several of these in rapid succession, then stood beaming, his pots of wine glistening with sweat. "I learned this from a Russian in Shanghai!"

It turned out that Pocky had been a local opera singer in his hometown of Suchou, where he was famous for his witty performances as a clown. He reprised this role in the department, providing comic relief whenever Luomin got too serious by making outlandish faces behind his back. Or bursting into song when everyone's eyes would grow heavy during their night shifts at the radio station. He kept awake by drinking strong, black tea from the spout of a clay teapot. Each time he tilted the teapot toward his face to drink, a tiny clay dragon's head would spring out of its lair in the lid; Pocky would reciprocate by popping his one good eye and sticking out his tongue. The effect of this clownish countenance on such a disfigured face was so incongruous that Wang Kun found himself laughing nervously each time Pocky reached for his teapot.

Wang Kun observed that, each day after lunch, a small group would gather and follow Pocky into the hills. Always in search of a good view, Wang Kun began tagging along on these afternoon expeditions and soon discovered the attraction. On these outings, Pocky would teach them songs from his beloved Suchou opera.

One day, Pocky hatched a plan. "We have so much time

on our hands," he proposed, "let's perform an opera for the department!"

He jumped up on a rock ledge and sang an aria that Wang Kun recognized immediately. *The Song of Everlasting Sorrow.* The tragic love story about the Tang emperor who was so enamored of his concubine that he forgot his duties to the kingdom and, facing revolt, was forced to watch as his soldiers put her to death, trampling her under their horses' hooves.

"Her golden hairpin fell to the ground, and nobody picked it up," Pocky intoned, his good eye fixing Wang Kun with a mournful gaze.

But singing was not one of Wang Kun's talents. "I can play the erhu," he offered. "I'll be part of the orchestra."

"But we need a female lead." Pocky had clearly given thought to this problem. "And your chin is so smooth, and your lips so red!"

"But I can't sing," Wang Kun protested, though he was flattered to be singled out in this way.

"Anyone can learn to sing. Just open your beautiful mouth."
It was impossible to refuse Pocky when he said things like
this.

In the end, Wang Kun didn't have to sing the part himself.
Pocky persuaded the only woman in the department, a shy
beauty with a strong voice, to sing the female arias from
behind a curtain. Wang Kun merely had to wear the costume
and strike the appropriate postures. Pocky would play the
part of the lovestruck emperor. Even Luomin was persuaded
to play a minor role, that of the soldier who would lead the
revolt. Wang Kun was impressed by Pocky's ability to induce
people to do things that seemed out of character.

They built a stage in the clearing behind the radio station
and strung a large red cloth between two poles. Pocky made
a trip into Chungking to borrow costumes, makeup, and
instruments from a local opera troupe. He worked relentlessly
behind the scenes to make sure that everyone learned their
respective parts. He fussed over their costumes and fastidiously applied the makeup himself, contorting his own face accordingly as he painted on each of theirs. He taught them how
to exaggerate their every movement in order to make their
inner conflicts visible to the audience. "This is opera with a
moral!" he screeched at them from behind his emperor's mask.

Pocky taught Wang Kun how to move across the stage like a
woman who knows she is being watched. How to embody the
difference between being shy and being coy. How to artfully
pluck lychee from a branch that is dripping with blood.

On the night of the performance, Wang Kun glided across
the stage in an embroidered silk robe and elaborate head-
dress of sequins and jewels with long black plaits of hair

draped over his shoulders. He moved with willowy delibera-
tion, head tilting, lips parting, arms lifting, celestial sleeves
floating backwards as a haunting aria issued from behind the
red curtain.

I dream I am digging through stacks of books searching
for my father. I finally find him in a history textbook, the
sepia-tinted photograph slightly out of focus. He is wearing
his fedora and a long, wool coat and stands dead center in
the photo surrounded by a restive crowd. Behind them is
a train. Steam spews from the hot engine and their cold
mouths.

Finally some tangible evidence.

I find another volume with a fountain pen stuck between the pages about halfway through, as if someone had marked the place but never returned to it. The binding of the book is now permanently cracked open to that page. There is a passage underlined in blue ink. I can't read the words, but know that they implicate him, name him.

He has been found out.

There are other passages marked throughout the book. Someone has been stealthily tracking him, noting his every move, his presence at This Time or That Place with These People.

I must hide the book. I must protect him.

There is a slip of paper wrapped around the pen, and I carefully unroll it. It's thin, like tissue paper. The same blue ink. The tracker has left herself a note. Dates and names line up perfectly in two incriminating columns labeled "World History" and "Wang Kun's Life."

That's just circumstantial, I want to scream at the tracker, that doesn't prove anything! But the tracker is long gone.

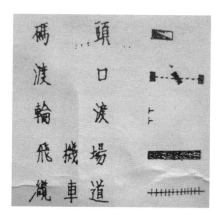

*During the weeks immediately following the performance—
which even General Tai attended, a tight little smile on his
face—there was a flurry of communication that would come
in at all hours of the night. Luomin asked the staff to put in
extra shifts at the radio station. The runners, who delivered
messages from the station back to headquarters to be decod-
ed, came more frequently, and would wait in the corner of
the room, cracking spiced watermelon seeds and spitting out
their shells. Their boorish presence only added to the pressure of a job that was becoming more demanding and more
tedious, and Wang Kun tried to ignore them as he concentrat-
ed on the sounds that were coming fast and furious through
his headset. Mistakes could be costly, as he'd witnessed on the
day the Director of Telecommunications had personally come
out to the station to reprimand Luomin for a transcription
error made by one of his staff.*

*After nearly three years at this job, Wang Kun had to invent
ways to keep his mind from drifting. He'd given up searching
the airwaves for his lover. There was no time for that now
anyway. So he entertained himself by trying to see how many
numbers he could recognize and decode. Recently, handwrit-
ten copies of codes had begun to circulate illicitly among the
staff, transforming their mundane work into a game of skill.
On hikes, they would talk in numbers and test each other's
decoding ability. They gave each other code names. Pocky even
began to write an opera in code. Though he knew Luomin
would not approve, Wang Kun was hooked. The codes stuck
in his head, transforming monotonous lists of numbers into
puzzles of meaning that he would try to work out on the page.
Some numbers he recognized by sound and could immediately visualize the associated characters: Hankow. Chungking.*

Japanese. Communist. When he met a number he didn't know, he wrote it down to look up later.

In this way, he came to string together meanings that might have better been left unstrung.

"Why are you writing this?" my father asks.

"Because it's a good story," I lie.

"Be careful," he warns, "some stories should not be told."

Two stalky plants stand side by side under a covered stall: 麻

A child with arms extended stands beside the stall: 子

The presence of the child ensures that the stall and its contents are not mistaken for flax or jute or any of the sturdy fibers that the hemp plant produces. The child's presence insists on the other meaning, turns the fiber into an adjective that describes its coarse, pitted texture, applies this texture to the face of the child: 麻 子

Mazi.

Pock-face.

/ *The pock-face is a spy.* /

Wang Kun knew the meaning even before he had written down the numbers. He heard the crack of watermelon seeds behind him and felt the eyes of the runners on the back of his head. Across the room, Pocky reached for his teapot, his seeing eye scanning the room for an audience. Wang Kun looked away.

He remembered a conversation he'd once had as Pocky was applying his makeup.

"I feel lucky to have lost the face I was born with," Pocky said solemnly.

"Why?" Wang Kun asked, walking straight into the trap.

"Because," he paused for effect, "I will never lose face again!"

Wang Kun marveled at Pocky's gift for turning tragedy into comedy. Even their opera had turned out to be more of a farce than a serious love story, much to everyone's relief. How could it be otherwise when the emperor was a clown!

But now even the clown was not whom he appeared to be.

Who do I appear to be, Wang Kun wondered?

He felt lightheaded. His heart was pounding so hard he could barely make out the sounds that continued to pulse through his headset. He dared not look around the room. He kept his eyes fixed on his hand and watched in horror as the pulse in his ear ran like an electric current down his arm,

moving the pen across the paper. A number emerged from the tip of his pen, then another, and another. The numbers swam before his eyes, transforming themselves on the page into pictographs. A covered stall. A child with outstretched arms. Go inside, he willed the child, hide behind the branches! But the child remained stubbornly planted in the open, unashamed to show his face. His pen continued to move, nailing the meaning like a coffin around the child.

/ The pock-face is a spy /

His pen did not pause at this but continued to spit out the code names of others, their little opera group, the voice behind the curtain, his hand and heart racing until he came to the end of the transmission and knew with relief that his own name was not among them.

His pen stopped moving. He took off his headset and wiped his brow. The runner was there, half-eaten bits of shells and seeds stuck to his mouth and shoes, ready to deliver the message to headquarters.

After all these years, my father still remembers the lyrics to the Song of Everlasting Sorrow and writes out the last verse—six lines, seven characters each—in shaky black strokes that roam from top to bottom and right to left over the surface of the rice paper. He can't control the size of the characters or gauge the distance between them, and they grow and shrink with the changing space on the page. He has to rely on me to reposition his arm each time he comes to the end of a line. I guide his brush back up to the top of the page, pausing to dip at the ink stone as needed. After all these years, he still knows exactly how long his brush needs to drink so that he can lay down each character boldly and lift off the page with a flourish.

He puts his brush down and inspects his work.

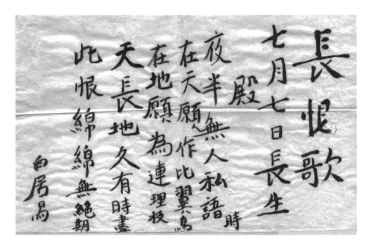

"Not bad," he says, "but not as good as I used to be." He looks relieved to see the characters fixed there, absorbed into the fibers of the paper. They'd been swimming in his head for so long.

He asks me to recite the poem.

Who do I appear to be? I wonder. But I obey, struggling with the pronunciation as my mother and the nurses clap approvingly.

Seeing that he has an audience, my father smiles broadly. "This is a famous Tang poem, an epic," he says, as if this will win us over, "very, very famous."

He tells the story of the emperor and his concubine, the

hairpin and the horses' hooves. He translates the poem, line by line, clearly at home and in control in his role as interpreter. He does not look or sound like a man who has just suffered a traumatic head injury. He does not falter or grope for words, but moves smoothly and judiciously between the Chinese pictograph and the English idiom, just as he has always done.

"Heaven endures, earth endures, someday both will end, but this everlasting sorrow goes on and on forever." He translates the last two lines and looks up expectantly.

"Oh, that's awful," says my mother, "he let his soldiers murder her! What kind of love story is that?"

"Love story? This is a tragedy!" His smile is gone. "The emperor had no choice. He had to sacrifice his own happiness for the good of the kingdom!" He speaks slowly and deliberately as if to a child. "Their sorrow will last for eternity. Sorrow is what lasts, even after we're gone. Don't you people understand?" He spits these last words at all of us.

You people! This is what he always called us just before he flew into a rage.

Now he is looking at me. You of all people should understand.

I am looking at my mother.

My mother is looking away. She is gesturing wildly at the nurses, trying to draw their attention away from her husband and his imminent rage. She has taken on his broad smile, as if to say, don't mind him, he's only joking. This is our happy family, just like the dish in the restaurant: our Happy Chinese American Family.

NORMALIZATION

He complains of a strange sensation at the back of his throat just seconds before the onset of a seizure. Then his body goes rigid and his arms retract, hands balling up, lips smacking and mouth working like a newborn rooting for the breast. He does not respond to the various cocktails of anti-epileptic drugs prescribed by the chatty neurologist with the Scottish brogue.

"Could be mesial temporal sclerosis," the neurologist speculates. "Scarring of the hippocampus. If that's the case, surgery may be the only hope for the normalization of your father's temporal lobe functions."

Normalization.

And right there in the rehab hospital, a temporal rift opens.

It's the winter of 1972.

I have just turned eleven, and Richard Nixon has just become the first American president to visit the People's Republic of China. My father keeps the television on the entire week, eating all of his meals on a tray table in front of it and chewing slowly with his mouth closed. I can't tell if he's happy or sad about the president's visit to China. Everyone on TV seems happy, all smiling broadly and shaking hands.

Outside the house, my father smiles, too, as friends and neighbors come up to offer their congratulations, as if he himself had single-handedly orchestrated this visit. I watch as he gamely takes the credit.

Back at home, he continues his close-mouthed vigil while I sprawl on the oval rug between him and the TV. The commentary confuses me, especially that word. Nor-mal-i-za-tion. I let it roll off the roof of my mouth and over my tongue. It sounds hopeful and damning at the same time, like the promise of a cure for a disease you didn't even know you were afflicted with.

"What does it mean?" I ask my father.

"It means," he takes a sip of tea and holds it in his mouth for a moment before swallowing, "we will start talking again after long silence."

"Who? Who will start talking?"

"The Chinese and the Americans," he says, gesturing to the TV.

I watch as the First Lady emerges from the plane wearing a long red coat with what looks like a fox wound around her neck.

"Which one are we?" I ask.

"I am Chinese, you are American," he answers, not taking his eyes off the TV.

His reply stuns me into silence. After defending all those Chinamen on the fence, how could I not be Chinese?

I turn my back on my father. I decide that I do not like the way the fox lady shakes hands, holding her fingers out stiffly in front of her and bending them ever so slightly at the knuckles. Like a queen offering her hand to her subjects. This is in stark contrast to the man they call the Premier, whose handshake is so wide and effusive that I can imagine my own small hand tucked warmly inside of his. I cannot take my eyes off him. His arresting black eyebrows like two fat, wooly caterpillars wriggling toward each other across his brow. The way his mouth laughs widely at one moment and seconds later rearranges itself into a thin, grim line.

The disease and the cure latent in the same man.

For a brief moment, I entertain the fantasy that my father is related to the Premier. That the Premier is really my grandfather waiting for the return of his son and family. I imagine descending the steps of the plane wearing my favorite tie-dyed t-shirt and bell-bottom jeans. The way the Premier opens his arms as I run to him for a bear hug. The way my father, who never gives hugs, hangs back at the edge of the tarmac, waiting to see if he has been forgiven.

As in a dream, the memory ends abruptly there, at the edge of the tarmac.

Still sprawled on the oval rug, I fight to dream myself into the next scene, when father and son will surely begin talking after a long silence.

But the rift has closed.

The seizure has passed.

His fists unfurled, my father sleeps fitfully.

The way he has always slept.

I search my memories, trying to recall the exact moment when China came out of the closet and became a voluble presence in our home. When my father began to speak of China in the future tense rather than the past. When Chinese was no longer merely an adjective describing the food in the freezer or the carpet under foot, but became a reference to certain habits of the heart and mind and tongue that surfaced as he set about preparing for his return.

I am Chinese, you are American, he'd said, surprising maybe even himself.

He liked to quote Nixon, saying that that was the week that changed the world—and the course of the Zhang family, he would always add.

Yet it would take another seven years of talking before the Americans and the Chinese would be able to hammer out a mutual agreement establishing diplomatic ties between the two countries. Seven years before relations were officially normalized and my father's return could even become possible. Seven years during which he must have been quietly preparing for this eventuality. Sending out feelers. Testing the waters.

Did my father, like Nixon, have a go-between, I wonder? Did he send an emissary ahead? There must have been many late-night phone calls and long letters. Both sides reading between the lines. Normalization could not have come quickly or easily. His return must have been as carefully orchestrated as his departure.

But I cannot recall those seven years, at least where my father is concerned. Those painful progression-from-middle-to-high-school-years, when skin and hair and eyes became the cloistered center of my existence. Those were the years when I turned my back on the Laughing Chinaman and slipped out my bedroom window to escape the alternately hot and cold war escalating in my home. I stole off down the street to drink and smoke with boys who had once taunted me, who now respected me for my fists.

A long-haired boy named Marcus, sporting a black leather jacket with a dirty grey hoodie underneath, stole my heart. He was one of those tough guys who slouched when he walked and smelled of smoke. One of those who would never look you in the eyes when you passed him in the hallway. I would watch him steal out of school in the middle of the day, and my heart would beat faster. I finally worked up the courage to go up to him and ask where he was going and could I come along. He looked startled at first but his mouth broke into the sweetest grin I'd ever seen and said, "Sure, cool, come along."

We sat inside his battered purple van and drank Coke laced with rum. He was so gentle and unassuming, his burnt-tobacco kiss so soft, I couldn't believe he had a reputation for being a tough guy. He told me he was afraid of dying young and only the pot could take the edge off. When he was high, he liked to unclench my fists one finger at a time and trace the lines on the palms of my hands. I wore his black leather jacket and played greaser girl that year, going to parties with him and feeling invincible.

When Marcus died in a car crash that summer, his van bouncing off the sunlit guardrail and rolling down a grassy embankment, I threw his jacket away, but the smoky smell lingered. I figured I might as well start smoking myself. Each drag tasted of him, his burnt-tobacco lips and tongue. I liked to chase it with the sweet swill of rum and Coke. The smoke emptied my head of the sound of breath and blood, and the drink made me sleep so soundly I no longer dreamed of escape.

When my father finally decided to return to China, he asked me to go with him. Just in case. He also took along his best American buddy, Bob, who had taught him how to eat ice cream, how to talk football, how to court an American woman. My father called Bob his "shoe horn," failing as he so often did to get the idiom right.

My father's invitation caught me off-guard. I'd just returned from Israel, where I had spent a year on a kibbutz studying Hebrew. I'd gone there on a whim, the fancy of my then-Jewish boyfriend, and ended up staying the year, thoroughly diverted by the land, the language, and the music of Zionism. I was ripe for the cause. I might even have converted if my father had not asked me to go to China with him that summer. It hadn't occurred to me that I should want to go.

I remember that first trip in images only. Muted greys

and blues of a country still emerging from revolution. I play these images back now, trying to figure out how I arrived at certain misunderstandings.

I remember disembarking from the train and being surrounded by faces of people who all seemed to know me, though I recognized no one. A skeleton of a man with a toothy grin. A woman with bangs cut bluntly over sad eyes and the softest hands that wouldn't let me go. A gaunt man with razor-sharp cheekbones and a tall nose who averted his eyes every time I looked at him.

Qing Ming, they greeted me in voices thick with emotion. I knew my Chinese name but had never been called by it before. It sounded like a question as much as a declaration. Qing Ming? You are here at last, but are you who we imagined? It sounded so intimate, so full of expectation, as if they knew things about me that even I didn't know about myself.

I remember the bus pulling up in front of a crumbling cement building, a small, round bundle of a woman stooped over a cane in the doorway. I remember my father getting off the bus, a slight swagger in his step as he approached the woman. How tall he suddenly appeared. I remember the way they took each other's hands, cupped each other's faces.

"Ma?" he asked.

"Erzi," she replied.

And for the first time, I saw my father as a son.

Back in the U.S., I heard Bob tell the story of my father's return in words that didn't match the pictures in my head. In Bob's version, mother and son pressed their palms together in front of them and bowed deeply and respectfully to each other.

Everywhere we went, we moved in a huge, amorphous entourage. My grandmother in an antiquated wheelchair that was pushed from behind by Fatty, the wide-faced, wide-bottomed peasant woman who cooked and cleaned and cared for her. My father strutting along beside them, drinking in the spectacle of his return. A curious crowd of relatives and friends and neighbors, whom I could hardly tell apart, much less know their relation to me, trailed us everywhere.

I tried to be inconspicuous in the cut-off shorts and tank tops I wore everywhere that summer, bandana tied around my head to catch the sweat that was a constant trickle down my body. My tongue felt heavy and my limbs clumsy and out of proportion next to these spare figures that bore not a trace of perspiration. Unable to speak Chinese, I hung onto the edges of conversations, waiting for my father to throw me a fragment of meaning. The entire trip was mediated through him and the man with the razor-sharp cheeks, whom my father introduced as my cousin.

He wore a white short-sleeve shirt untucked and open at the collar, his long, skinny arms dangling loosely at his sides. "Welcome to P.R.C.," he said, articulating each syllable with staccato-like precision. "But you do not look like an American." He sounded disappointed. "Your eyes are not blue and your hair is not gold."

"Not all Americans have blonde hair and blue eyes," I snapped.

"The famous ones do," he replied, and proceeded to espouse his theory of why the fairer race ruled the world.

His pronunciation was flawless, but I could not catch his meaning. He spoke with a causal logic that I could not follow, citing statistics to support his claims as if orally defending a thesis. He knew many more facts about the U.S. than I knew about China, and made it brazenly clear how eager he was to go there to study. He seemed to have been preparing for this moment his whole life.

"What college do you attend?" he asked and, when he did not recognize the name of the small liberal arts college in upstate New York, again looked disappointed.

There was no equivalence between his language and my experience. In the labor of our conversation, I felt myself twisted and squeezed into as few utterances as possible. I was horrified by this reduction of self, but could do nothing about it.

I went for a boat ride on the lake with my cousin. He rowed and fired question after question at me about my life in America: the size of my house, the make of my car, the dollar amount of my electric bill. Questions I could not answer to his satisfaction. He seemed to know, or at least to assume, so much more about me than I could about him. I felt as if I were being held accountable for a crime I had no idea I had committed. When I could bear his interrogation no longer, I shouted, "I'm hot, let's go for a swim!" and leapt fully clothed over the side of the boat. I laughed out loud at the terror-stricken look on my cousin's face, reveling in the rashness of what I had just done. The cold shock of the lake against my hot skin. The buoyancy of my body in the water. I kicked hard away from the boat and swam toward the shore where my grandmother sat watching in her wheelchair, surrounded by the rest of the entourage like an empress holding court. The old woman was laughing as this strange hybrid fish emerged from the water shivering with pleasure.

When I finally set about formally learning the Chinese language in college, it came with remarkable ease, the four tones rolling off my tongue and lips with perfect intonation as the other students in the class struggled to even hear the difference. Was it those late-night phone calls, my father's voice floating up through the register, at once foreign and familiar, rousing then lulling me back to sleep?

He never spoke to me in Chinese, even during those combative years when he forced me to attend Saturday morning Chinese school, dragging me away from the television set just as Bugs Bunny popped out of a rabbit hole on the other side of the world wearing a coolie hat and a goatee and spewing strange sounds I swore I would never make. I resisted him with a terrible will, declaring "You are not my father!"

But after that first trip to China, I discovered sounds my mouth already knew how to make.

When I returned to China the following year, a college graduate and alone this time, I kept a small, black notebook in which I wrote down characters that I repeatedly encountered.

斗争 (dou zheng): to struggle
培养 (pei yang): to cultivate
发展 (fa zhan): to develop

How strange to meet these familiar words in another language only to discover that I didn't know what they meant. Civilization. Modernization. Progress. Ideas that even in English felt foreign on my tongue. When I tried to use them in Chinese, I felt like an outsider inside my own body.

I collected characters in my notebook that would help me distinguish between like and different things, to know where the lines were drawn. What was out of bounds and what was possible.

范围 (fan wei) : scope, limit, range
包括 (bao kuo): to include, comprise, consist of
坚持 (jian chi): to persist, persevere

I would repeatedly ask: What does this consist of? What are the limits of that?

I will persevere in learning Chinese, I told my grandmother, the sounds emerging so perfectly formed that no one suspected me of being other than who they thought I was.

努力学习 准备为社会主义现代化贡献力量
专心听 勤思考 认真完成作业

When the person I thought was my cousin left for the U.S. on a scholarship to my father's alma mater, I stayed on in the city that my father had been borne out of. I landed a job teaching English to semi-retired professors of engineering and mathematics who spoke English with a Russian accent and dreamed of going to the Beautiful Country, if only to bring back a refrigerator. On weekends, we would go on class excursions, biking out of the city and hiking into the hills, a dozen or so aging intellectuals strung out behind me, eager to practice their English with this American girl. We would spread our lunch of tea eggs and steamed buns on newspapers on the ground, and they would tell me stories of what my father might not have lived through had he remained in China. I would correct their English and teach them useful idioms.

What it means to beat around the bush.

How it feels to be caught between a rock and a hard place.

In between semesters, during the cold winter months, I lived with my grandmother, who had neither refrigerator nor heat, clothing my body in so many layers of cotton that I hardly recognized myself when I looked in the mirror. My face had grown round after a year on a diet laden with meat and starch and oil, excesses of the New China that I voraciously indulged in. Eating and keeping warm consumed me that winter. I spent the days in bed piled under quilts, devouring books on the Chinese Revolution and waiting for Fatty to serve up the next meal. Before I could even get out of bed in the morning, Fatty would be there making her mental list for market and asking me what I wanted to eat that day.

Steamed buns or sesame balls for breakfast?

Soup noodles or fried rice for lunch?

Stewed chicken or steamed fish for dinner?

My grandmother watched me eat through cloudy eyes that never missed a beat, her chopsticks rooting through each dish to find the choicest morsel for her insatiable, foreign grandchild.

I was rescued from my torpor by a 15-year-old boy who lived upstairs, a student of the ballet in Shanghai who was home for the winter break and bored. He wore a long rabbit-fur coat and a matching fur hat over an angelic face that at first I mistook for a girl's. "Little Japanese," Fatty whispered, telling me all about the illicit union that had produced him. Every morning, when his mother came downstairs to play majiang with the other women in the building, the boy would coax me out of bed and off to the park, where we rowed boats and rode go-karts and played hide-and-seek in the elaborate rock gardens. He showed me how to foxtrot under a pavilion where middle-aged couples danced discreetly to music pulsing from an oversized boombox. I taught him to recite my beloved Eliot, always behind closed doors. I did not understand the meaning of Spiritual Pollution, even in English, but I knew well the thrill of the forbidden. I found a kindred spirit in this exuberant creature who was not quite a boy, not yet a man, not fully Chinese.

I stand in the designated smoking area just outside the hospital entrance and shake my head at the silver-haired gentleman who just offered me a cigarette. There's something about the way he taps the carton lightly and extends his hand that makes me think he might be a mainlander. He reminds me of those aging professors who, in their zeal to practice English, would vie with one another to be the first to offer me a smoke.

China in the '80s, it turned out, would not be the place to try to quit smoking.

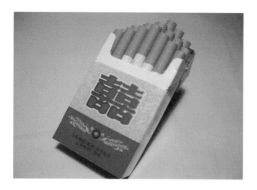

Double Happiness. Wild Horse. Dragon & Phoenix. The brightly labeled cartons and flip-top lids were essential starters to any conversation.

Since so few women smoked publicly, when I accepted my first light, word quickly spread on campus that the American teacher was a smoker. In the evenings after dinner, I would find on my doorstep at the foreign teachers' quarters some of the university's most prominent professors, their hands in the pockets of their Zhongshan jackets and their desire for modernity on their sleeves, ready to draw a light. They introduced themselves to me as Jackson and Henry, Clarence and Martin, Howard and Franklin. They left their shoes at the doorway and squeezed stocking-footed into my tiny room, racing for the chairs and piling onto my bed in the manner of excited schoolboys. As I poured the hot water, they plied me with their favorite smokes so that by the time I sat down there would be a pile of cigarettes stacked like little logs next to my teacup. They chain-smoked and sipped their tea noisily, spitting the leaves back into their cups while trying to mimic my American accent and gestures. I was flattered by all the attention and looked forward to their nightly visits, mistaking their interest in me as an American for their acceptance of me as a Chinese.

When the dinner invitations started rolling in on a weekly basis, I felt as if I had finally come home. One by one, Jackson and Clarence and Howard invited me to visit their homes and meet their families. One by one, Henry and Martin and Franklin cooked elaborate meals for me that lasted late into the evenings and were always accompanied by repeated toasts of the local beer, which they were impressed to discover I could consume in large quantities with little ill effect. As the night wore on, and my host would grow redder in the face and looser in the tongue, his wife would disappear behind closed doors and the confessions would begin.

"Do you know what is a rightist?" Clarence asked with a twisted smile on his lined but still handsome face. He held up his right hand to show me the missing digit.

"I am... reactionary," admitted Martin, a soft-spoken professor of aeronautics. He told me about his ten years of labor in the countryside, during which he ate only corn, explaining that this was why he had such an aversion to the vegetable now. He expressed his shy delight at learning the English word "tingle" to describe what it felt like to wash his hair with shampoo after all those years.

"Bad element," Henry pointed to his teeth and whispered so softly that I had to ask him twice to repeat himself. On a piece of paper, he explained that a micro recording device had been implanted in his teeth. He produced a stack of letters tied together with string and asked me to carry them back to the U.S.

"If your father had stayed," Jackson informed me, "he would have been a counterrevolutionary."

My father—a counterrevolutionary?

At the time, I had nodded sympathetically without fully comprehending what these men were trying to tell me. I looked up the word "reactionary" in my English-Chinese dictionary, but couldn't comprehend the meaning of the characters I found. So I went to the Chinese side of the dictionary and translated backwards into English. In this way, I came to understand the importance of 反 (fan), which means to overturn. When placed in front of another character, 反 abruptly turns over its meaning. When placed in front of the character for "movement," 反 could turn an ordinary person into a reactionary. Left could be turned into right. Esteemed teachers could be turned into class enemies. Even the self could be turned on itself.

But this was still only word play to me. Though moved by the confidence these old men showed in me, choosing me as the surrogate daughter who would bear their stories out of China, I didn't really know what they were asking me to carry. Clarence's missing finger. Martin's corn and hair. Henry's teeth and letters. Their stories were so fantastic, I wondered at times whether they'd all gone a little mad.

Back in the hospital, the neurologist is blathering on about the inverse relationship between epilepsy and psychosis. "It's widely known, of course," he says, "that seizures induced through electroconvulsive therapy can be useful in treating psychotic patients, essentially disrupting their brain wave patterns in order to jolt them back into reality. Conversely, when epileptic patients are treated with medication to normalize their EEG readings, some may experience psychotic symptoms."

Forced normalization, he calls it.

"In other words," he says very slowly to make sure I get the punch line, "some epileptic patients require abnormal brain patterns in order to live sanely."

"Crazy old men!"

When my father came to visit me in China, he quickly spied a problem in the making and sent me packing.

"Go home!" he decreed. "You have stayed too long!"

His words stung. I had expected him to be pleased that I was learning the language, finally showing an interest in China after all those years of defying him. But he saw the men lining up on my doorstep, old and young alike vying for my attention, and alarm bells went off. These men could be interested in only one thing. He warned me of the dangers of a marriage of convenience. I was shocked that he could even think such a thing.

"You are an American, you don't belong here. Go home!" he commanded. "You are spoiling here!"

If he had not used those words, I might have resisted him. I might have questioned his motives in treating his fellow Chinese with such rank suspicion. I might even have inquired what he knew about a marriage of convenience. Hadn't he married an American woman, I could have shot back at him. But his words were successful in deflecting me, turning the problem around so that I questioned my own motives. Turning my nascent sense of belonging into unearned privilege. It was time for the spoiled American to go home.

I did not notice the relief on my father's face as I packed my bags.

Now I rewind and play back that first trip to China with my father.

I see him rising from his armchair, the wheels already spinning, grimly composing himself for the task ahead.

I watch him make the obligatory purchases, one of each of the Eight Big Things, ensuring that his would be a glorious return.

I observe him as he steps off the train and notice where his eyes go first.

I trail him as he swaggers through the crowd, shaking hands and handing out spanking-new dollar bills to the children.

I pay attention this time when he introduces me to each of my relatives.

I grasp the hand of my so-called cousin and search his face as my father claps him on the back. I see the contempt that flits across my cousin's mouth before he rearranges it into a wide smile. I am surprised to hear them exchange terse greetings in English before my father pushes on.

I note who comes to our hotel room at night. Who eats dinner with us in the private banquet room. Who are the recipients of the munificent checks my father writes at the end of each day. Who is poised to receive the offer of a one-way ticket to America.

I know now that my father's return was never the story of

the prodigal child. That was my story.

In his story, there was no father waiting for him.

In his story, it was the fathers who ran away and the sons who were left behind

A WAY OUT

After a month in the rehab hospital, my father is finally released and sent home. I help my mother convert the living room into a bedroom, taking out the sofa and bringing in a hospital bed, portable toilet, and wheelchair. A visiting nurse stops by several times a week to check on him, and a home health aide comes daily to help him bathe and dress. My father is suspicious of these strangers who come into his home and try to be so intimate with him. He asks constantly whether the doors are locked, and warns my mother and me to be careful about whom we let into the house. He refuses any visitors. Eventually, we give up on the home health aide, and instead, I go half time at my job to help care for my father.

"So, how did you get out?" I ask him bluntly one day.

He is surprisingly forthcoming. "Luomin gets me a job teaching English to a general. This general, he likes me, he sees me as an intellectual person. He says, you don't belong here doing this kind of work. He says, you can make a contribution to your country by furthering your study. So I take the university entrance exam and, what do you know, I get in. And they let me go!"

This particular exchange is sandwiched on one page of

my notebook between my father's brief mention of his disappeared Communist colleagues and his condemnation of those corrupt Guomindang officials whose pockets were lined with American dollars.

And these words, scribbled verbatim in the margin: "I just want to get out. Anybody can help me."

The disappearance of Pocky and the other members of the opera group left Wang Kun with a queasy feeling in his gut. What a fool, he thought, to get mixed up with such stuff! And he nearly took me down with him! He was stunned that his own usually keen instincts had failed him this time. Of course it was that face—or the absence of one—that had tricked him into letting his guard down. You never really know anybody, he reminded himself. His own father, another fool who disappeared, had burned that lesson into him. He had to be more careful from now on. The Americans were coming to Chungking in droves now, and if he played his cards right, he would leave with them.

At night, however, that queasy feeling intensified and woke Wang Kun, sending him running to the outhouse, where he squatted over the trough as he tried to purge himself of the strange, troubling thoughts that assailed him. He thought of Pocky squatting there, shitting and singing in the early hours of the morning, and he wondered whether his friend had sung Suchou opera as he was being tortured. He'd heard from some of the runners about the prison in the old Bai Mansion, the former villa of a warlord who claimed to be a descendant of the Tang poet who'd penned the Song of Everlasting Sorrow. Now the runners joked about the never-ending anguish of those locked inside the mansion. They knew some of the

*guards who worked there and took great pleasure in passing
on graphic stories about the "tiger bench" and the "acid bath,"
the latter being the surest way to make someone disappear
for good. During the day, Wang Kun could easily dismiss these
tales as the lurid imaginings of those who are destined to spit
seeds and run in place. But the images stayed with him, and
at night, his belly burned with acid of his own making.*

*One evening, when the cramps were particularly prolonged
and painful, Wang Kun squatted for nearly an hour as he
vividly recalled the last time he'd seen his father. It was right
after his celebrated return from the boy scout jamboree. The
Generalissimo had just been released from his kidnapping
and had agreed to cooperate with the Communists in fighting the Japanese. There had been a big parade in Nanking
in which the returned boy scouts had been invited to march.
He knew it was a great honor to be chosen, and he had his*

uniform washed and pressed in anticipation of passing under the Generalissimo's scrupulous gaze.

The day before the parade, he'd received a telegram from a cousin in Shanghai telling him that his father was there and wanted to see him. He felt shame and rage wash over him as he read the words. This was the first communication Wang Kun had received from his father since he'd abandoned them over a year ago.

Your father would like you to pay him a visit.

Your father? What kind of father would steal from his family and slink away in the middle of the night? Before Wang Kun had even realized his father had gone, a new magistrate was pounding on their door with a warrant for the arrest of the corrupt tax collector who had been embezzling state funds for nearly five years. When Wang Kun's father was nowhere to be found, the magistrate had immediately proclaimed the house sealed and all its contents impounded. Wang Kun and his mother were not even permitted to dress. They had to walk through the streets in their night clothes, hisses and jeers following them until they reached his aunt's house.

The humiliation of his father's departure refused to go away, like bile at the back of his throat that he had to keep swallowing. The worst part had been watching his mother suffer. With her broken feet, she could not work outside the home, and had been forced to take a live-in position as a seamstress for a wealthy family, where she was treated as little more than a servant. Wang Kun felt himself torn between his duty to care for his mother and his desire to make a break, to make himself over, to prove that he was not his father's son. So when the scoutmaster invited Wang Kun to stay with him, he'd jumped at the chance. The boy scouts became his salvation, his ticket to America. He'd swallowed hard and left his mother behind, promising to come back for her one day. He'd swallowed even harder, relegating his father to a place inside himself where he could never again cause him shame. How cruel, then, that upon his return from America, his father should resurface and try to steal his moment of glory away from him!

The day of the parade, Wang Kun rose early, dressing and grooming himself with great care. Looking in the mirror, it was not the Generalissimo's eyes that shrewdly appraised him. He would go to his father that afternoon; he would show him who he had become.

He'd marched that day with all the dignity he could muster. When they passed in front of the reviewing stand, he held his head high and did not even glance in the direction of the Generalissimo. Afterward, still in uniform and glowing with pride, he took the train to Shanghai and then a bus, following his cousin's directions to an address that he was disappointed to see would take him nowhere near the International Settlement. It was dark by the time he found the street, but the sweet, smoky air and the skinny girls with their pale faces beckoning to him from the doorways told him immediately what kind of neighborhood his father lived in.

Inside the dank building, the air was even more cloying, and he brought a handkerchief to his mouth as he knocked on the door. The man who opened the door was unmistakably his father, with the same boyish good looks as ever but much thinner than Wang Kun remembered, his skin sallow and his eyes sunken into his face so that his cheekbones and nose stood out even more prominently.

He's dying, Wang Kun realized.

"Ba."

His father did not answer but merely stepped back to allow his son to enter the dimly lit one-room apartment. There was a mattress on the floor in the corner of the room, on which Wang Kun could make out a feminine shape. On the floor next to the mattress was a tall silver pipe and a tray with an assortment of small utensils. His father ignored Wang Kun's inquiring glances and pulled out a stool at the table on which a pack of cigarettes, a thermos of boiled water, and two teacups, the tea leaves already apportioned inside them, had been arranged. His father sat down across from him, poured a small amount of hot water into each cup, and put the lids on to steep. He offered a cigarette to Wang Kun, who politely refused, then lit one for himself. He did not look at his son when he finally spoke.

"I heard you went to America."

"Yes, I've just returned. I marched today for the Generalissimo in Nanking."

"You are a good boy," came the barely audible reply. "You make your father proud." He took a drag on the cigarette and immediately began to cough, a deep hacking cough that sent him running for the spittoon.

When his father spat, Wang Kun could see flecks of yellow and red floating on the surface of the dirty water. Instinctively, he brought his handkerchief to his mouth again. Then his father's watery eyes caught his and he saw the panic in them, the panic of a man who suddenly finds himself arriving too early at the end of his life with too little to show for it and too late to rectify his mistakes.

Had there been anything but panic in those eyes? Some sign of remorse? A plea for forgiveness? Crouching over the

*outhouse trough, Wang Kun searched this painful memory,
the spasms in his gut finally beginning to subside. No, there'd
been nothing else there. His father had not tried to explain
himself, nor had he inquired about Wang Kun's mother. If he'd
wanted his son's forgiveness, he did not ask for it. He'd merely
wanted to bask in the glory of his son's accomplishments,
Wang Kun decided. By the end of the visit, which had lasted
less than an hour and had ended abruptly when the woman
on the mattress began to thrash and moan, Wang Kun had
felt only pity and disgust for this man who claimed paternity
over him.*

*You never really know anybody, he reminded himself again
as he pulled up his trousers. The queasiness had passed, and
Wang Kun walked back to the barracks, poised for what he
had to do next.*

You never really know anybody.

Those exact words jumped into my head at the moment
of my father's confession and have remained with me ever
since. My feelings at that moment surprised me—not anger
or disappointment, but a sense of release that continues to
find expression in those five words. The pleasure of release
from all expectation. And then, unbounded possibility.

If my father was not the man I thought he was, anything
was possible—an idea both liberating and dangerous. An
idea that I knew, as a writer, could serve my purposes very
well.

The girl in rabbit fur could turn out to be a boy.

The boy jumping on the bed could turn out to be an old
man.

The old man could turn out to be a bad element.

The bad element could turn out to be nothing more than a word, which, once uttered, could invert all previous meanings.

Eraser!

Such are the reversals you learn to live with.

I am pleased to be able to use these five words now, to put them into Wang Kun's head as he pulls up his trousers. To see what he will make of them. What he will do next.

When the winter fog rolled back in, cloaking the city in a cold, dripping blanket of protection, Wang Kun finally got some sleep. He awoke clear-headed and confident one Saturday morning in November. Good, he thought, he needed to be clear for the job that lay ahead. He dressed smartly in a suit and tie, combing back his hair and whistling at himself in the mirror. He set out at 7:00 a.m. sharp, hailing one of the sedan chairs parked outside the entrance of the main office of the Department of Telecommunications. He was pleased to have recently been transferred to this post in the city, which afforded him more opportunities to come into contact with the Americans. He paid the two boys in advance, and they set out briskly through the west gate and along the main thoroughfare to the general's mansion on the opposite side of the city.

Wang Kun tried not to look at what lay along the roadside. After months of bombing, Chungking looked like a leprous body with whole pieces of flesh torn out and left to rot on the streets. Ash combined with other remains had merged with mud to create a foul, sludge-like substance that moved through the city with a life of its own, seeping into cracks and cavities in roads, buildings, shoes, feet, fingernails, eyes. Wang Kun clamped his mouth shut, but the putrid substance infiltrated his nose and clung to the back of his throat.

Upon arriving at the general's, he asked the servant who greeted him at the door for hot water and a basin to wash in. He would try to stay clean for this job.

The general was waiting for him at his desk with his hands laced across his round belly. The wide eyes on the thick neck appraised Wang Kun. "What a good-looking boy you are," he oozed with a glint of gold.

Wang Kun felt the game immediately. He knew he was being tested and could not show a hint of nerves. All business, he opened one of the English books he had carried with him and asked the general to repeat after him. His own pronunciation was perfect and he knew it, showed it off, seduced the general with it. The general tried but could not make the strange sounds that the English language demanded. "I welcome you to Free China," Wang Kun said proudly, imagining a room full of Americans in front of him. But of course the general could not pronounce the "r." Wang Kun could not contain his laughter. When he explained the joke, the general too burst out laughing and snorting until tears rolled down his cheeks. He could be surprisingly charming, Wang Kun thought.

At the end of the hour, the general thanked Wang Kun, saying that he was an honorable young man, the kind who understood the meaning of duty. Then he suddenly curled a hand around Wang Kun's shoulder and asked with a coy smile, "Do you have a girlfriend?"

The wide-set eyes were so close now that it was hard to look into both at once.

In a panic, Wang Kun shifted his gaze to the general's other hand to see if a sword might have magically appeared there, but was relieved to see it empty. He quickly collected himself.

"No, I prefer to spend my free time reading."

"Good," the general said, patting him on the back and leading him to the door. "Be careful, there are many pretty girls in Chungking these days who can lead even such a good boy as yourself astray!"

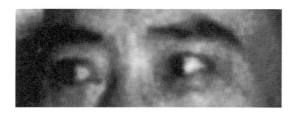

My father claims he cannot remember the name of the general to whom he taught English once a week. The same general, he thinks, who released him from the Bureau.

I can't help but entertain the possibility that this general was none other than Dai Li himself. Even though I know that's impossible. Such a man would never let a smart boy like Wang Kun go. Such a man would certainly have used my father for his own purposes. But who was using whom?

I read aloud to my father from a biography written by an American scholar whose obsession with the general rivals my own. "Listen, Dad, it says here that Dai Li did not permit anyone to leave his organization until they were sleeping in their coffins."

"How did he manage to get out alive?" my father marvels.

He has begun to refer to himself in the third person, sometimes even using the fictive name that I have given to the father character in my book. It's easier for both of us to talk about him in this way.

In my notebook, I compile a list of my father's maxims under the heading "Wang Kun's Guide to Survival and a Way Out of China":

1. Have no ideology.

2. Speak English.

3. Stay in the main stream, don't go against the current.

4. You have to be in the right place at the right time.

5. The best place to be is with the Americans.

And to this list, I add one of my own:

6. A faithful woman is vital to survival and an indispensable accessory to any escape plan.

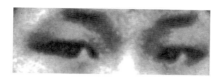
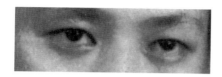
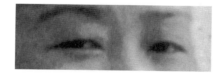

FEDORAS IN FLIGHT

Shapingba.

The name of the Chongqing suburb rises like oil to the surface of my father's mind.

I had given him a notebook to jot down any memories that might occur to him, and he had written those three characters: 沙坪坝. Shapingba. And next to them, two more: 洛民. "Luo," referring to a river in Western China, and "min," that most common of Chinese referents on both ends of the political spectrum, meaning "the people." There would be no more entries in the notebook after that.

I pull out my 1948 map of Chongqing, obtained from a taciturn librarian from the mainland who works in the bowels of the Chinese collection at Harvard. I follow the main road west out of the city, reversing Wang Kun's footsteps that foggy November morning. Just outside the city gate, I pause at #19 Luojiawan. There is no sign, but I know from my research that this is where Dai Li kept his private office. And perched on a rocky rise above it, the headquarters of the Department of Telecommunications under the direction of General Wei Daming, a.k.a. "the spirit of Dai Li."

On one of my father's rare clear days, he had blurted out this other general's name and told me three seemingly disconnected facts about him: (1) Luomin was this general's secretary; (2) This general had a girlfriend at the university in the same department as my father; and (3) I had almost met this general on our family trip to Taiwan in 1971. My father had invited the general to dine with us, but he was too old and sick to come. I felt a chill pass through me when my father told me this: just two degrees of separation between myself and the spirit of Dai Li!

I continue along the narrow neck of land between the two rivers until a sandy plain opens up before me. I see signs announcing the names of high schools and colleges, along with some of the more famous universities in China, including my father's. This is Shapingba, farmland turned cultural center by the schools, factories, and hospitals that relocated there during the war.

I keep tracking west until I find the destination I am looking for: Gele Mountain and the site of the Sino-American Cooperative Organization—SACO for short. Happy Valley, as the Americans who served there called it. A sprawling mountain complex that included radio stations, training grounds, villas for the Big Potatoes, and prisons for their enemies. Where the Americans served as advisors to General Dai's secret police. Just a few miles down the road from my father's university. The same mountain where he once worked the radio nightshift.

The complicity of it all astounds me.

The Saturday morning bus was packed as usual with a few locals but mostly with downriver folk desperate to get out of Chungking for the day. The stink of the city spilled out of the bus with the disembarking passengers, and Wang Kun backed up to wait on a grassy knoll. He saw the despair in their faces and momentarily felt guilty for his unthwarted ambitions.

*When the Americans entered the war, there had been a
brief moment of celebration and hope, but nearly five years of
bombing and blackouts, hunger and extortion and dysentery,
had left the residents of Chungking physically and emotion-
ally shattered and scornful of the Generalissimo's continuing
promise of New Life to those who practiced "self-cultivation"
and "correct living." Even at the university, where the Generalissimo had declared himself president, talk of KMT corruption was growing bolder by the day.*

*Of course Wang Kun didn't allow himself to participate in
such talk. Two years at university reading Blake and Yeats
and Eliot had only hardened his resolve to go to America.
Since his departure from the Bureau, he felt himself inching
closer and closer to his goal. This war could not last forever,
and when it ended, he would be ready for whatever opportunities presented themselves. In the meantime, he recited English verse whenever he went out in hopes of being overheard
by the American soldiers who ambled through the town. The
language cleansed him, elevated him, made him feel invincible. Even those Romantic poets whose melancholic verses
were not altogether comprehensible to him. He much preferred the spare, pragmatic verse of the Modernists. "Speak
only when you have something to say, only what you want to
say, and only in the way you want to say it!" he would preach
to his classmates, echoing the words of the Chinese ambassador to the U.S. who had recently visited the university. Now
there was a Modern Man!*

*"Little Beauty!" Luomin hailed him as always as he stepped
from the bus.*

*"Old Man!" Wang Kun replied and, noticing the dark circles
under his friend's eyes, asked, "Have you missed me so much*

you can't sleep?"

Ever since Wang Kun had enrolled in the university, Lu-omin would come nearly every weekend to visit him, usually under the pretense of delivering something. Once it was vegetable oil to burn in his dorm lamp, another time a winter coat. In the midst of widespread scarcity, Luomin always seemed to have something to spare. Today he carried a hat in his hands, one of those soft felt hats with a wide band and a brim that seemed to be worn by just about every man these days, from KMT soldiers in uniform to beggars on the streets to the university vice-president, who alternately paired his hat with pinstripes or a chang pao.

"Where did you get that?" Wang Kun asked.

"Oh, it just fell into my hands." Luomin shrugged and expertly pinched the top of the hat before placing it on Wang Kun's head. "There, now you look like a gentleman."

"And where is your hat?" Wang Kun teased.

"Such a hat does not suit me," Luomin answered glibly. "What are you reading?" He gestured to the book in Wang Kun's hands.

"An Irishman, the first to receive the Nobel Prize in litera-ture. My professor says..."

"Your professor is a fool! When will a Chinese man ever receive such a prize?"

"Maybe I will be that Chinese man?"

Luomin softened immediately. "Yes, maybe one day you will be that man. In the meantime, how are your studies? Did you receive your semester grades?"

"Are you my father now?" Wang Kun chided his friend. "I got all As in my literature classes," he said proudly, "but only... a C in Principles of Kuomintang."

```
Freshman:  (1942 - 1943)

     Principles of Koumintang              1    C
     Readings In Chinese Prose             3    A
     Freshman English                      3    A
     Chinese History                       3    A
     Logic                                 2    C
     English Conversation                  3    A
     English Grammar and Composition       3    A
     Politics                              3    A
     Biology                               3    B
     Physical Education                    1    B
     Military Training                    1.5   A

                          Total         26.5    A
```

Luomin burst out laughing. "Good, good! Then you really are a gentleman!" He reached up to push the hat back on Wang Kun's head so that his face was out of the shadows.

A gust of wind hits the knoll and lifts the hat off my father's head.

"I'll get it!" I chase the hat down the hill and across the terraced fields, zooming between Time Present and Time Past, in and out of This Story and That One.

The One about Luomin and the Hat.

The One about the General and the Girl.

"I might have made that one up," my father admits, "to make the story more interesting."

"So what do you remember about the girl?"

"Oh, you want to work on the romantic part!" My father laughs. "The girl, like me, left the Bureau and became a student. She has nothing to do with me. I'm not in their inner circle. I just observe through Luomin. He is my source of information."

"Why do you think he helped you get out?"

"He was my good friend."

"Do you think he had strong political beliefs?"

"No, it is just a job. Luomin always has this inner desire of disliking the Bureau. He doesn't like it, but he cannot get out. He cannot get rid of it."

"Do you think that's why he helped you, because he knew he couldn't get out?"

"He got stuck."

"He must have done some things he wasn't proud of."

"He didn't tell me."

"But he must have, right?"

"No. He is a very mild person, a very likeable person."

"What did he look like?"

"He's a little bigger than me."

"Was he good looking?"

My father laughs. "Is he the main character in your book?"

"He's definitely an important character."

It was not General Tai but General Wei whom Luomin approached about letting Wang Kun take the university entrance exam in exchange for English lessons. And it was not English that was the actual bargaining chip, but rather the general's mistress who was a student in the Foreign Languages Department. Wang Kun would be a good excuse to visit the university more often, Luomin had persuaded the general, allowing him to check in on the girl and make arrangements for their secret liaisons. The general's wife was a jealous woman who made frequent, unannounced visits to the general's office, putting Luomin in the un-

comfortable position of having to run interference for his boss. To make matters worse, General Wei's wife was the former mistress of that other general and could still command his attention, or at least make a show of trying to do so when she did not get her way. Luomin knew that he had to be extra vigilant in arranging places and times for his boss to meet his young lover so as not to draw any more unwanted attention to the department.

After the fallout from the Red Radio Incident, as it came to be called by those who survived the wrath of General Tai when he discovered Communists working under his own roof, Luomin had to admit to himself what a wild card the actions of others could be in determining one's own fate. No matter how prudently he tried to live his life, there were always the excesses of others to deal with. And to clean up after.

He had seen excess before, of course, had lived with it as a child in the opium den his father called home. His father didn't smoke but had capitalized on the habits of others, outfitting two rooms in their house with everything a man needed to comfortably and discreetly indulge himself, including a curtained bed and the finest brass smoking paraphernelia. As a child, Luomin had learned how to prepare a tray, lining up the instruments in their proper order and heating the oil lamp to just the right temperature before packing the waxy ball into the pipe bowl. His father required him to sit beside the reclining guest as he smoked, making sure the bowl of the pipe stayed positioned over the flame even as the one holding it drifted away. After the first few times, he knew what to watch for: the involuntary shudder as the vapors entered the body, the slackening of the jaw and rolling back of the eyes as the pleasure peaked. Grown men turned into clay dolls. The faces of excess. Later he would scrape out the sticky remains and polish the utensils and tray, observing his own dispassionate face in its shining surface. By the time the New Life Movement rolled into town, Luomin was ripe for the cause.

At first, he'd believed it was enough to cultivate himself, to put the Four Virtues into practice in his own life. When the Generalissimo spoke of such daily practices as an art form, he likened it to the brushwork he had mastered at school. He imagined his body as a brush, held upright and moving with deliberation, stroke by stroke, always perpendicular to the palette of the earth. Line was everything, yet there were so many ways to make a line! One stroke, one movement, which, once issued, could not be modified or corrected. Thus does a virtuous man move with clear intention and careful execution.

Luomin applied the principles of the brush to his life, lifting and pressing with varied force as the situation required.

Shu: the backbone of all strokes, the father of all lines, the virtue of verticality. Spine of man and brush lined up, equally unwavering in their moral carriage. Luomin perfected this stroke at school, filling notebook after notebook with these strong, descending lines like an army of literati.

Heng: a bold, horizontal gesture like an outstretched arm, a welcome or perhaps an invitation that is as innocent of its own beginning as its end. Join us, take my hand, let us work together to build this country! Thus did Luomin take the hand of the general when it was offered him and extended his own to the beautiful boy scout in whom he saw himself.

Heng Gou: a hook at the end of a line, a minor flourish, demonstrating not merely a sense of decorum but an understanding of what is needed to live in the world of men. One of the most difficult strokes to make without looking like a dirty, wagging finger. Luomin spent hours practicing Shu Wan Gou, a vertical line with a long cursive hook that reminded him of the talon of a phoenix, and Heng Zhe Gou, a horizontal line followed by a bent hook like a crossbow fully drawn and poised to release at the opportune moment. He did not imagine himself a phoenix or a crossbow, but he saw the potential of different kinds of hooks to arouse and activate different kinds of people.

 Xie Gou: a slanting line with a hook at the end like a sturdy branch of pine hanging over a precipice. The Red Radio Incident would give Luomin the opportunity born of crisis to perfect this stroke, to extend a sturdy limb to those hanging beneath him.

 Pie and Na: slicing diagonally downward, left and right, a major flourish requiring not only speed but acumen with the brush. Or the blade. A stroke deft enough to pass through skin, fat, tendon, ligament, bone. When Luomin saw the way General Wei wielded his blade like a brush, one movement which, once executed, could

not be modified or corrected, the blood spilling
gratuitously onto the floor, he felt his face burn
with comprehension of the Fourth Virtue: a
sense of shame.

I google Luomin's name, still looking for some trace of this man who would save my father but could not save himself. But there is nothing. Not on-line, not in the books, not anywhere. As if he never existed. As if he were just another one of my father's tall tales, grown taller by my own prolific speculations.

I stumble onto the blog of a writer from Chongqing, now living in the U.S., who returned to her hometown in search of the truth about American involvement in the massacre of 200 Communists in one of Dai Li's notorious prisons on Gele Mountain. Like me, the writer is suspicious of the stories she was told growing up. We have been reading all the same books, both of us earnestly trying to separate fiction from fact.

The writer tells me about a woman in Chongqing named Sun who is rewriting history. For twenty years, Sun worked as a tour guide for the Revolutionary Martyrs' Memorial on Gele Mountain before quitting to write a book to set the record straight.

I email Sun, and she responds immediately. She offers to show me around the mountain, says she'll tell me the true stories that go with each exhibit, from the American guard dog houses at the bottom, to General Dai's villa halfway up, to the Refuse Pit at the top. She also claims to know the site of the Guomindang radio station where my father worked, and offers to take me there.

Without a second thought, I book a flight to Chongqing.

Sun reminds me of a pit bull with her short, sturdy legs

and no-nonsense attitude. When she was a child, she tells me, her father was struggled to death as a rightist, and she was sent down to the countryside to work on a rural production team.

She gives me a personal tour of the mountain, stopping at each exhibit to tell me what is real and what is fake. The mountain resembles a theme park, with reconstructions of torture cells and graphic depictions of the deaths of each martyr. Inside one cell in the newly remodeled Bai Mansion, a brightly lit banner declares: "Die a Martyr Calmly with Noble Aspiration and Daring!" At the Refuse Pit, all variety of torture equipment is on display, including handcuffs bearing the caption "Made in USA."

"Jia de!" Sun dismisses the exhibit as fake with a disdainful thrust of her chin.

We drive, then walk, then drive again for hours in the stifling summer heat, searching for where the radio station used to be. It's been over a decade since Sun has been to this part of the mountain, now a maze of unpaved roads and half-finished buildings that she does not recognize. The driver is skeptical, but Sun is unrelenting. Finally she signals to pull over at a hilltop dotted with peppercorn trees. Follow me, she says as she vanishes down an overgrown path. A dog barks madly up ahead, and I feel a flash of fear. We are surrounded on all sides by lush green mountains while below, the city of Chongqing floats in the dizzying distance. The smell of peppercorns is intoxicating, almost numbing. It would be easy to disappear.

A man emerges from a house with a basket of freshly picked corn. He invites us to try some, but Sun is hot on the trail now. She scrambles up a rocky incline, and I hurry to catch up. At the top is a small plaza, where dozens of oblong stone monuments stand tall and stark white against a steel blue sky.

In the middle of the plaza, the largest of the monuments is engraved with red characters that declare this to be the Radio Station Martyrs' Memorial, the site of the murder of 29 Communists on November 24, 1949 at the hands of the retreating Guomindang. The surrounding stones bear their names. I begin reading them out loud one by one, still hopeful, even though I know I will not find Luomin's name among these martyrs.

Sun walks impatiently past the memorial and into the woods. With uncanny accuracy, she zeros in on what looks like a gravestone in the undergrowth, but which turns out to be yet another tribute to the Communist martyrs. She circles the stone slowly, shaking her head. There was another monument, she insists, one without names, for the Guomindang who were killed here, but she can't remember when she saw it or where it was. She pushes deeper into the forest, and I follow, completely under the spell of this woman and her dogged search for a nameless stone.

Finally we return to the plaza. Sun studies the monument in the middle, running her hands up and down the stone as if divining its truth. This is it, she declares triumphantly, the monument has been whitewashed! Her finger traces a white line down the side of the stone, incontrovertible evidence of one tale of martyrdom covering up another.

One month after my return to the U.S., I receive an email from Sun telling me that she made a mistake: There was no cover up. Attached to the email are two photos, both taken decades earlier. Figments of evidence of the past. In one photo, a youthful Sun the Tour Guide stands smiling next to the Radio Station Martyrs' Memorial, which appears exactly as it does today. In the other, she squats next to a smaller monument in a much younger forest than the one I'd visited with her. Behind her, in the distance, another stone is clearly visible.

What is necessary in order to live in the world of men?
Luomin pondered this question as he rode the bus back to the city. It was already dark, but he knew General Wei would still be in the office waiting for him. He would want a full report on the girl—and the professor. And of course he would have to make some mention of Wang Kun, though the general was not really interested in him. He hadn't even bothered with the English lessons. When Luomin had made his offer to the general, he hadn't anticipated that there might be more

than one person of interest at the university. As it turned out, the professor was even more of a hook than the girl—one that was rapidly slipping out of Luomin's control.

The girl was not a problem. She liked the attention and especially the gifts Luomin brought from the city, a scarf or some trinket of jewelry. Sometimes Luomin would take Wang Kun along on these visits, killing two eagles with one arrow as the saying goes, and the three would go for walks around the fish ponds that dotted the campus. Wang Kun and the girl hit it off right away, reciting English poetry and singing English songs as they strolled. They were a strange yet compatible threesome, each using one another to pursue their respective dreams, though they never spoke of this.

Still, Luomin worried about the girl. She was either excep-
tionally naïve or completely shameless for the way she went
along with just about anything the general proposed. Each
week, Luomin carried explicit instructions from the general
as to the girl's "assignment" for their next rendezvous. What
she should wear and what role she should prepare to play:
innocent schoolgirl or hungry farmer's daughter. This week it
was alluring Communist spy. As the assignments grew more
elaborate, involving props that Luomin had to discreetly pro-
cure, he grew more uncomfortable orchestrating these trysts.
Yet the girl never protested and seemed almost eager. At
times Luomin wanted to shake her into consciousness about
the dangers of this game she was playing, but he dared not.
After all, he was the one who had instigated it. As long as she
played her part, he would play his. This way, at least he could
keep an eye on her.

It was worth the risk, Luomin reminded himself as he
recalled his friend's shining face at the bus stop that morn-
ing. Wang Kun, having passed the entrance exam with flying
colors, was now well on his way to a college diploma. And a
new life that Luomin was certain would far exceed his own
flagging dreams. He had even found a way to add Wang Kun's
name to the special payroll, composed of people who didn't of-
ficially work for the Bureau but who received reimbursements
for "services rendered." It gave him great satisfaction to re-di-
rect money that would otherwise have gone into the pockets
of runners, smugglers, and assassins. The English lessons were
the public face of this arrangement, but the notion of "service"
held a more private meaning for Luomin—not reimburse-
ment but an offering. Each time he personally delivered the
payment into Wang Kun's smooth, clean hands, he felt as if he

were performing an act of penitence.

Ever since the purge of the Red Radio, he'd begun reading the Bible and had found solace in the idea of atonement. At first he had resisted the efforts of the Generalissimo and his wife to make a Christian of him. The idea of life everlasting was absurd, but the Bible offered him a way of living with his shame. If he could not rectify his past actions, his unwitting participation in the violent excesses of men, he could at least try to atone for them. If he could not extricate himself, he could use his position in the Bureau for the salvation of others. Wang Kun's release would be his first act of penitence. And each gift given after that would be an offering on the altar of a genuine new life.

Vegetable oil for blood.

A hat for the life of a gentleman.

Of course he knew that atonement could never be simply a tradeoff. He understood that this must be his life's work. But it had come as a shock to discover that his efforts to make amends could reproduce the very conditions that necessitated them in the first place. How could it be that in securing the freedom of one life, he now found himself compromising another? Perhaps this was the nature of atonement, he consoled himself as the bus pulled into the Chungking station, each offering containing within it the seeds of a further transgression. When the general had made his counteroffer, asking Luomin to keep an eye on a certain professor of Chinese literature, he should have responded more cautiously. But he was so eager to find a way out for Wang Kun that he had agreed at once without considering what was being asked of him or why.

At first it had been an easy, even enjoyable assignment. The professor was a well-known poet whose work he had read in school, and he was excited to have the chance to hear him speak in person. Though classically trained, the poet was famous for his bai hua style of verse, which used spare, everyday language to give voice to the struggles of the common people. Luomin knew that in recent years the poet had become an outspoken critic of the government, but he told himself that such a beloved public figure couldn't be in any real danger. What could he, Luomin, report on that everyone else didn't already know?

Looking back now, the answer was obvious.

The first time he had gone to hear the professor speak, he'd found himself in a standing-room only auditorium where he was just another admirer among a swell of adoring students. He was transfixed by the eccentric figure with long hair and beard, cigarette burning slowly between ink-stained fingers, speaking in free verse—even the professor's lectures were poetry!—about what the Chinese people must do to escape spiritual bondage. He felt as if the poet were speaking directly to him when he asked, who among you has learned how to dance with shackles on?

The next week, Luomin invited Wang Kun to go with him, though of course he did not share his official reason for being there. He knew his friend would be thrilled to hear this champion of the vernacular that he so loved. And contained in that simple but powerful form, the promise of a strong and unified China that was a salve to the fissure growing day by day inside Luomin.

Perhaps that was why, in his first report to the general, he had so foolishly shared his observations on the similarity between the words of the poet and those of the Generalissimo. The sudden sharp slap across his face made it clear to him that he should never again make such a mistake.

"The Generalissimo has nothing in common with this left-leaning, trouble-making element!"

At those words, he understood immediately: The poet was already a dead man. This was all a test to determine where he, Luomin, really stood. And he felt something cleanly and irrevocably separate inside himself as he fell to his knees in front of the general.

After that, he dreaded his weekly visits to the university. He tried to avoid Wang Kun, fearful of drawing him back in. He went alone to hear the professor speak, or brought the girl along as a safety measure. He knew what he had to do. The poet showed him the way.

Dutifully he attended each lecture, transcribing the poet's every audacious word and reporting back to the general exactly as he had been commanded. Exactly as the poet wished him to. As the poet's words grew sharper and more damning, both of the government and of himself, Luomin understood the sacrifice that he was being asked to make. When the poet raised his arms and asked who would come down to the front of the auditorium and smell these hands that could not hold even a chicken still, these hands that carried not a scent of blood, Luomin hung his head in shame.

Now, as he walked the crowded streets from the bus station back to his office to make what he knew would be his final report, Luomin recalled the last poem the professor had read that afternoon, just before he accused the Generalissimo of being an assassin. It was one of Luomin's favorites for the stark imagery and the rhythmic flow of the verse. He looked forward to reciting the poem aloud to the general exactly as he had memorized it in middle school:

Let the dead water ferment into a ditch
*   of green wine*
Pearl-like whitecaps floating all over
The laughter of little pearls will turn into
*   large pearls*
Before being bit burst by mosquitoes stealing wine.

He would deliver the poet's words to the general. He would
deliver the poet. And he would agree absolutely with the gen-
eral that the poet had nothing in common with the Genera-
lissimo.

Now, as he climbed the stairs, the ancient hollow cries for
order and frugality and cleanliness rang mockingly in his
ears: Buttons should be well-buttoned! Hats should be worn
straight! Wash out your mouth and keep your hair clean!
Walk and sit with erect posture! Drain ditches and gutters
frequently! Exterminate mosquitos!

And he wanted to shout out the window to the people hur-
rying through the streets: Even the ditches contain new life!

The poet never lived in Shapingba.

That was another professor, a political scientist affection-
ately known to his students as the Old Gentleman, who disappeared one foggy spring morning in 1944 while standing
on a dock waiting to board a ferry to attend a conference.
When the student who was accompanying him turned
around, the Old Gentleman had vanished.

It is I who places the poet there in Shapingba, at the
university, with my father during the war. For Luomin's deliverance. For my father's salvation. For the sake of the loss

contained in every act of liberation.

In my notebook, I keep a record of what really happened:

Both the Old Gentleman and the poet had studied in the U.S., returning to a country they did not recognize.

Three years after his return, the poet ceased to write poetry.

Twenty-one years after his return—the same year my father graduated from college and General Dai died in a mysterious plane crash—the poet was shot in the head just hours after speaking at the funeral of another gentleman.

Some say the silencers on the four guns that were used to kill the poet were provided by the U.S. Navy.

Some say the Old Gentleman's body, which was never found, was dissolved in a bath of nitric acid in Bai Mansion on Gele Mountain.

Some claim to have seen the Old Gentleman years later wandering the mountain wearing the robes of a monk.

The poet and the Old Gentleman both preferred to wear a chang pao rather than a suit and tie.

The poet liked to pair his with a long white scarf.

The Old Gentleman preferred a fedora.

Both the Old Gentleman and the poet, like Luomin, were beloved.

THE UTILITY
OF A WOMAN

"I met her on the boat, going back to Nanjing, after the war. The Japanese have surrendered. The whole country is moving back east. I notice her on the second day as we enter the first gorge. We are supposed to be heading downstream, but the current keeps pushing us up and turning us around. The trackers all jump out of the boat and are pulling like crazy to keep us on course. She cannot take her eyes off them, and I cannot take mine off her. She is leaning over the rail like she is harnessed to those naked, grunting men. When the lead tracker shouts a command, she obeys. She leans backward and then so far forward I think she will fall over. I reach out to catch her, and she turns around laughing. The other girls clap, and from then on, whenever we pass each other on the deck of the boat, they call out to me, 'Hero! Hero!'"

My father closes his eyes as if listening.

Hero! Hero!

On the boat, Wang Kun feels like a hero.

Diploma in hand, proof of his four years of study and recitation and mastery of English literature.

Blake, Yeats, and Eliot his companions now.

His break with the Bureau.

His ticket to America.

The war ending just in time for him to make his next move.

The boats lining up at the Heavenly Pier to bear them safely back through the gorges to reclaim the capital.

Another free ride, he chuckles.

Still, he can't forget the sight of those naked bodies straining in their harnesses, the frayed ropes that bear the boat grudgingly forward.

*He is embarrassed and aroused by her mockery of these
men.*

She, too, with a fresh diploma in her hand.

*Her hand, small and surprisingly pliant in his as he holds it
that last night on the boat.*

*They whisper their ambitions to a night sky that is finally
free of smoke.*

A few good, peaceful years.

That's how my father recalls Nanjing. A few good, peaceful years sandwiched in between one army's retreat and another's arrival.

In his new job at the U.S. Information Service, among the Americans at last, he watched the China Watchers. The daily comings and goings of important men, testing the wind with their index fingers cautiously raised. They were his weather vane, and he learned how to read them with remarkable precision.

"The Americans are easy to read," he tells me, "they wear a heart on their sleeve."

Yes, those were good years. My father basks in the memory. A few good years with his mother by his side. He brought her to live with him in the capital, in a compound surrounded by a high wall to keep the beggars out. On the weekends, she cooked for him and Luomin, whom she called Second Son. He recalls her tiny lake shrimp glistening like imperfect pearls, lightly sautéed with gingko nuts in a clear chicken broth.

My father does not have much to say about the girl on the boat. He would rather talk about more important things: the crash of the spymaster's plane, the assassination of a beloved poet. All this dirty business recounted to him through the wagging fingers and tongues of the Americans. All this dirty business that pales in comparison to his betrayal of the girl on the boat.

"This is the part of the story I think you shouldn't emphasize too much," he says.

"But did you love her?" I want to know.

"Love has nothing to do with it."

When she showed up that day at his office, he was surprised but pleased.

"Hello, Hero."

Wang Kun looked up from the film he'd been splicing. The girl from the boat stood arm in arm with one of her classmates, both dressed fashionably in tailored blouses and knee-

length skirts with stockings. There was something about her long, curving neck and wide, unblinking eyes that reminded him of an antelope about to leap. She's too eager, he thought, though he did not look down on her for this.

"We heard the Americans hired a Chinese who speaks perfect English, and we knew it was you!" She giggled behind her hand.

He felt a strong desire to grab that hand. Here was another moment of promise, standing before him in a skirt with a picnic lunch. There was no mistaking the signal this time.

"Let's go to the lake," he suggested, reaching for his hat.

They walked arm-in-arm through the wide, poplar-lined streets of the capital. Spring was just breaking and the trees were filled with tight buds waiting to burst at the first hot day. With his hat riding high on his head and a skirted girl on each arm, Wang Kun thought he too would burst. He could hardly believe his good fortune. A job with the Americans, a home with his mother, a dear friend with whom to eat and drink on the weekends. And now this doe-eyed girl who called him "hero"! He almost wanted to give up his dream of the Beautiful Country and settle into the beauty that surrounded him here. Why had he not noticed it before?

Maybe there was a future here after all? Maybe the reports of Communist victories in the north were exaggerated? Maybe the Americans would find a way to bring the two parties together? This had been the talk among his happy-go-lucky colleagues around the water cooler at the USIS. The optimism of the Americans was infectious, though at times he thought them naïve and reckless. The way they shared their opinions so freely, though he'd done little to win their confidence. The atmosphere at the USIS was so relaxed, so unlike the Bureau, that at first he'd felt wary. It unnerved him to observe these men cracking jokes and sharing confidences and slapping backs in his presence. But after awhile, realizing that they did not expect him to reciprocate, he, too, had relaxed. They rarely asked for his opinion, and only turned to him when they needed an interpreter. He did not mind. He was happy to be able to serve in this middleman capacity, a position that suited him very well. He took pride in his ability to move between the Chinese and the Americans, to be privy to the idiosyncrasies and confidences of each. Recognizing his talent, the director had recently promoted Wang Kun to head of public relations, putting him in charge of the library and reading room.

His would be the new Chinese face of America in China. What more could he ask for?

So the first time one of the staff, a freckle-faced young man several years his junior, called him "boy" and asked him to go for coffee, Wang Kun took it as an honest mistake. He himself often had trouble guessing the age of Americans or even telling them apart. When it happened again, however, he couldn't ignore the sting of that word. The term called to mind those naked bodies tethered to the boat. Or the beggars that stood outside the embassy gates. As if he were that kind of Chinese! How little the Americans understood him! Yet he understood that this was precisely his advantage, and so he went along with the game, even bowing slightly as he poured the coffee.

When the girl from the boat showed up calling him "hero," her timing couldn't have been better. Feeling his blood surge and the heads turn and the eyes follow them out the door, he realized how useful a woman could be.

He'd never considered this idea before: the utility of a woman. He did not despise women (he was too modern a man for that!), they simply never figured into his dream. Or they threatened to distract him from it. Like his mother. Whenever he thought of her, he felt heavy with the knowledge that he too would one day abandon her. There was no getting around this eventuality. This was his Destiny, his Duty even as the only son. His sister had died as an infant from lack of milk while he, still nursing hungrily as a toddler, had been afforded the unending supply of a wet nurse. And for what? Not to remain at his mother's side. She expected more of him than that. When she put the steaming plates of shrimp and pork and chicken on the table, she would order him with fury to "eat!" as if this were his obligation to her: to fill himself up and go forward into the world. Why just last week she had hobbled all the way down to public security to ask for a permit for her *son to go to Hong Kong to care for a fictitious sick uncle.*

A woman's destiny is so different from a man's, he thought. But still he felt weighed down by the knowledge that she had no one but him.

He would not slink away in the night.
He would find a way to leave like a hero.

"What is your question?"

My father's back in the thick of it, I can tell by the glow on his face. His head is cocked as if listening—to what? The traffic blaring outside his window at 358 Zhongshan Lu? The phone ringing off the hook as he fields inquiries about this English book or that American film? Hello, Mr. Zhang?

He looks at me with surprise. "What is your question?"

"Why did you marry her when you knew you were going to leave?"

"Isn't it obvious?" he answers impatiently. "To take care of my mother."

"But how could she take care of your mother if she was planning to follow you?"

I can see that my questions make no sense to him.

Yesterday I had pulled out his old passport and showed him the stamps on it with the dates of his departure from Hong Kong and his arrival in the U.S. There's no exit stamp from China, I pointed out.

Of course not! The British just open the gates and I walk through!

But I wanted to know: How long after the Communists arrived? How long after the Americans pulled out? How long after your marriage did you leave China?

"How long did you wait for her in Hong Kong?" I ask now.

"When did you find out what happened to her and the baby?"

"Baby? Who would that baby be?"

One question sends him back and the next jerks him forward.

Still, I can see that he is trying to stay with me, to follow my logic. He has always loved my logic, so linear like his own. More like a man than a woman, he used to say. Maybe that's why, when he could carry the secret no longer, he chose to tell me. I know more than he himself can remember now.

"The Guomindang is evacuating, the Americans are leaving," he says, trying to make his memories line up for me. "Luomin gets me my passport. My mother is living with me. I am anxious to get married, it could be anybody... You are interested in this? What is your question?"

I hold the passport gingerly in my hands. It is the only

tangible evidence I have of my father's passage through the world, the only means I have to fix him in time and place. It is surprisingly intact, the deep blue cloth cover only slightly frayed at the edges. I pull at one of the loose threads and watch it unravel until it reaches the corner, where I snap it off. I open the passport and press it against my nose, surprised to find a sweet, smoky scent lingering there.

Inside there are sixteen pages, all filled with the red, blue, or purple chops of this immigration inspector or that consul general. On the second page, my father's youthful face is embossed with the 12 points of the Guomindang star. On page 7, the Minister of Foreign Affairs of the Republic of China declares that my father, at the age of 28 (I note that he has already knocked three years off his age), is going to the U.S.A. "via all necessary countries en route" and requests all foreign states to please "let him pass freely" and "afford assistance in case of necessity."

I study the binding. The pages are held securely in place by two rusty staples. Upon closer inspection, I find a third hole no bigger than a needle point running through the center of each page. As if they had once been held together by a different means.

The pages arrived in four separate envelopes, each postmarked from Canton, addressed to Mr. Wang Kun c/o the USIS. When he opened the first envelope and saw the white star illuminated against the blue sky, his heart began to pound. Luomin had done it!

He'd been waiting for this since Luomin's departure over two months ago, anxiously checking the mail, his hopes growing dimmer with each passing day. He feared he had asked too much of his friend this time. In the midst of the Kuomintang's hasty retreat, he had burdened Luomin with this one last selfish request. He knew that without a passport, he would never get farther than Hong Kong.

He also knew that such a document would be coveted by many, yet granted to only a select few. Since his break with the Bureau, he had no other recourse but to ask for his friend's help.

But Luomin had been hard to find. For several weeks, he'd stopped coming to dinner on Sundays, causing Wang Kun to wonder whether he'd done something to offend him. The last time he'd come to dinner, the girl from the boat had joined them, and Wang Kun remembered how Luomin had eaten little and spoken even less. Then he just stopped coming. He wasn't at home or in his office. The government was in such a state of turmoil that Wang Kun didn't know where to look for him. With each passing week, he felt more certain that something terrible had befallen Luomin, thereby sealing his own fate.

Then one day there was his dear old friend again, standing in the doorway with a wan smile on his face, asking whether he was too late for dinner. His mother had immediately sent the servant to the market.

They ate with relish that evening, his mother bringing out dish after dish in slow succession, as if she knew this would be their last meal together.

Luomin did not mention where he had been, and Wang Kun did not ask. They did not speak of the girl from the boat

*or the gold ring that now decorated Luomin's finger. They
toasted each other and his mother and her lake shrimp and
all the cooks and poets and artists in the world who knew
how to appreciate something so simple as the beauty of a
shrimp.*

*"A beautiful mind needs a beautiful country," Luomin
declared as he raised his glass toward Wang Kun. "To your
Beautiful Country."*

"It is not my country yet."

"What have your American friends promised you?"

"They cannot help me if I do not have a passport."

He did not have to say another word.

*How did he do it? Wang Kun wondered now. He searched
inside each envelope for a note, but there was none. Carefully,
he put the pages in order and inserted them into the stiff new
binding. He lifted the heavy-duty stapler from his desk, and
as he was lining it up along the center margin, noticed the
tiny pinholes where the document had originally been held
together, probably by strong thread.*

*He imagined Luomin painstakingly cutting and pulling
each strand, and an involuntary shudder passed through
him. In that moment, he realized the enormity of his friend's
actions and felt the pettiness of his own desires.*

*With great care, he lined up the stapler with the pinholes
and firmly planted two bolts of metal into place. Holding his
freshly minted passport in his hands, he turned the pages one
by one, looking closely for any sign that the document had
been tampered with.*

*On page 7 he stopped. "Let him pass freely and afford as-
sistance in case of necessity," he read aloud, the sound of his
voice speaking English a balm on his anxious heart.*

Some indisputable facts as recorded in my notebook:
The passport was issued on April 12, 1949 in Guangzhou, where the Guomindang had set up a temporary government.

Nine days later, Communist troops crossed the Chang Jiang and two days later took control of the city of Nanjing.

The Americans hung on until August, still waiting to see which way the wind would blow, before the ambassador finally threw in the towel and the embassy relocated to Hong Kong. Sometime before they left, the Americans threw a wedding reception for their Chinese director of public relations and his new bride.

Sometime between the fall of one regime and the rise of another, my father paid a visit to the registrar's office of his alma mater and left with a transcript typed up with his own two hands.

On September 20th, the director of the USIS wrote a letter

"to whom it may concern" stating that my father "is a loyal and reliable employee whose character is beyond question" and recommending him "without hesitation for a similar type of work in any organization."

Sometime in October, just days after the birth of the People's Republic of China, a baby was conceived.

Sometime between conception and birth, my father boarded a train that would bear him out of China.

He thought he had more time.

The day after the pieces of his passport arrived in the mail, the People's Liberation Army crossed the river and marched spiritedly into Nanking. Watching from the rooftop of his office building, Wang Kun was surprised by how different these Communist soldiers looked from the Kuomintang, how clean and orderly they were, courteous even as they swept the streets and offered food to the beggars. Why, they reminded him of boy scouts! He felt a pang of nostalgia for that heady young scout returning from the jamboree who had stood swooning in front of the Generalissimo. But he had not succumbed even then. And now, thirteen years later, instinct and experience told him that it was only a matter of time before the purging would begin. He had not escaped one regime only to risk execution by another.

He threw himself into wooing the girl from the boat.

She worked for the Department of Transportation just down the street from his office. Since that first picnic by the lake, they had spent many lunch hours together, talking at a nearby tea house, walking hand in hand through the park, kissing and fondling each other in a wooded pavilion. Wang Kun felt he knew her about as well as he could know any girl.

Compared to him, she had grown up in the relative comfort and security of a middle-class family in Shanghai. He wouldn't call her spoiled, but he knew she had ideas about the kind of life she would like to live. A life not that different from the one he wanted. A modern life. Their courtship was fueled by this shared dream of modernity. Her stockings and heels aroused him in the same way he knew his white suit and tie and fedora did her. He knew that, with his American connections and U.S. dollars burning a hole in his pocket, she considered him a good catch. Who wouldn't? But the more he saw his desire mirrored in her eyes, the more he worried for his future. He still hadn't mentioned his plans to go to America. He hesitated, suspecting that the only way for him to realize his dream was at the expense of hers.

The arrival of the Communists forced his hand and hers. For the first few days, they holed up together at home with his mother, playing majiang and waiting to see what the new masters would ask of them. Wang Kun had insisted that she stay with him until the situation stabilized, and she was quick to accept, offering to sleep with his mother and help out around the house. The apartment had only one bedroom, on one side of which Wang Kun slept, while his mother occupied the other. Both beds were hung with mosquito netting, and at night, he could see the girl's shadowy figure as she undressed and got into bed. He watched her comb his mother's short hair, then brush out her own in a long, black curtain that he longed to crawl inside. During the day, he observed the way she attended to his mother, pouring her tea and lighting her cigarettes and running for her spittoon. His mother seemed pleased to have the attention of this younger woman and made all kinds of intimate requests of her: to cut her hair *and clip her toenails, to wash and massage her crippled feet, to sew the torn lining of her tiny, handmade cloth shoes. She even asked the girl to read the newspaper aloud to her, a task that had been Wang Kun's since he was a boy. Was his mother testing or training her, Wang Kun wondered? Either way, it didn't take him long to recognize the utility of this arrangement.*

In the weeks and months that followed, as life in Nanking resumed a brief semblance of normalcy, Wang Kun looked like and acted with the urgency of a man in love. He made several trips to Shanghai to visit the girl's family. He went shopping for a wedding band and ended up buying four gold rings, three gold chains with lockets, and two pairs of gold earrings, much to the delight of the old shopkeeper. He had a new suit made for himself, a wool coat for his mother, and a silk qipao for his wife-to-be. He purchased a case of Maotai that he kept in his office and from which he withdrew individual bottles each time he went to visit a friend. And there were many visits paid to old friends and former teachers at the university, as well as lunch and dinner invitations extended to his colleagues at the office.

Noticing Wang Kun's comings and goings with his hands full of packages, Freckle-Face teased him: "What's your hurry? Got a bun in the oven?"

Wang Kun, ever the student of English, appreciated the nod to his virility and retorted: "Yeah, but will it have one egg or two?" He was sure this American boy, ignorant of the subtleties of Chinese cuisine, would not get the joke. He was dismayed that the Americans neither understood nor shared his sense of urgency. Assured of their own safe passage out of China, they seemed quite content to stay put as long as

possible, fingers to the wind, while Wang Kun rushed about
orchestrating his own daring exit.

"One day these two girls from Shanghai walk into my
office," my father begins again. "You know girls, they always
come in pairs."

"I thought you said you met her on the boat, coming back
from Chongqing, after the war?"

"Nah, that wasn't her, that was another one."

COLLABORATION

We speak in hushed voices, the door between the bedroom and the living room closed tight. On the other side of the door, my mother waits. When she knocks on the door and asks whether we would like some tea or juice or something to eat, my father and I freeze like children caught in some forbidden act. We are quick to reply—no thanks, we're fine, we don't need anything—and send her away.

I hear her restless footsteps in the hallway, the rattling of pots and pans and slamming of cupboards, sounds so familiar to the girl in the attic room. Then my mother calls out, I'm going for a walk, and a door bangs shut.

My father and I look at each other with relief.

Where were we?

It's like this every time I go over to the condo now. My father and I hoard our time alone together while my mother hovers about trying to find a way to break in.

He lies in bed all day, pillows propped behind him and blankets piled high on top, waiting for my arrival. My mother sits alone in the living room doing crossword puzzles and sweating because he forbids her to open the windows. The air inside is stale and thick with what has gone unspoken between them all these years.

"How's Dad?" I ask as I move past my mother and make my way down the hallway to my father's room.

I am not unsympathetic to my mother's predicament. To roll over in bed and discover that the person you have slept with for forty years is a stranger! But I am impatient to get back to my father, still trying to get at whatever truth is left in him. My mother would prefer not to know any more truth than is absolutely necessary. She talks and talks but does not ask a single question of him. When she comes knocking on the door offering food and drink, she seems more intent on interrupting us than on trying to find out what we are talking about. As if she suspects that her husband's confession was only the tip of a monstrous iceberg. As if she is trying to stop the two of us from giving birth to this monster that she fears will tear our family apart.

But there is no monster.

There is only the Baby.

And the deliberate, concerted effort to bury him while he is still alive.

I have become an accomplice to my father's memory.

No matter how I try to do otherwise, no matter the traps and trials and temptations I throw in his path—the bundle in the water, the cock on the table, the bodies on the steps, the girl on the boat, the spymaster and the codebreaker and the pock-face and the freckle-face—I end up writing a hero's tale.

The One about the Forward-Looking Scout.

The One about the Reluctant Recruit.

The One about the Single-Minded Student.

The One about the Shrewd Culture Broker.

The One about the Practical Lover.

Wang Kun emerges doggedly from each of my tales, bruised but unwavering in his pursuit of his goal, zeroing in on that little window, still clearly in sight.

I did not set out to write my father in this way.

I thought to get underneath, behind, inside his bravado. That perpetual bravado that charmed and goaded me. Even now.

"You still haven't gotten into the real Chinese mind," he counters when I question him too strongly.

Familiar words. Fighting words. With those words, my father casts me out and turns himself into a foreigner in his own family. You people!

Now I fight the urge to run. China is the goad, poking and prodding me and driving me away when I get too close.

"Go home, you are spoiling here!"

China is the smoking jacket. The silk cap and the silk pajamas and the never-fucking-ending supply of dumplings. All this oriental kitsch designed to entertain his fellow

Americans, to shunt would-be pursuers of the truth off the track.

I am the only one he ever really needed to divert.

He saved his best performances for me.

No wonder I can't write him any other way.

"You were asking too many questions," my father says in defense of himself. As if I am the reason he had to lie.

On that first trip to China, I wanted to know my relationship to every person I met. I was not satisfied with those loose American terms: uncle, aunt, cousin. Especially cousin. I was determined to learn the more complicated Chinese kinship terms and to use them correctly. I needed to know exactly where I stood.

So my father obliged me with a family tree. He recruited his Father's Father's Younger Brother's Third Son, the only one of his generation left, to help. Together they recalled their ancestors, going back three generations, including even the names of the sisters who married out and the women who married into the family. When they presented me with the tree, penned in fine blue ink, I was pleased to see my name written there in Chinese beneath my father's. Running parallel to my name, I noticed a long string of characters in which I recognized the name of my cousin.

That's your grandfather's affair, my father said, better not to talk about that.

Now I dig the tree out of my file marked "Primary Sources" and begin translating that string, character by character, in order to see just how they hid my brother from me. How they folded him into a story about my good-for-nothing grandfather, the corrupt tax collector who fled the magistrate and abandoned his family for Shanghai, where he took a second wife and produced a second son. This son, so the story goes, died before he had a chance to sow his seed, but his widow remarried and luckily gave birth to a baby boy. Unluckily, her second husband also died, and it was decided that this boy should be raised as a member of the Zhang family since there were no other male descendants—my father having gone overseas where no one knew whether he lived or died. As I translate this last sentence, I can't help but laugh at this dramatic flourish.

But I can't wrap my mind around the lie. Why he needed to turn his First Born Son into his Father's Second Wife's Son's Wife's Son. Why he needed to concoct such a twisted tale to hide such a simple truth. And how he managed to get them all—my great uncle, my grandmother, even my brother himself—to be a part of this elaborate ruse. They forged a whole line of fictive kin, then killed them off one by one, just for me, First Born American Daughter with a heart on her sleeve. All because, as my father still likes to remind me, I was asking too many questions.

Did you know she was pregnant when you left?
When did you know you had a son?
I keep returning to these two questions.
I have started to audio record our conversations again. The recordings give me something solid to return to when my father starts to lead me in circles.
"Who is pregnant?" he asks.
Transcribing the tapes, I notice how many different ways I have tried to ask these questions and how many different ways my father has found to answer them.

"Look, there's a picture here," I show him. "There she is, with the baby."

"That's nothing to do with me."

"But it was sent to you!"

"How do you know?"

"Because I found it in your files. You kept this picture. Did your mother send it to you? How did you find out about your son's birth?

"Oh, there was nothing..."

"But you must have known something! Because you were communicating with your mother, you were exchanging letters for years, right? Your mother must have been keeping you informed."

"About what?"

"About your wife and baby."

"No."

"She never mentioned it?"

"Never mentioned it."

"So there was no communication at all?"

"No, I was entirely in the dark."

"But this picture means that your mother was communicating with you about your wife. So you must have known, at that point, that you had a son."

"What's your question now?"

"Well I was trying to figure out, when did you know you had a son?"

"The baby was born after I left."

"So you knew."

"My mother helped him, she went to Nanjing."

"She took care of him?"

"He couldn't grow up by himself."

"So that means you knew about him, your mother told you. Because you said before that, when you left China, you didn't know. You didn't even know she was pregnant, did you?"

"Say it again?"

"When you left China, did you know your wife was pregnant?"

"Oh, that wasn't, she didn't... not yet."

"Well she had to be, Dad, because you got her pregnant and then left, right? But maybe you didn't know she was pregnant. Is that what happened?"

"That didn't ever occur to me."

I follow my father around and around, trying to separate what he knew then from what he knows now. I can't tell whether his confusion is real or just another performance. He is trying, I can see that. "Let me get this straight," he says, and I see his eyes like headlights searching the inside of his head, but I don't know whether that's what remembering or what lying looks like. Or whether, for him, there is even a difference.

"Any new information I give you today?" my father asks as he always does at the end of each interview.

Is he hopeful or afraid? I wonder.

I am neither. I have begun to consider the possibility that there is nothing more he can tell me. Our conversations repeat: I ask versions of the same questions, and he tells versions of the same stories. Or increasingly, I find myself telling his stories back to him. I have even begun to finish his sentences for him, much to my father's relief.

"I am glad you are writing this," he tells me.

And as I transcribe these words, I understand. He is looking to me to write him free.

I return to the task of transcription. I transcribe every word and utterance, every pause and interruption and overlap in our conversation, every attempt to ask and to reply, to tell and retell, to cloud and clarify. All the ways that one tries to say what one means.

WAITING

In the absence of memory, I dream.

I walk the streets of Hong Kong with my father. He is giving me a tour of the neighborhood where he spent nearly a year, in between countries, in between lives, waiting. Block after block of office buildings, tenements, and warehouses lean into one another.

I want to show you something, he says.

He leads me inside one of the warehouses and up a dripping cement stairwell. This way, he says, surprising me by bounding up the stairs. On the next landing, I catch him urinating in the corner. I am disgusted until I remember his age and that he can't control his bladder anymore. I regret that I forgot to bring along his urinal.

Relieved, he continues up the stairwell at a more leisurely pace.

On the top landing, a tall, thin man with a shock of wavy black hair on the crown of his head greets us in a dialect that sounds just like my father's.

Ga lai le! You've come back!

Curly, my father says, this is my daughter, she is writing a book about me, she wants to know what happened in Hong Kong.

Curly nods his head knowingly and beckons us inside.

A cavernous room is filled with boxes that take up most of the floor space and climb all the way to the ceiling. The boxes are all stamped with the same two characters: 出口. For Export. One corner of the room has been converted into a bedroom, with two mattresses on the floor and a box serving as a table in between. On the box is an electric fan, which sucks in hot air from an open window and blows it back and forth between the two beds.

This is where I wait, my father says.

He takes off his shirt and trousers, folds them neatly, and lies down in his undershirt and boxers. Curly does the same, stretching out on the other mattress and patting the empty space beside him. I glance over at my father, but his eyes are already closed. I feel suddenly sleepy. I lie down next to Curly on the bamboo mat that covers the mattress and am relieved by how cool the wooden slats feel against my sticky skin.

This is how we wait, says Curly, reaching into his shorts. His breath reeks of garlic.

I turn away and become aware of a ticking sound. It is coming from the fan. It ticks like a clock each time the blade completes a rotation. I am fighting to keep my eyes open, wary of the man pleasuring himself next to me, but the ticking of the fan and the cool bamboo put me to sleep.

I am awakened by the trembling of the mattress beneath me. Curly is still working himself vigorously with one hand and pointing with the other to where the ceiling used to be. The sky is blinding white and there is a rushing, roaring sound coming at me. It's not just the bed, but the whole room that is shaking. The stacks of boxes wobble and teeter and threaten to tumble down on top of us. Curly waves his one free hand as a massive airliner with an American flag on its tail soars over us so close I can taste the jet fuel on my tongue.

When I look over at the other mattress, my father is gone.

I dream my way back to Hong Kong night after night, looking for my father. I know my way around the city, the way the streets rise and fall, where to cross over and when to go underground. I go out of my way to avoid the vendor men with their slick offers of fake brands and forged documents—everything a girl needs to make a person for herself. I recognize the distinctive scents of each neighborhood. Durian. Curry. Jet fuel.

I have come this way before.

Four decades after my father, I came to Hong Kong like so many Chinese Americans in those years leading up to the Handover. I was recruited by two greying men in suits who interviewed me in the lobby of a Days Inn just outside New York City. One, a political scientist, and the other, a professor of literature, both lured away from their second-rate academic posts in the Not-So-Beautiful-Country and come back to the Motherland to shine. Reversal of Brain Drain, they declared by way of introduction. They were looking for fresh talent for a brand-new university being built on the cutting edge of the Pacific Rim. I figured this was as good a way as any to get back to China.

They wooed me with forward-looking phrases like "state of the art" and "world class." Words that a girl might use to fashion a future for herself. They showed me fantastic photographs of a Lego-like structure at various stages of being built—bright blue towering rectangles, radiant red archways, dazzling white triangular spires—all connected by glass-covered bridges and walkways that spanned the steep, rocky cliffs and stretched down to where the land crashed into a cerulean sea. The photos had a surreal now-you-see-it-now-you-don't quality about them, as if the university had been photoshopped onto those cliffs and might vanish with the click of a mouse.

I was unimpressed by the architecture, but did not doubt the sincerity of their offer. I appreciated the formal, courteous way they spoke to me. They seemed more interested in my family background than my academic qualifications. What university did your father attend, they inquired politely. When did he come to the U.S.? And why do you want to go back to China?

At the time, I thought the answer obvious. I am Chinese, I stated matter-of-factly.

They looked pleased with my response, nodding their heads and giving each other affirming sideways glances. A warm filial current buzzed across the table.

I came to Hong Kong not because I was Chinese, but because I was not Chinese enough.

I came like so many before me, imagining that Hong Kong would be the sanctuary I had been searching for. Not the Middle Kingdom, but the Middle Ground. Middle men and middle women everywhere, hoping to capitalize on their dislocated hearts and minds, turning refuge into fortune. People like me and my father and Curly with middle backgrounds and middle tongues who could easily slip between the cracks, across the border, over the threshold of those categorical truths: Nation, Race, Culture. I came to Hong Kong because deep down I craved such truths, even as I tried to live defiantly outside them.

I came to Hong Kong knowing that it had never been my father's destination, so overpowering was his dream of America. But I thought I could still see him there making his way through the streets, tailor-made jacket slung over his shoulder, moving always forward, slowly and deliberately, the same way he swam, so as not to break a sweat. Whenever I moved in for a closer look, he disappeared into the crowd.

In order to get there, to get to that place where my father cannot take me, I must go by way of a past that is always conditional.

A past that is dependent on the present.

The present perfect and continuous as it endlessly unfolds backwards.

All this time, I have been looking to the past to illuminate the present.

Now I understand that it's the other way around.

I return to the place where I started and begin again.

When my father was lifted out of the masses and onto the train that spring day in 1950, desperate to catch one of the last trains out of China, he must have known exactly what he was leaving behind. Though he prided himself on being a man who looked ahead, it's likely that at that moment he could not avoid dwelling on where he had come from. He could probably still smell the oil of his wife's skin on his hands and shirt. His mother's cigarette smoke in his hair.

Given his wife's condition, he would certainly not have permitted her to see him off at the train station; they would have said their good-byes at home. Though not a man who typically showed much affection, it's not hard to imagine that he hugged each of them in turn, stooping to encircle his mother's small frame and feeling the tight drum of his wife's belly as she pressed against him. He may have comforted himself with the thought that these two women would take care of each other as women everywhere have done during times of war.

Fare forward, he may have whispered into his wife's ear. Not fare well, but fare forward. Whether in his suitcase or in his mind, the unforsakeable Eliot was surely already his travel companion. He might have read those words aloud to his wife as they lay in bed their last night together. Even if her English was not as good as his, she would have appreciated the sentiment. He might even have pressed his lips to her belly and spoken those words to his unborn son. He would have wished for a son, a boy who would become a world traveler just like his father. Fare forward, my son!

Earlier that day, it's likely his wife helped him to pack, folding his new suit so that it would be wrinkle free and ready to wear on the other end of the journey. Then together they must have hid the gold and other valuables in the house.

Knowing my father, he would have rehearsed one last time with his mother and wife what they should say if the People's Liberation Army soldiers came looking for him, laughing at his mother's feigned disapproval: "If you find my son, you let me know!" He may have reassured himself of their safety by recalling that so far the Communists appeared to be after only those who had actually worked for the Guomindang. Everyone else could be rehabilitated. He may even have felt an inexplicable trust in those stalwart Communists, hoping that they would treat these two women, one pregnant and the other crippled, with courtesy and respect.

If he worried about anyone, it was Luomin, whom he hadn't heard from since he'd received the pieces of his passport nearly a year before. By this time, the Communists had begun to hunt down all those deemed to be counter-revolutionaries, with graphic photographs of their executions appearing in the newspaper every day. If Wang Kun had been a Christian, he might have prayed that his friend had gotten out safely through Guangzhou. He may even have been expecting to see Luomin in Hong Kong.

Once on the train, he would have felt the inside pocket of his suit jacket for his passport and transcript. Or maybe his wife had sewn these documents into the lining of his suitcase, just in case he was stopped and searched. Or he may have mailed the passport in pieces to a friend in Hong Kong, in yet another version of the story.

As the train pulled out of the station, he may have felt light with relief or heavy with grief, or he may have felt nothing at all, numb with exhaustion. He may have mused over what might have been and what had been, trying to consider the future and the past with an equal mind.

Whether the man leaving the station and the man arriving at the terminus would be the same or different people. He might have entertained himself with the thought of the astonishment on the faces of the Americans when he showed up at the consulate in Hong Kong. More likely, he could not shake the disquieting thought that the train could be stopped and boarded anywhere along the route to Guangzhou, changing the course of his life irrevocably.

As the train left the city limits and began to pick up speed, the momentum would have thrown my father first forward and then backward, pressing him up against all those other hopeful, swaying bodies being slowly borne out of China.

The Curly of my dream probably bears only a superficial resemblance to the man who offered my father a place to sleep in his import-export business during that year of interminable waiting in Hong Kong. They came from the same hometown, *where Curly survived the Japanese occupation by offering free haircuts and manicures to the Japanese soldiers. For years, Curly's family had run a small salon, and when he took it over from his elderly father, he became known for his skill with the Three Blades: scissors, nail clippers, and knives (this last for cooking, at which he was also quite adept). The Japanese soldiers would wander into his salon looking for female companionship, but would soon discover a different kind of pleasure in Curly's skillful shampoo and massage, the steaming cloths and soaking tubs that washed the blood from beneath their fingernails, the deft moves of his blade around ears and toes that sent shivers up the spines of even the most hardened men. Curly gained such a reputation that after the war, KMT officials and generals were soon frequenting his salon and taking him into their confidence. He did not encourage this, of course, wary of the dangers of knowing these men and of knowing too much. But his touch was so light and his manner so disarming that they came to him in droves, and, under his blade, confessed to all sorts of horrific deeds. It was said that if General Tai were to pay a visit to Curly's salon (though there is no evidence that he ever did), even he would have left feeling cleaner and lighter: a new man.*

In Hong Kong, Curly continued to ply his trade, but he also ran a small business on the side selling the three kinds of blades plus a variety of personal care products such as the peach-wood combs and boar-bristle brushes that were native to his hometown. Before the border closed completely, he managed to stockpile these products, which he sold not only locally, but also increasingly to British and American businessmen who had returned to Hong Kong after the war and were trying to regain a foothold there. He was surprised to discover that these foreigners were interested in such crude local products, especially the brushes—it was pig's hair after all! But he was good at reading faces, and when the eyes of these men lit on the brushes, he saw that they were hungry for a fantasy, so he learned to package them accordingly.

Chinese Goddess Brushes for the Americans.

Royal Princess Styling for the British.

He named his business Lucky Blades and Brushes and had these words imprinted on the packaging:

Ancient Chinese Grooming Instruments:
Fit for Emperors and Empresses, Kings and Queens,
Concubines and Commoners.

By the time Wang Kun arrived, Curly had several boys working under him in the salon, and demand for his auspicious brushes and blades was growing faster than he could keep up with.

Even after he disembarked from the train, walked across the footbridge that linked the mainland with the so-called New Territories, and stood at last on British-occupied soil, Wang Kun felt as if he were still moving. The ground hummed beneath his feet, and a faint wind blew in his ears. He felt the constant purr of a motor somewhere—was it outside or inside him? Hong Kong was like a moving train to Wang Kun.

He commented on this sensation to Curly, who laughed and said, "You'll get used to it."

Wang Kun couldn't get used to the planes roaring in like bombers about to drop their load at all hours of the day and night. Or the hundreds of thousands of refugees who descended on the city day after day, squatting along the roadways and building their ramshackle huts any place they could stake a claim. Or the way the streets rose and fell sharply, forming strangely acute angles where the buildings met the earth. And the mountains, undulating in the background—as if the whole city were a moving mirage.

He had to keep moving to combat the fear that he would be left behind.

Whenever he went out, he wore his new grey suit with the smart, wide lapels, a starched shirt, and a striped tie, all of which he was careful to take off and hang up as soon as he returned to Curly's office. The office was in Kowloon City, a good hour and a half by public transport from the U.S. Consulate, perched high up on the rocky climbs of the island. Each day finished promptly at 5:00 p.m., and then Wang Kun would take the tram down to the pier, ride the ferry across the harbor, catch the bus uptown, and walk the last few blocks to Curly's. Each change of transport brought with it a

conspicuous transformation, not just in geography, but also in his fellow travelers, both growing more coarse and churlish with his descent into the city. By the time he hit the teeming streets of Kowloon City, with its distinctive odors of over-ripe fruit and medicinal herbs, he was desperately looking forward to Curly's ministrations—first a visit to the salon just below the office, then an evening of eating and drinking and talking that would usually go on late into the night.

Curly kept Wang Kun's hair trim and his nails filed and his body nourished. He was an unflagging source of information about what was happening on the mainland. His KMT clients had mostly left for Taiwan, but he still had reliable sources over the border. He expertly chopped meat and vegetables into the finest of slivers, all the while telling Wang Kun the latest news from their hometown.

There was still no news of Luomin. He was not to be found in Hong Kong, and Curly's contacts in Taiwan had not seen nor heard from him. Curly joked that he'd heard rumors that Luomin had married a local girl from the Chungking area and gone back there to be with her. Wang Kun did not laugh.

It was Curly who broke the news to Wang Kun of his son's birth.

"Congratulations!" Curly greeted him at the door with an opened bottle of Maotai.

Wang Kun's tears surprised them both. When, in the midst of his preparations to leave, he first learned that his wife was preg-nant, he had felt only a minor irritation. But now the confirmed presence of his child in the world stunned him. And the realiza-tion: I am a father! He was a tangle of emotions—pride and joy laced with an alarming concern for the welfare of his son.

For Curly, this was reason to celebrate. He prepared their favorite hometown dish of Lion's Head Stew, pounding and then mincing the fatty pork with fresh ginger and rolling it into fist-sized balls before dropping them into his special broth. Over dinner, they drank the rest of the bottle and began to make plans.

"There's not much time," Curly told him. "Very soon the border will be closed for good."

Wang Kun let Curly do the talking. He did not dare give voice to the thoughts roiling inside of him. Just that morning, Freckle-Face had let it slip that the Americans had a leftover Fulbright and no one to give it to. Now he couldn't help but think through all the possible permutations of his future.

Fatherhood.

Fulbright.

Freedom.

He felt the building tremble as another jetliner soared overhead.

During the seven years that I lived in Hong Kong, I would go on Saturday mornings to the Kowloon City shopping plaza next to the airport, which was soon to be closed and replaced by a state-of-the-art bubble well outside the city. Once there, I would take the cargo elevator up eight stories to the rooftop. There was just one tortuous flight path into this airport, with its single, narrow runway that started where the tenements left off and extended only as far into the bay as the land that could be reclaimed. I would stand in the northeast corner of the roof directly in the path of the arriving planes. I never had to wait long for the approach of a plane, with its precipitous descent and last-minute, razor-sharp turn that threatened to pass right through me. Though at this point in my life I'd given up smoking, I would suck in the hot exhaust with a long, slow drag to get my Hong Kong high.

It was in Hong Kong that I began to collect stories.

At first, it was just a job. I was part of a university research team whose task it was to study migration in and out of Hong Kong. As the colony prepared to return to the mother-land, we would follow all kinds of people to see where they would go, what they would do, who they would become.

We were divided into two teams: the Demographers and the Ethnographers.

The Demographers were mostly middle-aged men from China and Taiwan, trained abroad in the science of popu-lation movement, still basking in the glow of their return. They worked in their offices with their carefully calibrated instruments and data sets, trying to enumerate the push and pull factors that brought people to the territory, the independent variables that correlated with a person's decision to stay or leave: job opportunities, political freedom, family ties. From their desktops, they could model mobility and produce dazzling charts and graphs that showed an order and reason to the way people move and why.

The Ethnographers were a less polished lot. There was just myself and a British man whose family had once been part of the empire, both of us trying to right the wrongs of a past that was still hiding from us. We were suspicious of models. Our instruments were our mouths and feet and hands. We set loose upon the city, looking for what we thought migration looked like.

In Hong Kong we discovered there were many words for talking about the manner in which one moves through the world. Refugee. Migrant. Expatriate. We discovered fine distinctions among terms that signalled whether one was looking from the perspective of the sender or the receiver. We discovered that each word was a clue to the direction from which one had come: refugees and migrants flocking from the South, businessmen and tourists descending from the North, expats hailing from the West. And if you knew the direction, you could predict what kind of job a person held, how many rooms he lived in, what she carried with her and what had to be left behind. It was like the winds in the game of majiang that my father loved to play. If you knew which wind someone was holding, you could predict their chances of winning.

We were all kinds of people moving through Hong Kong, but some of us had better chances than others. At the dinner table, my father used to ask: What makes it possible for some people to succeed while others are destined to fail? He was fishing with these questions, sounding into the distance he had travelled to measure the person he had become. And he could always count on me to take the bait. Now I wanted to know: What kinds of opportunities are born out of crisis? How is it possible to separate pull from push?

I took my questions up a steep flight of stairs to a tiny house atop a hill that overlooked a fishing village where women from the South gathered on their day off. The same women who cooked and cleaned for me and my colleagues and our families, which had traveled with us from the North and the West. On Sundays after church service, the women would cook vast plates of food on a single gas burner and one old elephant of a rice cooker, then pile into a steamy room hung with oversized crucifixes and images of the Virgin Mary to tell me stories about their lives. The one about the girl who was born dreaming of Hong Kong, who grew up and got married and left behind her infant daughter so she could care for the newborn baby of her American employer. Who said she could feel the milk harden in her breast when she spoke of her daughter's untimely death. The one about the two sisters who loved women, who left behind their parents and good-for-nothing brothers to make a life for themselves in this not-so-fragrant harbor, who, after two decades of sending money, finally built an enormous house back home that they would never live in.

I collected these stories with a micro-cassette recorder that I'd bought at an electronics shop in Kowloon City along with reams of cassette tape. To protect the tapes from humidity, I stored them with packets of desiccant inside of mooncake tins that were embossed with the faces of famous beauties and that still smelled faintly of red bean paste. I filled sweet-smelling tin after tin with the stories of people who had traded one life for another, always making their way toward something better.

Stories of people with plans and stories of people whose plans had gone awry.

"We had a plan. I would go first. She would follow."

Of course my father had a plan.

It must have been as carefully wrought a plan as any he had devised thus far. He would not have left something so important to chance. He would have used every contact and connection he had to ensure the safe passage of his wife and son out of China. He would have studied the train schedules and consulted with those who knew what was happening on the ground. He certainly would not have trusted his wife to make the arrangements on her own. He would have gone over and over the details with her to make sure she understood exactly what she had to do.

The idea of a traveling companion had probably not been his. It must have been Curly who proposed it, casually introducing the idea into their conversation: *There's someone else who wants to get from Nanking to Hong Kong, a man who used to work with you at the USIS. Maybe you can help each other.*

"The Communists are helping your cause!" Curly announced one evening as he was giving Wang Kun a shave. "They are so eager to catch those KMT bastards, they have restored rail service all across the country! There are more trains running now than ever!"

Wang Kun appreciated Curly's attempt at humor. Train

service under the Nationalists had been notoriously unreliable. Now there was even a schedule, which Curly miraculously produced and spread out on the countertop.

"She will have to change trains twice, here and here," Curly pointed with his razor to the two cities. "But she will have hundreds of traveling companions, it will be difficult to get lost!"

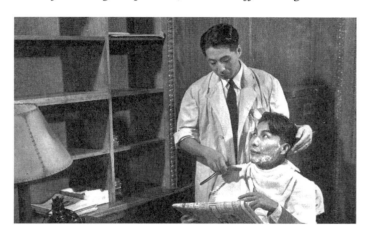

Wang Kun was relieved by the simplicity of this plan. All she had to do was go with the tide. Thousands of people made the same trip successfully day after day.

Lately he had turned a more sympathetic eye to these new arrivals, especially the women with babies slung against their chests. Yesterday, passing by a squatter settlement on his way home from work, he had come across a young woman nursing her baby by the side of the road.

The sight of the sweat trickling down her engorged breast into the child's mouth had elicited a chain reaction from him:

first physical arousal, then fear for the safety of his own wife and child, then guilt over his inability to protect them. The whole plan suddenly felt out of his hands.

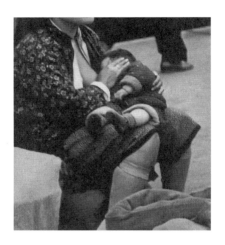

The Fulbright was his for the taking.

"Don't wait too long," Freckle-Face had goaded him. "Those Commies to the north might invade Hong Kong any day now!"

Curly laughed when Wang Kun told him this.

"Listen to me," Curly said as he dropped a steaming hot towel over Wang Kun's freshly shaven face. "It's not the Communists you have to worry about, it's the Brits. They don't like all these mainlanders swarming into their colony. They will seal the leak very soon."

Wang Kun let himself relax into Curly's practiced hands. Thank god for friends, he thought. Always one step ahead of everyone else.

This is how he waits.

This is how he waits.

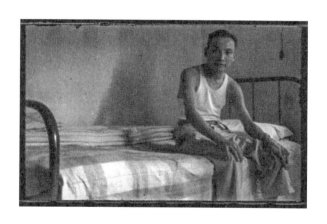

"Rice Christian!" Curly teased as he pressed the shutter.

"One more!" Wang Kun called out as he leaned back into the arms of the white-robed priest.

He felt slightly foolish standing there bare-chested, waist-deep in the harbor. Curly was right of course, his decision to convert was largely instrumental. If there was a God, he wanted to be sure that he was standing on the side of the faithful. Just in case he needed a little help down the road. The Christians he met in Hong Kong were good, kind people who would help a man if they could. He was sure there would be Christians like this in America, too. He understood the value of having friends in the world.

And just in case, he purchased a hand-carved ivory Buddha, small enough to slip into his pocket. Throughout the day, he reached into his trousers and stroked the Buddha's smooth, round belly with his thumb.

I still carry the little book my father gave me with the names, addresses, and phone numbers of his contacts in Hong Kong and China.

Curly is in there. Luomin is not.

I tried several times to call Curly when I was in Hong Kong, but there was never any answer. I found the street in Kowloon City where generations of Shanghai barbers had set up shop. I even got a haircut from a boyish-looking man with long, wavy locks who earned his living using only a razor blade. With deft movements of the blade that sent shivers down my spine, he gave me the best haircut I ever had.

Now you look like a Chinese girl, he said as he held up the mirror so I could see the way he had angled the hair to accentuate my cheekbones and draw attention to the shape of my face.

I am, I said, shifting into Mandarin and telling him the

story that my father had told me about the last train from China. He looked so captivated that I thought I might as well ask: Do you happen to know a barber named Curly who came to Hong Kong just after the revolution?

The long-haired man grabbed his chest and said in barely a whisper: You must be the daughter of Wang Kun.

This, too, is all a dream.

"Let me see... what happened?" my father gropes. "I was waiting for her. Then she somehow... disappeared. She's not on the scene anymore. I am entirely in the dark."

I stand with my father on the border between countries, between lives, scanning the horizon.

Something is moving there.

Something that is necessary for the forward motion of life.

Something that at the time must have seemed expedient but would forever after feel like betrayal.

"What if she and the baby had made it out?" This time I put my question to him in the conditional past.

"You have to clarify all this," he implores.

"The Communists have rebuilt the railroads," I say, shifting to the present perfect, then into the past continuous. "She was following you to Hong Kong."

"She is following me?"

"Yes, on the train."

With my index finger, I trace the route from north to south on the 1951 map of the rehabilitated railway that I'd miraculously found in an academic journal. The map uses dashes to indicate where new sections of track have been completed and dots to show where new lines have been projected.

Between Nanjing and Hong Kong, there is only unbroken line.

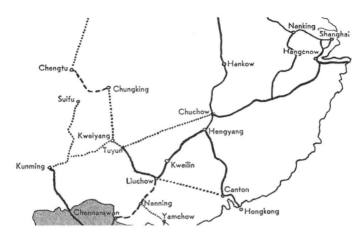

At the end of the line, my father is surely waiting.

He is waiting like he used to wait for me on walks when I was a child, hands clasped behind his back, lips pressed together, humming the only tune he could carry. Twinkle, twinkle, little star, how I wonder what you are? He would pick me up and carry me home, humming twinkles all the way.

I can see him now, waiting and humming on the Hong Kong-China border, in the designated area just outside the makeshift customs building that flies the Union Jack, behind a line of barricades erected to separate new arrivals from those who have already arrived.

He can't be missed in his immaculate suit and tie and natty new hat. He takes the hat off each time a group of arrivals pours through the double doors of the building. His brows shoot up and his eyes widen as he scans their faces in anticipation. He opens his mouth, then closes it without making a sound. When the crowd passes, he puts the hat back on his head and resumes his waiting.

In between trains, he practices English with the British border guards.

By late afternoon, he has shed his jacket.

By nightfall, the hat remains in his hands.

Even in the dark, my father is humming while he waits.

WHAT HAPPENED
ON THE TRAIN

Impossibly, it's the Baby who claims to know what happened. Even though he was not even a year old at the time, still suckling at his mother's breast as she tried to follow her husband to Hong Kong, the border sealing up between them. The Baby, it turns out, is a storyteller, too.

He appears one day, fully grown, on my doorstep. His cheekbones have softened with age and his hair has thinned after twenty years in the Beautiful Country, twenty years of biting his tongue and swallowing the bitter blood.

The one they called cousin.

The one who, with a stroke of blue ink, had been turned into my Father's Second Wife's Son's Wife's Son.

The one who used to taunt me: "Someday I will tell you a story about our family."

The first time the Baby spoke those words to me, I was perched precariously on the rear rack of his bicycle as we bounced over the rutted road leading out of Nanjing. It was the week before his long-awaited departure for the U.S., and he had offered to take me into the countryside since, as he put it, this would be his only chance to show me the Real China. Even though his offer was issued more as a command, with the usual flecks of disdain in his voice, I was moved by his reaching out to me in this way. I sensed a tiny crack in the aloofness I usually felt emanating from him. It felt like a small victory on my part.

When he came to pick me up on his bicycle, a single-speed, jet-black Flying Pigeon with a shiny metal rack mounted over the rear wheel, I was unnerved at first at the thought of having to be so physically close to him.

"The ride will take at least two hours, and the roads are not smooth," he advised, "so hold on tightly."

Though I had grown accustomed to this intimate mode of transport in China, with my cousin I felt vulnerable. What if he started interrogating me again, and I had to jump off?

But the day had turned out fine for the most part. He rode at a leisurely pace and inquired from time to time whether I was comfortable. I was surprised just how comfortable I felt sitting there on the rack with my face pressed against his back to avoid the dust and fumes that gusted around us. As we crossed the Great Nanjing Bridge, with its majestic statues of the proletariat, their fists raised to the sky, he panted and pedaled more slowly and told me how the Chinese had built the bridge during the Cultural Revolution without any outside help, and, in the same heavy breath, how much he hated the Communists for taking away his youth.

"I am one of China's lost generation," he shouted into the wind.

On the other side of the bridge, we dismounted. He pointed north to a wide, desolate stretch of land and told me that that was where he had been sent to be re-educated.

"I lived there for 11 years," he announced, then turned abruptly and got back on his bicycle. "Come!" he commanded as he began to pedal away.

I had learned from the boy in rabbit fur how to mount a bike in motion and was pleased to be able to demonstrate this, running alongside and hopping lightly onto the rack with perfect timing as I grabbed his waist to steady myself.

And that's when he flung those words over his shoulder at me: "Someday I will tell you a story about our family."

I was so intent on the mount that I almost didn't catch them. "What story?" I shouted back.

"Not now!" he retorted, contempt creeping into his voice. "You would not be able to understand."

Now that my father has opened the secret, the Baby has come to claim his rightful place in the family. First Born Son. Eldest Brother.

"First, it was in my own interest to keep the secret. I didn't do it just for our father and his American family. Second, I don't blame him for leaving or for not going back. Only that he did not acknowledge our suffering."

I notice how the Baby speaks in bullets.

I notice the pleasure he takes in narrating the story.

I notice when he says "your father" and when he says "our father" and how difficult it is for him to say "my father."

I reach for my recorder.

For the first sixteen years of my life, my true identity was hidden even from me.

I thought myself an ordinary boy from an ordinary family. My parents were both teachers, and though we were not rich, we had a stable life in Nanjing.

At the age of three, my mother and father sent me to live in a boarding kindergarten. At the time, I did not think this strange. I believed they wanted to give me the best education possible. The only hint that something was not normal was that my parents did not show me much affection, though I often saw them hugging and kissing my sisters. But I was never wanting for toys or books or clothes. They gave me everything I needed to succeed. At school, I studied hard, especially English. I was very good at languages and I made them proud.

However, during my last year of middle school, I experienced two blows that changed the course of my life. The first blow was when I learned that the man I called "father" was actually my step-father, and that my biological father—our father—was in America.

My mother probably never would have told me this if history had not compelled her to do so at that moment. The Cultural Revolution was about to begin, and my mother was forced to expose me as a product of her illicit union with a counterrevolutionary who had escaped to America. Even if I did not want to believe my mother, it was all there in the government files for me to read. Reading those files, I learned about my jiating chusheng—my bad family background—and I discovered my true identity. I was sent down to the countryside along with thousands of other youth to begin my re-education.

Then, one year later, the second blow came. My whole family, including my mother, my step-father, and my sisters, was sent to one of the poorest parts of the province to live and labor for eleven years. Eleven years!

We managed to stay together, but we lost everything—our home and all our possessions—all because of MY bad family background.

My sisters and step-father did not blame me. They just shook their heads and said "dao mei," how unfortunate!

I thought, how could this man whom I have never even met have so much influence on my life from so far away?

Someday I will tell you a story about our family.

The Baby had continued to taunt me while we were in graduate school together. At the time, it did not seem strange to me that we both ended up at my father's alma mater. Of course my father wanted to help him. Isn't that what overseas Chinese do, reach a helping hand toward their compatriots?

Freshly returned from China, I had gravitated toward the Chinese community at the university. I befriended one old professor who reminded me of Henry with his bad teeth and delusions of being watched. Hanging out with these crazy old men again was a strange comfort. And besides, it was the one place on campus where I could still smoke freely. I would occasionally cross paths with my cousin, and we would make small talk, but I did not go out of my way to see him, nor did he seek me out. We treated each other with the combination of friendliness and formality that one might expect of distant cousins.

He must have said those words to me again on at least one or two more occasions, once even putting it in an email. Each time I demanded that he elaborate, he would shake his head dismissively, "not time yet." Even in the U.S., he continued to act as if he knew more about me than I knew myself. I couldn't imagine what kind of a story he could possibly tell me about my own family. I suspected him of conceit rather than duplicity.

I didn't know then that each time the Baby spoke those words, he was performing a small act of defiance against my father. I didn't know that my father had threatened to disown him if he ever dared to open the secret himself. That he almost told me that day on the bike, but was stopped by fear of what my father might do. That his coming to America was contingent on his silence. And that he had willingly accepted these terms.

"You have to distinguish between the lie your father told and the one we told," the Baby says now. "They are different."

"How?"

"We did that at the request of your father. And also out

of our own interest. Because if I am against your father, if I open this, your father won't help me to come here. That's part of my interest also. Not to deliberately lie for your father, it's upon the request of your father."

"What's the difference?"

"Our father made a request to all the relatives. He says, this matter we settle in this way. You tell the American family in this way. It was all for the stability of this American family."

"Why should you care about us?"

"If there is instability here, our father will be in trouble, right? Then they may lose, because your father is sending money."

"So my father is paying everyone to keep his secret?"

"No, not like blackmail," he replies patiently. "OK, without opening the secret, so far so good, everybody's happy. Your father tried to please everyone by helping everyone a little bit. But what if there is instability on the American side, and your father stops doing this? I believe this is one of the major reasons everyone is against opening the secret."

"So would it be fair to say that some people had an economic interest in keeping the secret?"

"Yes, on the Chinese side. The Chinese are more practical than the Americans," he says coolly, his bravado as necessary for his survival as it had been for his—my—our father.

In the spring of 1951, just after I celebrated my first Lunar New Year, a big event happened to this family.
This is the story I have been waiting to tell.
My mother is taking me to Hong Kong to join my father!
We have spent many weeks packing and getting all the documents we needed, and now it is time to leave. My granny

hugs me so tightly, I spit up a little milk on her shoulder. Xiao
Bao, she cries, calling me by my nickname, Little Treasure.

    I am excited to ride the train for the first time—and to see
my father! But at the train station, there is a strange man
waiting for us. My mother seems to know him. She calls him
Lao Li and gives him her suitcase. I stare at this man. I think
I have seen his face before, on the wall in the building where
we live. Lao Li says he will go with us to Hong Kong. He prom-
ises to take care of my mother and me, but only if she will
cover for him. We will travel together as a couple, he says, and
you must say that I am your husband. My mother agrees.

    On the platform, Lao Li walks in front of us so quickly that my
mother cannot keep up. She calls out to him in a strangely tender
voice, and he stops to wait for us. He takes my mother by the
arm, and we walk together, more slowly this time, like a family.

We get on the train and find our seats. Lao Li sits very close to my mother. I do not like the smell of him. I begin to cry. Sshh, sshh, my mother whispers as she bounces me in her arms. It is hot on the train, and there are many people standing in the aisle. They are staring down at us with unhappy faces. My mother puts her finger in my mouth, and I suck and suck but do not fall asleep. I keep my eyes on Lao Li.

Suddenly the train stops and a group of men in uniform get on. They are carrying guns. As soon as he spots the men, Lao Li starts twisting around in his seat. Get out, get out, he hisses to my mother. But the train is too crowded to move. He grabs me out of my mother's arms and pushes her toward the window. Let us out, he shouts, this baby is sick! I open my mouth and let out my strongest cry yet.

*The men surround us and pull us from the train. They put
handcuffs on Lao Li and my mother. They take us back to
Nanjing and throw us into Laohuqiao Prison.*

*Laohuqiao! It is a very famous prison in Nanjing. When I
was in school, the teachers would threaten the children: If you
are not good, we will send you to Laohuqiao!*

"Was my father expecting her to come to Hong Kong?"
"I believe so, because otherwise we wouldn't make that
trip, right?"
"So they really did have a plan."
"It's everybody's decision, it's a family decision."

*We were in Laohuqiao for almost a month. They interro-
gated my mother for hours every day, asking her the same
questions over and over. How do you know this man? What is
your relationship to him?*

*During those days, I was always with my mother, nursing
at her breast. Whenever a stranger tried to take me out of her
arms, I cried very loudly. And during her interrogation, I cried
so out of control that the interrogator grew impatient and
left the room. So I cooperated very well and helped my mother
while she was in prison!*

*Through all of this, my mother was in shock. Lao Li was
sentenced to eight years for counterrevolutionary activities.
What would happen to her? The cadre who had interrogated
her came again and said, there is nothing wrong with you
trying to join your husband in Hong Kong. If you still want to
do this, we will give you a new passport. However, the new
China needs people like you to help with socialist reconstruc-
tion. You are only 25, a college graduate, do you think you*

have nothing to contribute to this country?

My mother was frightened. She had been threatened over and over by this man. How could she trust him now? So she chose to stay in China. We were released and went home and then everyone knew what happened to us. We had been missing for a month with no news. On both sides, Hong Kong and Nanjing, no one knew what had happened. We just disappeared. When we reappeared, everyone was happy at first.

However, my mother had suffered a lot, she was alone without money, so from that time on she began to rethink her life. The first thing was to find a job. Recruiting was going on everywhere, and she got many interviews, but no one would hire her because she was married to a man who worked for the Americans. At each interview, they told her, if you divorce him, the job is yours.

So she consulted with a good friend, a chemistry professor whom our father greatly admired because he got a Ph.D. from the U.S. And even he advised my mother to divorce. Everybody agreed except my granny and me! So we went to court, and granny represented our father, and my mother represented herself, and they fought over me, and in the end, my mother won. She divorced our father. And after that, she got the first job she applied for.

My mother wanted my granny to stay with us, but she refused. My granny loved me very much, but she couldn't accept this arrangement. Before my granny left, she let my mother read the last letter our father wrote from Hong Kong. He wrote: jia po ren wang, qi li zi san. The family is broken, the wife and son departed. I believe he was very sad.

When my mother told me this story, I felt a new idea growing inside me. During those years in the countryside, I saw through this society. I felt I did not belong to this country. I knew that someday they may not let me go. I listened to the Voice of America every night and knew I was just like our father. I knew my end goal had to be in America.

My father claims to know nothing about what happened on the train or its aftermath.

"Why did he wait until now to tell me this?" he demands when he hears the Baby's story. He is furious at having been kept entirely in the dark for so long. He is suspicious of the Baby's motives in bringing this out now.

"There is something fishy here," he warns me.

The Baby doubts my father's claim to ignorance. "One of the biggest events in his life, and he says he can't remember? Before your father fell down the stairs, he knew exactly what happened. There are two possibilities," he says. "Number one, he is pretending to forget. Number two, he has suppressed this memory for so long that he has in fact forgotten it."

I do not doubt the Baby. I am transfixed by his orderly recounting of events. The way he is able to make the past line up for him. The way his story fills in all the remaining holes. He is such a persuasive narrator that at first I forget that this is not—cannot be—his story.

When my mother told me this story.

This was her story. The one about the woman who, even after Nanjing had fallen, married and conceived a baby with a man the Communists loved to hate. Who dared to strike a deal with a wanted man—another Nationalist who had worked for the Americans—in order to follow her husband to Hong Kong. Who welcomed the crying of her baby in prison and was not fooled by the promises of her interrogator. The one about the woman who chose to stay.

She is as much an accomplice to this story as I am.

I continue to press my father, trying to discern when he knew what. As if timing could explain everything. But I have been asking the wrong kind of questions.

"How did news travel over the border back then?" I ask now.

"There must have been a letter or something," he offers.

This is as close as he can come to speaking about her.

I go back to his files to find it. It's been there all along. Faded blue grass script that was until now indecipherable.

Now, with the Baby's help, I translate the letter.

"In order to stand steady…" I translate out loud, "no, to take a steady stand, a steady standpoint…"

"*Political* standpoint," the Baby interjects, "in order to *stabilize* my political standpoint…"

"OK," I try again. "In order to stabilize my political standpoint, I went last year to the Nanjing City Court… to apply for divorce from you… and they granted it to me."

The letter is a declaration of love. She opens with her reason for letting him go: not by her own will, but in order to live in the world of men. She wanted to make sure he knew this before all else.

"You wanted a copy for your records…" I continue to translate. "Of course you should. In my own hand, I write you this letter as proof of our divorce."

The letter is a proof. He asked for it. She gave him what he needed in order to start over again in the Beautiful Country.

"Regarding the Baby… of course he is the bone and the

meat of us two… Since you are far overseas… from now on I have the responsibility to care for him."

The letter is a promise: I will care for our son.

"Regarding the problem of your mother… according to my feeling… I can care for her. But my salary is limited… the Baby is young… there are many expenses. Do your best to send money to support your mother. But just in case the money does not go through… or something unexpected happens… rest assured I will do my best to take care of her."

The letter is a release: No matter what happens, I will do my best.

I go back to the recording of the Baby to listen for her voice.

She chose to stay in China.

She began to rethink her life.

She divorced our father.

He was very sad.

A possibility I had never considered.

A love story I never thought to tell.

That *she* released *him*.

That my father left Hong Kong a free man with a broken heart.

Is a broken heart, I wonder, reason enough to lie?

FARE FORWARD

At first, he probably felt frustration when she didn't show, maybe even a touch of anger. Had she missed her connection? Did she get on the wrong train? Maybe she decided to stop in Shanghai to see her parents one last time? Such were the ways of women, always making men wait.

The apprehension would have come later. The next day perhaps. Or after several days without any word. Curly's assurance that his contacts in Nanjing saw her get on the train, the baby strapped to her chest, would have only added to his growing anxiety. His thoughts likely turned to her travelling companion. He probably began to imagine more unspeakable possibilities.

Did he consider going back after them? How could he not? But surely Curly or Freckle-Face would have talked him out of it. Everyone would have agreed that going back was not an option.

He must have felt an impotence in Hong Kong that he had never known before. Unable to act as husband or father. Unable to move forward or backward.

No little window in sight.

When word finally came, it must have been brief. Like

those neat coded transmissions he had learned to send and
receive during the war:

/ *She was arrested.* /
/ *She has been released.* /
/ *She has denounced you.* /
/ *You are a free man.* /

Each message a bullet, delivered with precision so there
could be no doubt as to its meaning. Relief and remorse
spilling like blood from the same wound.
One message followed by another.

/ *He went back to his wife in Szechuan.* /
/ *They were hiding in the mountains.* /
/ *They were arrested and branded counterrevolutionaries.* /
/ *They were executed by firing squad and buried in a mass
grave.* /

If these messages arrived within weeks or even months of
each other, as I imagine they did, how could my father fail
to appreciate the terrible irony?

*Curly always knew more than he let on. That was his lot in
life: to listen and remember, then use what he knew sparingly
and always in the service of giving pleasure. He did not see
himself as a political creature, but he understood that from
the most desperate to the most influential men, physical
comfort was a source of power—both for the giver and the
receiver. Words could cut or caress just as much as the blade
of his razor as it moved over the contours of a man's face.*

*With all the bloodletting going on, he just wanted to provide a
little relief.*

*So he felt terrible when his efforts to help Wang Kun ended
up hurting him. He should have known better than to use a
man like Lao Li. He was one of those people the Communists
loved to hate. They should have put their plan into action
sooner, but they were waiting for the baby to be born. By the
time she could travel, the Great Terror had already begun.
Xiao Mie. Annihilation. Curly knew more than he wanted
to about this. About the killing quotas. About Luomin's fate.
When the telegram arrived, he had not shown it to Wang Kun.
He did not want this knowledge to disrupt their carefully laid
plan.*

*Over the next few months, Curly pieced together the story
from the men who sat in his chair. They were trickling over
the border in much smaller numbers now, and each had a
horrific tale to tell. One man had come from Szechuan, where
he told about the regional boss, a man named Deng, who was
vying to be the first to achieve his district's quota of one per
thousand. Whole villages were razed in the search for one
counterrevolutionary.*

*Luomin was staying with his wife's family in a remote
village outside Chungking. He had disguised himself as a
farmer and spent his days working the fields. He became
quite skillful at this, producing some of the biggest cabbages
in the region. But the land reform had begun, and farmers
were turning against each other. They became suspicious
of Luomin. They didn't like the neat, geometrical look of his
fields, the smoothness of his hands and feet, his tendency to
recite poetry while planting or plowing. And then there were
his cabbages, larger and sweeter than their own.*

At public gatherings, they denounced him and his wife. They didn't know about his KMT background, but that did not matter. His whole demeanor smacked of bad class.

When Luomin and his wife realized what was happening, they felt they had no choice but to out themselves and ask to be rehabilitated, hoping this would spare her family and their son. Their plan didn't work. The whole family was taken by the regional boss as an opportunity to exceed quota. They were forced to publicly dig their own grave together. Then the six adults—Luomin, his wife, her mother, father, and two younger sisters—knelt beside the pit they had dug. Their hands were tied behind their backs with wire and, one by one, they were shot in the back of the head. Their one-year-old son was sent to a reformatory along with the children of other bandits, secret agents, and enemies of the people who had stood in the path of revolution and new life.

In hindsight, Curly realized that he should have told Luomin's story to Wang Kun as a warning. One should not follow one's heart during times of war. 600,000 Kuomintang were evacuated to Taiwan, yet Luomin chose to stay! Curly had been afraid that Wang Kun would read the wrong moral into this story. Thankfully, his wife knew the right thing to do. Better that she should denounce him than someone else.

Now as Curly broke the news to Wang Kun, he was careful with the words he chose, the order of the messages. The meaning had to be clear.

/ He went back to his wife in Szechuan. /
/ They were executed by firing squad and buried in a mass grave. /

One message followed by another.

/ She has denounced you. /
/ You are a free man. /

A letter never written:

> *November 30, 1950.*

> *My Dear Little Beauty,*

> *Can an old friend still call you that?*

> *Not much has changed here in the five years since
> we hiked these hills together. The fog still comes
> 100 days a year. The rivers turn brown when it
> rains. One dynasty has fallen and another has
> sprung up in its place. Seasonal change, that is all.*

> *You are probably wondering why I came back. We
> were in Canton for six months before the city fell.
> Many in our group decided to cross the border
> and try to make their way to Taiwan, but I felt a
> pull from the north. You may have heard that I
> married. Her family is from outside Chungking.
> We met at the university. I'm sorry I did not tell
> you at the time, but there was so much at stake.
> When I heard the Generalissimo was regrouping
> in Chungking, I decided to go back. You will think
> me a fool for following this clay man, but really
> it was for her. It seems I am a romantic after all.
> And now I am a father!*

*You would be surprised to see what a family man
I have become. Since the Generalissimo fled, we
have stayed on the farm and do not venture into
the city. Everything we need is here: rice, vegetables, even shrimp and crab in the nearby lake. If
this small patch of earth is my prison, it is also
my sanctuary.*

*I did not imagine the Kuomintang would fall so
fast—or so far. Upon my return from Canton, I
saw what a man will do when his back is against
the wall. I am no exception. But I have always
tried to seek redemption where I can. At Bai
Mansion, there were so many prisoners that we
had to work in batches. We started just as the sun
was rising, and by dusk there were twenty men
left, the last batch scheduled for execution. When
I saw that we had run out of kerosene, and they
could not be burned, I simply let them go. Twenty
lives saved in exchange for 200 taken that day!*

*Now every morning from our old lookout, I watch
the city below. I see the PLA soldiers pouring in
and out of the gates. Sometimes they come into
the village looking for the so-called enemies of the
people. I don't know whether to laugh or cry when
I hear these familiar words. The soldiers have a
daily quota to fill. At night the sharp chorus of
their guns rebounds off the hills and awakens my
son. His life is all that matters now.*

Do not worry about me! Strangely I have found peace here. I do not fear whatever justice awaits me. I am looking forward to the next life.

I have entrusted this letter to someone in whom I place nearly as much faith as I do in you. I hope that by the time it reaches you, you will be safely across the border and in the good keeping of old friends. Please give my regards to that other hometown boy. I know that you are not a religious man, but I pray you will soon arrive in your Beautiful Country. It makes me happy to think of you there.

You ask when I am coming,
I do not know.
On Bashan Mountain the night rain
is flooding the autumn pool.
When can we trim wicks again
by the window?
When can we...

Yours always,

Luomin

When can we...
...talk all night while the mountain rains?

I reply to Luomin on behalf of my father. I have learned to play the game as well as him, maybe even better. No wonder, since I am the one who invented it. Along with

Luomin's fingers and feet, his Christianity and his cabbages, his shame and his dignity.

I dream I am on the road with my father. We are traveling together in China. He is taking me to the house where his life history has been stored. Finally!

The house looks just like the villa on Gele Mountain where General Dai Li lived. Yellow plaster with red shutters. There are two rooms on either side of the house. One contains materials in English, the other in Chinese. Inside each room are photographs and documents that provide proof of my father's life. Everything I have been looking for. There are people who can attest to the validity of these documents. They know him. Look, they say in Chinese in the Chinese room, holding up a photo of my father lying on his back, his face spattered with blood. See, they say, he was hurt. They are incredulous that I did not know. You cannot blame him for this!

On the other side of the house is a bank. The teller is a young woman in a qipao who speaks perfect English. She is trying to explain to me how the money is converted from English to Chinese and from Chinese to English. It makes no sense to me, but she patiently tries to help me understand. This has something to do with my father, this conversion back and forth. If only I could understand.

September 6, 1951.

Four days before his departure from Hong Kong, my father made a final trip up the island tram to the U.S. Consulate to pick up his visa. The immigration officer on duty was Edward C. Ingraham. After spending two years as a Political

Officer in Bolivia dealing with anti-American terrorism incidents, Ingraham had put in for a transfer and landed in Hong Kong. He was one of fifty consular officers whose job it was to interview Chinese applicants for American visas and to try to distinguish the real claims from the false ones. In his on-line biography, Ingraham admitted that he did not agree with his country's racial exclusion laws, but he saw it as his job to uphold them.

Ingraham had only been in his post for a year, *but already he liked the Chinese, he really did. They were a proud people, and he respected their stubbornness in the face of adversity. Kinda like the Americans, he thought. Still, he was getting tired of having to ferret out their lies. It had taken him all morning and a good part of the afternoon to break the two 16-year-old boys pretending to be twins and claiming their mother gave birth to them nine months after their father, now a naturalized U.S. citizen, had left for what they called the Gold Mountain. What a web they'd woven before he'd finally trapped them in it! He was not unsympathetic to their plight and didn't mind letting a few get through now and then. He reasoned they wouldn't hurt the country, and some of them would make damn good citizens. But ever since his own wife and son had been forced to evacuate Hong Kong— impending threat of Communist takeover, the consulate forecasted—he had little patience for the elaborate family fictions of the Chinese.*

Thankfully Mr. Wang was an altogether different case. No need for trick questions to determine whether or not his story was true. No paper sons or forged fathers here. Here at last was a man who really did rest on his own impressive credentials.

Ingraham stamped a large purple immigration visa on the

*first available page of the R.O.C. passport of Mr. Kun Wang,
signed his name, and blew on it briefly to dry the ink. "Congratulations on your Fulbright, Mr. Wang!" he said heartily
as he handed the passport back to the well-dressed Chinese
gentleman standing at his window. Though he had never met
Mr. Wang before, he'd heard all about him from his colleagues
who had worked with him in Nanking. He really was quite
the dandy in his white suit and polka-dotted bow tie! But at
the moment he didn't seem to fit the happy-go-lucky profile
Ingraham had been given. He certainly didn't look like someone who'd just gotten his ticket to the Promised Land. The
man just stood there, turning the pages of his passport with a
pained expression on his face.*

*"Is everything OK, Mr. Wang?" Ingraham asked with genu-
ine concern.*

*Mr. Wang shook his head and gave a nervous laugh as he
continued to turn the pages of the passport one by one. When
he reached the end, he looked up and said in a barely audible
voice, "Could you please check my passport to make sure it
hasn't been tampered with?"*

*Strange request, thought Ingraham, but he'd heard stranger.
So he obliged, expertly flipping through the pages and dou-
ble-checking the dates.*

*"The binding," Mr. Wang spoke up, his voice cracking,
"please check the binding."*

*If this man hadn't come so highly recommended, with a
Fulbright granted by the consulate itself, Ingraham would
have politely but firmly asked him to step into one of the
interview rooms in the back. His emotional comportment
was the kind of red flag that this experienced vice consul was
attuned to. If he didn't know better, he'd say Mr. Wang looked*

like a guilty man. Or at least a man who had made one too many compromises to get where he stood today. Poor bastard, Ingraham thought, he's been through hell and back.

"You have a valid passport here, Mr. Wang," Ingraham assured him. "It'll get you to any city in the U.S. of A. So where are you headed?"

"Syracuse, New York," Mr. Wang replied, regaining his composure.

"Well, whaddya know, I'm from upstate myself! It's a fine part of the country." Ingraham suddenly felt the need to bolster this man's confidence. "The winters are cold there, but the women are warm—I think you'll find exactly what you're looking for."

"That's a Chinese curse, you know," Mr. Wang came back as he pocketed his passport.

Ingraham laughed, relieved to know that this gentleman really was who he appeared to be.

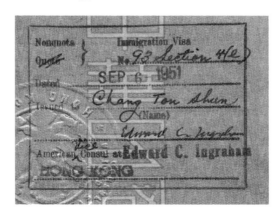

September 9, 1951.

On his last Sunday in Hong Kong, my father rose early to attend church service at the Ling Liang Free Church in Kowloon, which opened its doors for the first time that morning.

In a series of black and white photographs shot that day, the church shimmers in the morning sun that has just risen over Lion Rock Mountain. Heat radiates off the newly cut bricks and freshly laid cement. Churchgoers squint as they make their way across the courtyard. Inside, sunlight streams through tall, rectangular windows onto a packed congregation. Long, spindly ceiling fans descend from wooden rafters. A relief map of the world is embossed onto the wall above the altar where the clergy sits, ten men clad in immaculate white suits. A new global ministry in the making.

My Hong Kong friend, a devout Christian, showed the photographs to his pastor, who identified the church by name. Incredibly we find the church, since rebuilt in the same location, a nondescript building with a towering white cross, crammed onto a corner next to a busy intersection where double-decker buses and red and green taxis swerve precariously past.

Inside, Reverend Wong is waiting for us. He takes us into the chapel, where I am transfixed by the world map still hanging above the altar. I show him the photo of my father's baptism, and he immediately identifies Reverend Timothy Zhao, the founder of the evangelical Chinese church, a man who spread the gospel in Shanghai to twenty thousand Jewish refugees before going into exile himself in

Hong Kong.

Reverend Wong excuses himself, then returns with a sagging clothbound book that he presents to me with a quizzical smile. Are you a believer too, his smile asks.

I stare in disbelief at my father's name carefully scripted on p. 25 in traditional characters in faded blue ink. My father is number 161 on the Believer's Roll. He is the one-hundred-and-sixty-first person to be baptized in Hong Kong by the legendary Reverend Zhao.

This was a moment of Christian revival in Hong Kong, my friend tells me excitedly, something most people today are not even aware of. Your father had good timing and a sharp eye.

He also had a new camera, a Canon Rangefinder with a smart brown leather case. In Hong Kong, my father shot roll after roll of himself and his fellow sojourners, passing the camera back and forth between them with a kind of religious fervor, a witness to each other's rebirth. In the water. On the mountain top.

For each roll of film that he shot, my father made a contact sheet. He would cut the sheet into strips, then dissect each strip into individual thumbnail images, so that any durable sense of time unfolding or trace of movement was lost. He kept these tiny squares in unmarked sealed envelopes, which, upon opening, would spill their contents like so many pieces of a jigsaw puzzle. Only the contact sheet from September 9th, the last roll he shot in Hong Kong, remains fully intact.

Judging by the photos he took that day in the church, my father must have been moving around the back of the pews, trying to get the perfect shot. In one image, the whole church seems to be tilting, the windows threatening to fall in on the congregation.

    I imagine him there, making his way up to the balcony through the swaying crowd of believers, the blood pounding in his head as he tries to convince himself.

    The laying of hands.

    She has denounced you!

    The washing of feet.

    You are a free man!

    The promise of new life.

    When my father finally found his way to the highest point in the church, the world was righted.

September 10, 1951.

In a final set of images that my father shot before leaving Hong Kong, three men appear with him, all dressed in white. Smooth-faced charmers with their hair smartly coiffed, striking a jaunty pose in front of the British Overseas Airways Company. Then standing casually at the Hong Kong airport in front of the Pan Am twin-engine that would soon be winging them westward. Three little beauties, looking for all the world as if they hadn't just sacrificed everything they loved to get to where they stood.

/ *To my wife:* / I write in my father's hand.

/ *I received the good news from my mother that you and our son have safely returned home.* /

/ *I am very happy to know that you are both in good health.* /

/ *My mother told me of your intent to file for divorce.* /

/ *Of course I will not refuse you this request.* /

/ *You must do what is necessary to make a life for yourself.* /
/ *Please do what you can for my mother.* /
/ *I will do my best to send money.* /
/ *The family is broken, the wife and son departed.* /
/ *Fare forward.* /

Go, go, go, a bird named Eliot whispers in my father's ear, human kind cannot bear very much reality.

WHERE MEMORY LIES

    In his boat-bed, adrift on what body of water he cannot tell, my father waits to see how the story will end.

    "Why don't you just finish it?" he asks.

    He has imagined many endings in his lifetime, but somehow he managed to outlive them all. Such a talent for life! But he knows he can't outlive this one. He feels his time winding down, his body relinquishing its needs and desires. Even the food his daughter prepares does not entice him anymore. A spoonful of pork, finely diced with peppers, fills him up.

A single bowl of rice overwhelms him. The labor of chewing and swallowing and digesting and defecating. He wishes she would cook less and write more. But she is still asking questions. Probably she still doubts him. A liar is not believed even when he tells the truth, he reminds himself, remembering the fortune cookie he had received the last time the family went out to eat together.

I find the fortune on the floor while cleaning his bedroom and keep it as evidence of my father's remorse. Yesterday he had called to say only this: "It was not intentional, but I regret what happened." He rarely gets out of bed these days. And now there is this cancer growing on his leg, getting bigger every day, consuming the little nourishment that he takes in for its own wanton advancement. He refuses to have it amputated. Having kept all parts of himself intact all these years, why would he give up his leg at nearly 90?

He never expected to be around this long. He never expected to live to tell his story. When he first let out the secret to his daughter, he was afraid. He did not know whether this would ruin the story he had told so far, the life he had made in America. Would this make of his life a tragedy instead of a success story? But now he thinks it should be a happy ending. The secret has been opened and everyone has accepted it, even his wife. Maybe some suffering, but the children are doing well. Father and daughter have lived through and successfully concluded their life together.

"Why do you hesitate?" he asks. "If you already have the story in your hand, why do you doubt? I would say, finish it! Put it into words! I would like to read it before it's too late."

He wants to see his life in print. It's fiction, of course, but no one will know the difference. Especially the Americans. That's what makes the story so interesting, he tells his daughter, the reader won't know what is true and what is made up. He himself doesn't even know any more. When she reads her stories back to him, he can't remember if that's what happened or that's what he told her or that's what she made up. He's not sure about Harry or Pocky, but Curly seems familiar, and wasn't there another guy who helped him in Hong Kong?

And Luomin. She dared to use his real name. What does it matter now? Just tell the story! It's a good story, worth telling—and publishing!

My father of all people should know a good story when he sees one. After all those years as a small-town roving reporter. Five times he changed newspapers trying to make it to the big city, but somehow small-town America wouldn't let him go.

Just as well, otherwise he might have ended up another Chinese reporting on China. Instead he got to report on the Americans! How many Chinese could do that? He covered their births and deaths, their accidents and crimes and natural disasters, their wrangling over school boards and labor unions and public works. All their strange manners of being in the world. Human interest stories, he liked to call them. The one about the butcher who married a vegetarian. The one about the two brothers who always dressed alike and refused to be separated, even upon joining the army. The one about the all-girl dynasty: one great grandmother, ten great grandchildren, all girls, all delivered by the same doctor, all blonde. Everybody Has A Story To Tell, he called his weekly column. Yes, he certainly knew how to turn a phrase, even in English.

Maybe it was all those novels he read as a boy. What was the one where what was real and what was a dream was

*all mixed up? Even the names of the two families were Real
and Fake. His daughter needs to understand this novel. It's
important somehow, but he can't remember why. It was
definitely a romance, but was it a tragedy? There was a
sentimental boy, like a girl, who was born with a piece of jade
in his mouth. He lived with his granny and his girl cousins
in a big mansion with many rooms and many dreams. In one
dream, a fairy queen tries to teach the boy how to be a man. A
wet dream, he chuckles. What happened to the boy after that?
He can't remember.*

"Look," my father points to an oversized fan hanging on
the wall. On it are the names and faces of the Eight Eccentrics, those infamous painters from the same town as him
who broke with tradition to show the world in all its absurdity. Across the top of the fan are four characters:

难得糊涂

"Nan de hutu. Difficult to be confused," he translates.
"It's easy to be clever, but difficult to be confused. The Eight
Eccentrics knew this. You of all people need to know this."

I am confused.

"Hutu is an important stage of life. If you can, declare
yourself stupid!"

During all the years that my father lived in the Beautiful
Country, he did not speak of what had happened in Hong
Kong to anyone except an American lawyer, who told him to
forget about it.

Don't open a box of worms!

The perverse imagery would stick with him. It wouldn't help anyone to speak of it, and it might hurt his chances of getting citizenship. It certainly wouldn't help his chances of finding an American wife, the savvy lawyer advised him. Which, by the way, wouldn't hurt his chances of citizenship.

Who would take me with a wife and son?

This is where I imagine the lie began.

As with all such necessary lies, it must have arisen inadvertently from the conditions of life itself, at first so small and benign. He simply never mentioned his wife and son. And by excising them from his speech, he was able to keep them in a warm, dark place well outside his everyday awareness. Along with the Bureau and Luomin and Chongqing and the other unspeakable truths.

What else could I do? The doors of China were closed entirely, nobody gets in or out. That part of my life was gone.

It was the Americans who invited the lie. They took one look at him and wanted to know how he got out. They even gave him the words with which to speak about it.

One chop-chop ahead of the executioner's axe!

He was invited to give speeches at the Rotary Club and the Women's Society, where he spun masterful tales of escape while cracking jokes about himself and getting a free meal out of it all.

OK, you want a curiosity, fine, what's wrong with that? I have to eat some place!

The food, like the words in his mouth, tasted artificial but he ate it anyway.

Learn to play the game!

And once a year, he made a trip to New York City to the

Consul General of the Republic of China until every page in his passport was filled with the unfulfilled promise of citizenship. Then, when deportation loomed, he sought the help of a freedom-loving congressman who introduced a special bill to grant him permanent residency. Deduct one from the immigration quota! And just like that, my father became an American.

What's wrong with that?

It was not until he remarried that the lie began to divide and grow. When he took his marriage vows for the second time. When he held his second born for the first time. That's when I imagine the carefully kept silence began to mutate into something else.

It was all for the stability of this American family.

When the door between the two countries finally swung open, the lie would divide yet again in carefully worded letters and promises exchanged across the Pacific.

Somehow the Chinese have a way of doing these things.

By the time I stepped off the train with my father in China, the lie had grown into a mass of such proportions that excision in the form of confession was not an option. He would carry that mass for another twenty-five years before he could bear its weight no longer and turned to me to carry it for him.

You are the strongest in the family. I thought that maybe you of all people can handle this.

He was relieved when I took it from him.

But even outside him, it continued to grow.

Fed by my questions and imaginings, my own elaborate confabulations.

This, too, is the nature of such lies, which are born of

teeming, irrepressible life. Cut them out and keep them in a clear, well-lit environment where they can be cultured and observed, and they will flourish and proliferate, outliving even those who spawned them.

I tenaciously probe this one. With each jab of my finger on the keyboard, the lie mutates yet again, and with it my father, alternately hero and rogue, bystander and victim, perpetrator and survivor.

This is why I hesitate.

My father's remarkable ability to abscond one step ahead of the most dire circumstances has infiltrated my blood like a mysterious pathogen, leaving me with my own uncanny doubts and suspicions.

I dream I am on the lam again.

All this time I thought it was my father who was on the run, when in fact it has been me. I am the one they are after. I have been telling too many stories.

He had warned me about this. When you write the book, he'd said, be careful, some of this may be tinged by something unknown. It may have the opposite effect from what you intended.

Now when I close my eyes, they come, the men in suits speaking Chinese, trying to recruit me. I have the skills they are looking for. The ability to cross over. To know when to go under. How to blend in. I am the perfect hybrid, they coax me, the ideal double agent.

I am flattered and terrified. I ought to correct their impression of me, but sense the danger in doing so. I sense the trap, that barely discernible lever of restraint in their smooth voices that could flip at any moment, turning polite conversation into ruthless interrogation. My Chinese is not good enough to play their game. I cannot hide my heart beneath my shirtsleeve. As soon as I mention my father's name, they have me.

In prison, they question me relentlessly. Why did your father leave China? Why do you keep going back? Which are you really: Chinese or American? Throwing my own damning questions back at me.

I try to impress them with my knowledge of Chinese history, thinking this will win them over. But this only proves my guilt in their eyes. See, they say, I understood them all along.

Where memory lies:
Between my father's need to forget, his inability to remember, and my desire to know.
Between the spoken word and the unspeakable truth.
Between sound and pictograph and alphabet.
Between the hither and the farther shore.
Behind the bamboo curtain.
Up the sleeve of the smoking jacket.
In the cracks in the sidewalk and the door in the ceiling and the chink on the fence and the tongue in the water.
In the dirty little crevasses between crisis and opportunity.

"Do you think of yourself as a survivor?" I once asked my father.

"We do not call ourselves survivors!" he replied sharply.

I have been reading stories of other survivors. Not those who lived through the Holocaust, but their children. The stories of the second generation trying, like me, to write their way backwards into the past. Maybe we have something in common. Same war, different silences. The same impossible struggle to know. There is even one man who turned his father into a mouse in order to write about him. Such are the fantastic lengths one must go in order to try to excavate what has been buried. Decomposed memories. That box of worms.

The children of survivors, I read, are afflicted with a strange condition that makes it difficult for them to distinguish between fact and fiction, though they are certain that a clear line can be drawn between the two. They crave truth yet are beset by doubt and suspicion of anything that smacks of it. This is equally true of the children of perpetrators as of victims since, thanks to their parents' talent for survival, these too are indistinguishable. In some cases, this affliction takes the form of memories of experiences that never happened. Like a phantom third limb that never existed, though one clearly recalls the pain of falling out of the tree and breaking it or the pleasure of holding another's hand in it or sweeping a strand of hair back from a lover's brow. The condition even has a name: Prosthetic Memory.

When I hear about the traveling exhibit of a second-generation artist who made plaster casts of her formerly interned parents' arms, I have to go see it. I feel a strange excitement as I open the handmade wooden boxes and lift out each arm in turn—first the father's, then the mother's, their respective camp numbers cut into the pink papery flesh—holding the desiccated limbs as if they were my own terrible birthright.

"So what do you think is the moral of your story?" I ask

my father, still searching for an ending.

"It depends on whether I want to tell the truth or make it up," he replies, still the artful narrator of his own life even as he is preparing to leave this world.

"Well, what do you want to do at this point?"

"Let's visualize," he says helpfully. "A book in the form of a novel... the writer is you, you are making it up. No, not making it up, narrating, leading to a conclusion. You already did it! This is not fiction anymore, it's telling the story of a person, my story. You just follow the facts!"

The next night, I get back on the boat with my father.

He is sitting in his wheelchair waiting for me at the foot of the ramp. He is wearing the padded silk jacket I bought him on one of my trips to China and the hat with the two brims that he used to wear as a tour guide, taking scores of Americans back home with him after his retirement. One brim of the hat points east, the other west, always looking in two directions at once.

Where have you been? He is agitated. Hurry, we've got to get going. There's not much time left. Did you bring the tickets?

There is some place he needs to return to. The house with the sealed doors. He left something there. Something he brought back with him on that first trip to America as a boy scout. He wants me to go with him to the house to find it.

We will have to break in, he says.

But something doesn't make sense to me. Whatever he left there, it couldn't be from that trip, which, according to my timeline, occurred nearly a year after the house was sealed. I argue with him for several minutes before giving in and pushing him up the ramp.

Do you recognize this boat?
I look around.
The Pearl of the Orient!
*It's the cruise ship he used to take his tour groups on, the
one with the colossal ballroom and the shrimp cocktail piled
high on a table of ice and a jazz band of elderly winking
Chinese men in sequined jackets and bow ties, blowing their
lungs out under a revolving mirror ball. I had met him and his
group once in Hong Kong and circled the harbor with them.*

*Where are all the other people? I ask as I push him through
the empty hall.*

*Oh they'll board later, he replies knowingly. We have a lot of
stops to make.*

*We take the elevator up to his room on the second floor.
Imagine, a boat with an elevator, he remarks.*

*The room is newly refurbished with a hospital bed for him
and a pullout sofa bed for me. I will stay with him until the
end.*

*We go out onto the deck. The sky is clear and the moon is
nearly full, illuminating the landscape like a beacon.*

*A woman in a white pantsuit comes out carrying a tray,
and, for a moment, I think she is going to take our drink
order. But of course she's there to take my father's blood
pressure.*

Are you in any pain, Mr. Zhang?

*He shakes his head impatiently, trying to look past this
woman, toward something on the horizon.*

*I'll need to change the bandage on his leg tomorrow, the
nurse says to me. We may have to sedate him beforehand.*

Is that really necessary?

We only want to make him comfortable.

Look, my father points over the railing, we're moving!

I feel a surge in the well of my feet. I look up and see that we have already left the city far behind. Fields of tall grasses billow in the moonlight.

Are we headed upriver or down?

We'll see, depends on the current.

Are you cold, do you want to go inside?

No, we have to watch for the first pass.

What's at the first pass?

A sign, to tell us if we're headed in the right direction.

I strain to see ahead of myself. The landscape around us seems to be transforming, the grasses growing taller and less yielding. The boat is moving with unusually quiet speed for such a large vessel, as if the river is pulling us along toward its own purpose.

Then I see it. Up ahead, a giant banner hangs over the river, bold black letters on an auspicious red background:

Truth becomes fiction when the fiction's true,
Real becomes not real where the unreal's real.

I laugh at the absurdity of finding this quote hanging here in English. This is from The Story of the Stone, *I exclaim. This is how the story begins, when the two monks descend into the world of men carrying the immortal stone that will become the human boy. I am happy to be able to show my knowledge of the book.*

Yes, yes, he is beaming. This is the way back. He closes his eyes.

Now I can clearly make out rock formations rising up on either side of the river. And tucked here and there among the rocks, rice fields cut into neat geometric units and pooled with water, each one reflecting its own moon.

There's a wilderness there, he says with his eyes closed.

Where?

In the field, behind my house... a garbage dump, all kinds of junk there...

What are you doing there?

We play there after school... that's where they do the executions... the whole neighborhood comes running to see the show...

What do you see?

My father... he is wearing a summer gown...

What color is the gown?

White! A long white gown... ironed very nice, very stylish... like a gentleman...

Is he watching the execution too?

No, he is in jail... doing all those dirty things...

What happened?

Our house is seized... a big house with a courtyard and many rooms...

Which one is yours?

In the innermost corner... you have to pass through two courtyards to get there... and across the hall the room is rented by a landlord, another one of those corrupt guys connected to the government... When the house is sealed, his stuff is stuck inside too... It is his idea to break into the house!

How?

You have to dig a hole in the outside wall and crawl through.

Where?

Here, where the wall is soft. He reaches with both hands, feeling for the surface in front of him. Here. He takes my hands in his and guides them to the spot.

I am surprised how quickly the wall gives. My fingers sink into the crumbling plaster and pass easily through the porous clay. Is this what memory feels like? A sweet, pungent scent rushes through the hole, reminding me of pickled turnips, the kind my grandmother fed me with congee during that long, cold winter of reversals. Is this what memory smells like, sweet and sour, like an old pickle? It is the same redolent odor that has been emanating from my father over the last few days. A chemical transformation resulting from the inexorable passage of time.

How long have we been on this boat together?

I turn around with a question on my lips.

My father is sitting up in bed as the nurse gives him a drink of water on a sponge stick. She dips the stick into a paper cup, presses out the excess water, then slides it into his mouth. He sucks contentedly like a boy with a lollipop, waving me forward, daring me to commit this crime without him.

Dig! Dig!

For once I do not argue. I turn back to the hole, which is now blowing a steady stream of cool, preserved air that I find irresistible. The smell of the past as it comes into contact with the present. Using both hands, I pull whole pieces of plaster and clay and dirt and stone from the wall, widening the hole until the opening is just large enough for me to crawl through.

Back in his boat-bed, Wang Kun hears music. The band must be back from break. The tune is familiar, an old melody from his school days, a farewell song about drinking with old friends to keep the cold dreams at bay.

We are a product of some force we don't know, he murmurs to his daughter, pleased to see her still sitting by his side. We are molded and changed.

Dad, where are you now?

I'm pretending to sit here with you on a boat eating dinner. You'll remember this conversation someday. You talked to your father while he was alive.

FROM A DAUGHTER'S NOTEBOOK

"Not only must historical circumstance create a new existential situation for a character in a novel, but history *itself* must be understood and analyzed as an existential situation."

—Milan Kundera, *The Art of the Novel*

Prologue: Borne out of China

p. 1 "the last train out of China"—On October 1, 1949, the People's Republic of China was founded, ending 22 years of civil war between the Nationalists (see note for p. 4) and the Communists (see note for p. 1). During the months leading up to and following the Communist victory, many people associated with the Nationalist government fled China for Hong Kong on overcrowded trains and steamers. Even after the border closed, the flow of refugees continued.

p. 1 "the Communists"—Chinese Communist Party, CCP, 共产党. Borne out of clandestine meetings between Soviet cominterns sent to China and Chinese students radicalized and returned from Europe, Japan, and the U.S. Repeatedly purged by the KMT (see note for p. 4), they championed the art of guerilla warfare, peasant mobilization, and class struggle. Following the Long March, Mao Zedong (Mao Tse-tung) emerged in Yan An as the Great Helmsman (see David Henry Hwang's play of the same name). Extolled by left-leaning American writers fleeing the Depression who came to China looking for agrarian revolution.

p. 2 "Hong Kong"—香港, southern Chinese port city caught perpetually between China and the West. Declared a "free port" by the British Empire following their victory in the Opium Wars with China. Colonized by Britain from 1842-1941 and 1945-1997, occupied by Japan from 1941-1945, and reclaimed by the People's Republic of China in 1997, each conquest producing a fresh wave of migration in and out of the territory. Slippery middle ground for people moving both ways: refugees from China looking for a way out and foreigners seeking a way in.

p. 2 "the Republic"—of China, ROC, 中华民国, 1912-1949. The end of 2,000 years of imperial rule and the beginning of modern China. Founded by Sun Zhongshan (Sun Yat-sen), who did not live long enough to see his three offspring, the Three People's Principles—People's Nationalism, People's Democracy, and People's Livelihood—grow to maturity. A period marked by warlordism (1916-1928), Japanese occupation (1931-1945), and civil war between the Nationalists and the Communists (1927-1949). Also Russian organizing, American intervention, and a World War against fascism. A heady time of New Youth and New Culture and New Thought movements (see note for p. 58). A provisional time when no one knew which way the wind would blow and nothing was certain and anything was possible.

p. 4 "Guomindang"—the Nationalists, National People's Party, Kuomintang, KMT, 国民党. Established by Sun Zhongshan after returning from exile to unite the country around his Three People's Principles. Collaborated with Soviet and Chinese Communists to form the Whampoa Military Academy and fight the warlords. Reinvented after Sun's untimely death by his protégé Jiang Jieshi (Chiang Kai-shek, a.k.a. the Generalissimo—see note for p. 55) as the party of New Life (see note for p. 58): the marriage of

Confucian virtues, Christian values, and devout Anti-Communism. Under the Generalissimo, the KMT steadfastly resisted the Japanese while waging relentless war on the Communists. Supported by American evangelical Christians, *Time-Life Magazine*, and the U.S. Congress.

p. 18 "the Kennedys of China"—My father could not recall the exact names of the sisters who taught him English literature in Chongqing and admonished him in Hong Kong to "go back" to China, but he remembered their brother, Yu Dawei (俞大维), a KMT general who escaped to Taiwan where he later became defense minister. A large elite family, they served their country across generations, albeit from radically different positions along the political spectrum.

p. 20 "Chinese boy scouts"—童子军, tongzi jun, boy militia. Not the boy scouts of Norman Rockwell's paintings. Established by the YMCA in China in the early 1900s. Embraced by students returning from abroad as a form of patriotic physical training to counter the image of the "sick man of Asia." Gathered with their global brethren in Washington DC to prove that they, too, could be modern men. Reinvented by the Generalissimo as a wartime feeder into the KMT Youth Corps, with German youth groups as their model (see Margaret Mih Tillman, "Engendering children of the resistance: Models for gender and scouting in China, 1919-1937," *Cross-Currents: East Asian History and Culture Review*, E-Journal No. 13, December 2014, http://cross-currents.berkeley.edu/e-journal/issue-13). Student, scout, soldier, spy. How physical education turns into military training turns into espionage.

p. 22 "Heroes don't make history, history makes heroes"—An idiom attributed to Mao and Hitler. Often posed as an ideological litmus test: Do historical circumstances make the person, or does the person make the circumstance? 时势造英雄，还是英雄造时势? The correct Marxist response: the former. My father's response to my question about whether he feels regret.

The Fall

p. 30 "both possibilities were contained in one word, 'weiji'"—危机. Crisis = Danger + Opportunity. An orientalism popular among Americans over the last century, adaptable to any alleged crisis and regularly used in motivational speeches by missionaries, businessmen, and politicians. Most recently, a favorite trope of Al Gore when talking about the climate crisis.

p. 31 "the need for cooperation between the Nationalists and the Communists"—From its inception, the Republic was threatened from within by powerful warlords and military cliques, each with their own regional armies, and from the outside by the increasingly aggressive territorial expansion of Imperial Japan. Under this pressure, the KMT and the CCP reluctantly came together twice to try to unify China. The first United Front took place in 1926 against the warlords (a.k.a. the Northern Expedition), and the second in 1936 against the Japanese. Both parties had their own ideological motives. Both efforts were short-lived and doomed to fail.

p. 37 "Society for Vigorous Practice"—力行社, 1932-1938, secret KMT society whose members admired fascism, opposed communism, and pledged their loyalty to the Generalissimo. Patron of the Chinese boy scouts (see note for p. 20). (See Frederic Wakeman, Jr., *Spymaster: Dai Li and the Chinese Secret Service*, Berkeley: University of California Press, 2003).

p. 37 "Three People's Principles Youth Corps"—三民主义青年团,
Youth Corps named after Sun Zhongshan's three ideo-
logical offspring, formed in 1938 in an effort to mobilize
Chinese youth and reinvigorate the KMT in response
to growing factionalism within the party. (See Frederic
Wakeman, Jr., *Spymaster: Dai Li and the Chinese Secret
Service*, Berkeley: University of California Press, 2003).

p. 37 "Bureau of Investigation and Statistics"—调查统计局.
There were two branches of this intelligence organization:
the Central Statistics Bureau or Zhongtong (中统) and the
Military Statistics Bureau or Juntong (军统). The Chinese
FBI vs. the Chinese Secret Service. Under wartime conditions, the latter, which controlled all forms of telecommu-
nication, grew exponentially with the growing authority
of General Dai Li (see note for p. 104). How statistics
become code for espionage. (See Frederic Wakeman, Jr.,
Spymaster: Dai Li and the Chinese Secret Service, Berkeley: University of California Press, 2003).

Postcards from the Moon

Nixon

p. 43 "Normalization"—of relations between the U.S. and the
People's Republic of China took place on January 1,
1979. After thirty years of severed relations between the
two countries following Mao Zedong's 1949 declaration
of victory by the Communists over the Nationalists, the
Generalissimo's hasty retreat to Taiwan, and the Americans' pledge of allegiance to the latter against the
former. The end of three decades of dissociation between
Chinese and Americans—and within Chinese American
families. The One China Policy became the new normal,
as a consequence of which the U.S. broke with the KMT,
renounced the ROC (a.k.a. Taiwan), and declared the PRC
to be the Real China.

Daring

p. 53 "the Blitz....bombing Chongqing" —轰炸重庆, Hongzha Chongqing, the Great Bombing of Chongqing. Though the Japanese were never able to occupy the wartime capital of China, they relentlessly assaulted the city from the air for five years. Beginning with trial raids in the winter of 1938, through the first sorties of May 3 and 4, 1939, until the final barrage on August 23, 1943, the Imperial Japanese Air Service dropped 20,000 bombs, destroyed 20,000 buildings, and killed nearly 30,000 people (Chang Jui-te, "Bombs don't discriminate? Class, gender, and ethnicity in the air-raid-shelter experiences of the wartime population of Chongqing," *Beyond Suffering: Recounting War in Modern China*, edited by in James Flath and Norman Smith, Vancouver: UBC Press, 2011, pp. 59-79).

p. 55 "12-point star" —Actually a sun, blinding white against a stark blue sky, with twelve rays representing the twelve months of the year and the twelve Chinese units of time (时辰). A symbol of unstoppable progress toward a new modern China under the KMT. The red of the flag was added later by Sun Zhongshan to signify the earth stained with the blood of revolutionaries.

p. 55 "the Generalissimo" —Chiang Kai-Shek, Jiang Jieshi, 蒋介石. An Italian military superlative that Americans liked to call the supremely fastidious leader of Republican China. He eventually won over the Americans with the help of his U.S. educated wife (see note for p. 83), who wisely advised him to convert to Christianity. Admired in the U.S. for his staunchly anti-communist stance and feared in China for his dictatorial ways. "To foreigners his outer reserve argued stability, a sweetly rational quality in a mad society. But sometimes Chiang erupted from his expressionless calm into a rage in which he threw teacups, pounded on tables, shrieked and yelled like a top sergeant" (Theodore White and Annalee Jacoby, *Thunder out of China*, NY: Da Capo Press, 1946, p. 127).

p. 57 "the Japanese had taken Shanghai"—a.k.a. the "Fall of Shanghai," November 1937, four months after the Imperial Japanese Army invaded China proper (having occupied Chinese Manchuria since 1931). With no support from Western powers, the Generalissimo's National Revolutionary Army held Shanghai for three months before surrendering the port city to the Japanese and retreating to Nanjing (see Rana Mitter, *Forgotten Ally: China World War II, 1937-1945*, Boston: Mariner Books, 2013).

p. 58 "New Life"—新生活运动. The Generalissimo's sincere yet misguided movement to turn China from a backwards-looking nation into a forward-looking one through daily hygienic rituals. No spitting! No swearing! No smoking! No littering! An erect posture and a clean well-buttoned shirt became synoymous with the attributes of a modern Chinese gentleman. Cleanliness and orderliness as not merely godliness but a form of national salvation. How hygiene can turn into fascism. (See Arif Dirlik, "The ideological foundations of the New Life Movement: A study in counterrevolution," *Journal of Asian Studies*, 34(4), Aug. 1975, pp. 945-980).

p. 58 "kidnap the Generalissimo in his pajamas"—Xian Incident, December 12, 1936. "The Communists are a disease of the heart, the Japanese a disease of the skin," the Generalissimo famously said. His kidnapping by his own marshal was an attempt to force him to join with the heart in fighting the skin. As a student in China in the 1980s, I climbed the steep slope to the cave where the Generalissimo had hid from his captors, sans shoes and false teeth, urged on by my tour guide to feel his shame.

p. 59 "They will send their planes to fight the Japanese"—Even before the Americans entered the war, a volunteer force of U.S. fighter pilots under the command of General Claire Lee Chennault (an ardent fan of Madame Chiang, see note for p. 83) had been training the Chinese Air Force and downing Japanese planes over Chongqing. Although they were known as the Flying Tigers, the noses of their outdated planes (sold second-hand to the Chinese by the U.S. government) were painted with the toothy grin of a shark.

p. 61 "little Japanese"— 小日本. What my grandmother called the occupiers of China from 1931-1945, along with the offspring of their forced relations with Chinese women. Hearks back to 3rd century Chinese records, which referred to the Japanese kingdom as 倭, wo, literally meaning dwarf, and Ming dynasty references to 倭寇, "dwarf bandits," a derogatory term resurrected by the Generalissimo during the War of Resistance against Japan (see note for p. 80).

p. 61 "ship bearing an American flag"—For nearly a century, from 1844-1941, U.S. naval gunboats patrolled the Chang Jiang (Yangtze River) to protect American treaty ports, the result of a series of unequal treaties between China and the West. Since these and other foreign ships sailed with relative impunity, it was not uncommon for Chinese vessels to fly the flags of other nations as a form of protection.

p. 64 "the Rape of Nanjing—December 1937 to January 1938, as painstakingly documented in Iris Chang's 1997 book, *The Rape of Nanking: The Forgotten Holocaust of World War II*. Haunted by graphic stories of her grandparents' escape, Chang tracked down elderly survivors in Nanjing and poured through the diaries of foreign residents. Her book met with international acclaim along with accusations of lying by Japanese ultranationalists. On Nov. 9, 2004, in the midst of doing research for her new book on veterans of the Bataan Death March, Chang purchased a revolver, put it in her mouth, and took her own life. "I can never shake my belief that I was being recruited, and later persecuted, by forces more powerful than I could have imagined," she wrote in one of three notes she left behind. "Whether it was the CIA or some other organization I will never know. As long as I am alive, these forces will never stop hounding me. . ."

Romantic Hankou

p. 75 "Romantic Hankou"—"History, grown weary of Shanghai, bored with Barcelona, has fixed her capricious interest upon Hankow. But where is she staying? Everyone boasts that he has met her, but where no one can exactly say. Shall we find her at the big hotel, drinking whiskey with the journalists at the bar? Is she the guest of the Generalissimo or the Soviet Ambassador? Does she prefer the headquarters of the Eighth Route Army, or the German military advisors? Is she content with a rickshaw coolie's hat?" (W.H. Auden & Christopher Isherwood, *Journey to a War*, NY: Random House, 1939 pp. 50-51)

p. 78 "Revolutionary youth, quickly prepare..."—From "Song of the Linli Training Class," Military Affairs Commision, Bureau of Investigation and Statistics (Frederic Wakeman, Jr., *Spymaster: Dai Li and the Chinese Secret Service*, Berkeley: University of California Press, 2003, p. 250).

p. 79 "Changsha has been burned to the ground"— by order of the governor of Hunan Province on Nov. 12, 1938, in a panicked response to the false rumor that the Japanese were about to attack the city. Based on a similar tactic used by the Generalissimo earlier that year when he ordered the destruction of the dikes of the Yellow River without public notice, resulting in nearly half a million dead and 3-5 million refugees (Rana Mitter, *Forgotten Ally: China World War II, 1937-1945*, Boston: Mariner Books, 2013, p. 163).

p. 79 "That's what one historian called the city"—Stephen MacKinnon, historian of wartime Republican China, enamored like me with American journalists who were enamored with China. Truth seekers, all of us, trying to get the real story behind the romance of resistance, in spite of our own latent infatuations. (See Stephen R. MacKinnon, *Wuhan 1938: War, Refugees, and the Making of Modern China*, Berkeley: University of California Press, 2008).

p. 80 "Jewish refugee from Hungary with a Hollywood name"—Robert Capa, dubbed the World's Greatest War Photographer (he'd rather have been unemployed). Born André Friedman in Hungary in 1913, fetal caul around his head and an extra finger on his hand, both immediately excised. Champion of the 35 mm camera, so up close and in the face of war that he was accused of staging death.

p. 80 "Anti-Japanese War"—a.k.a. the War of Resistance against Japan, the Second Sino-Japanese War, 抗日战争, 1937-45. The result of a reluctant alliance between the KMT and the CCP in response to Japan's invasion of China. Chinese fighting Chinese fighting Japanese. Scorched earth tactics all around. 15-20 million dead. 90 million refugees. After Pearl Harbor, the unsung Pacific Theatre of WWII. Without such Chinese resilience, some say, the Allies might not have won WWII. (See Rana Mitter, *Forgotten Ally: China World War II, 1937-1945*, Boston: Mariner Books, 2013).

p. 82 "the train that will bear him safely into the interior"—On July 5, 1938, military advisors to the Generalissimo left Hankou on a train draped with the flag of the Third Reich to ward off Japanese bombers.

p. 83 "the First Lady"—Madame Chiang Kai-shek, Song Meiling, Soong May-Ling, 宋美齡. Wellesley grad, right-leaning Song sister, embodiment of New Life. Darling and Dragon Lady of Hollywood and Congress. Her visit to the U.S. in 1943 resulted in American support for the Nationalist cause and the repeal of the 60-year-old Chinese Exclusion Act, giving foreign-born Chinese such as my father the right to seek naturalization.

p. 84 "a freak snowstorm in March"—"In early March 1938, Capa found the local children enraptured because a rare snowstorm had blanketed the city (of Hankou). The resulting photograph is one of the most joyous of his career" (Richard Whelan, *Robert Capa: The Definitive Collection*, London: Phaidon Press, 2001, p. 148).

The Reversals You Live With

p. 93 "Bamboo Curtain"—Cold War term demarcating an ideological divide between communist Asian states and the capitalist West. A more malleable and therefore durable metaphor than the Iron Curtain.

p. 93 "Red Master"—The McCarthy Era had ended by the time my father took his oath of U.S. citizenship in 1963, but images of "red peril" and the fear and hysteria unleashed over the threat of communism spreading to the U.S. persisted well into the 1960s and 1970s. Films such as "China: The Roots of Madness" perpetuated this view of the seething minions of Red Chinese, "one quarter of the human race, who are taught to hate, their growing power is the world's greatest threat to peace and life" (written by Theodore White, directed by Mel Stuart, 1967).

Into the Interior

p. 104 "gold-mouthed Spymaster"—General Dai Li, Tai Li, 戴笠, a.k.a. the Hatchet Man, the Generalissimo's dagger, the Himmler of Republican China. Chief of the Chinese Secret Service (see note for p. 37). Noted for his horse-like appearance, post-nasal drip, tiny hands, ubiquitous network of agents, ruthless tactics, and dogged devotion to his master. "He might have been a witch or all of the things that they accused him of being, and an assassin, a poisoner, a saboteur of the first water, but… he was the only man that was allowed in the Generalissimo's bedroom armed at any time of day or night, and that showed a great deal of trust in China, if you know what that means" (U.S. Navy Vice Admiral Milton Miles in his talk to the Conference of NYS Association of Police Chiefs, Schenectady, NY, July 24, 1957).

p. 105 "Blue-Shirted Men"—Members of the Blue Shirt Society, 蓝衣社, right-wing KMT paramilitary group that sought to exterminate Communists along with all other enemies of the Generalissimo. Front for the Society for Vigorous Practice (see note for p. 37). (See Frederic Wakeman, Jr., *Spymaster: Dai Li and the Chinese Secret Service*, Berkeley: University of California Press, 2003).

p. 105 "Free China"—An embellishment used by the KMT (as well as some Americans) to refer to those parts of Republican China not under the control of the Japanese or the Communists.

p. 106 "one of humankind's greatest mass migrations"—After the fall of Hankou, from October 1938 through Spring 1939, "Free China" retreated inland to Chongqing. "They came by bus and sedan, by truck and rickshaw, by boat and on foot. Peddlers, shopkeepers, politicians all ended their march in the wall city… It was as if a county seat of Kentucky mountaineers had suddenly been called on to play host to the most feverishly dynamic New Yorkers, Texans, and Californians" (Theodore White and Annalee Jacoby, *Thunder out of China*, NY: Da Capo Press, 1946, p. 8).

p. 106 "Three Gorges"— 三峡, 120-mile middle stretch of the Chang Jiang between Yichang and the outskirts of Chongqing, known for its steep sheer slopes, treacherous waters, and for being a natural barrier to the interior of China.

p. 106 "an old novel in which the narrator is an ambitious American engineer"—*A Single Pebble* by John Hersey (NY: Knopf, 1956). Born in China to YMCA missionaries, Hersey was both a journalist and a novelist of the inhumanities of war, blurring the distinction between the two in order to get closer to the truth.

p. 109 "Hongzha Chongqing"—See note for p. 53.

p. 109 "The Fourth Department"—The Telecommunications Department, 电讯处, of the Bureau for Investigations and Statistics. Headed by General Wei Daming (see note for p. 158). Famous for its infiltration in 1942 by a Communist espionage ring (see note for p. 208). (See Frederic Wakeman, Jr., *Spymaster: Dai Li and the Chinese Secret Service*, Berkeley: University of California Press, 2003).

p. 109 "the 8th Route Army"—八路军, Communist army during the 2nd KMT-CCP United Front. Famous for their guerilla tactics in fighting the Japanese while reaping widespread peasant support. Sympathetically portrayed by left-leaning American journalist Agnes Smedley in her book, *China Fights Back: An American Woman with the Eighth Route Army* (NY: The Vanguard Press, 1938).

p. 110 "mathematician whose hobby is cryptography"—James Reeds, see https://www.njstar.com/tools/telecode/jim-reeds-ctc.htm for his brief history of the Chinese Telegraph Codebook, though the link to the codebook is no longer available.

p. 112 "the training camp"—Dai Li's organized effort to recruit educated patriotic youth into the secret service. A stepping stone from the boy scouts. "If you first slip the chain over their neck, then you have got them by the leash," wrote Shen Zui, one of Dai Li's top aides, quoting his former master in a memoir that earned him praise and royalties in the PRC. In his in-depth study of the Chinese secret service, historian Frederick Wakeman warns his readers "to take everything that Shen Zui tells us with a dose of salt" (*Spymaster: Dai Li and the Chinese Secret Service*, Berkeley: University of California Press, 2003, p. 386).

p. 112 "the campaign to catch rats"—According to one wartime refugee in Chongqing: "The rats in the Mountain Town are gigantic. Large ones are the size of cats. Moreover, they are extremely fierce and cruel. They are always gnashing their teeth and smacking their chops ready to go have a taste of anything, no matter what it is…" (Lee McIsaac, "The city as nation: Creating a wartime capital in Chongqing," *Remaking the Chinese City: Modernity and National Identity*, 1900-1950, edited by Joseph W. Esherick, Honolulu: University of Hawai'i Press, 2000, p. 177).

p. 117 "the Great Tunnel"—Tragedy of June 5, 1941, 重庆大隧道防空洞惨案, in which thousands of people (reports range from 1,000-10,000) suffocated inside Chongqing's largest public air raid shelter due to inadequate ventilation. In a 2015 interview with the *Chongqing Daily*, 92-year-old Gao Rongbin remembers working as a 16-year-old volunteer for three days and three nights, going deep into the tunnel to look for his teacher and pulling out the bodies one by one.

p. 117 "the Heavenly Gate"—朝天门, Chaotianmen, literally to look toward heaven or the seat of the emperor. The name of the largest gate in the old walled city of Chongqing, perched atop steep cliffs at the tip of the peninsula where the two great rivers, Jialing Jiang and Chang Jiang, come together.

p. 120 "the blue-greens of the Jialing Jiang and the yellow-browns of the Chang Jiang"—The Jialing Jiang (嘉陵江) is a tributary of the Chang Jiang (长江), the longest river in China, which flows westward from the Tibetan Plateau across the width of the country, gaining power as it moves through the Three Gorges (see note for p. 106), and depleting as it empties into the East China Sea at Shanghai. At the confluence of these two rivers, waters are deep, currents are swift, and banks are steep. Chongqing rises above, a mountain town, a fortress town, a witness to this perpetual collision of bodies. Only in early Summer or mid-Autumn can the separation of colors be witnessed.

The Maverick

p. 139 "this man whom I call Harry"—Based on the prolific writings of Herbert O. Yardley, poker-loving, code-breaking, truth-serum-testing, rogue cryptologist who went to China in 1938 to work for Dai Li. (See Herbert O. Yardley, *The Chinese Black Chamber: An Adventure in Espionage*, Boston: Houghton Mifflin Company, 1983).

p. 143 "Pop's"—There really was a Pop, surname Neilson, a Danish-German munitions maker and innkeeper memorialized in Herbert Yardley's book, *The Chinese Black Chamber* (see note for p. 139).

Entwinement

p. 151 "femme fatale"—Zhang Luping, 张露萍, 1921-1944, leader of the so-called Red Radio Incident (see note for p. 208). Initially branded as a counterrevolutionary by the Communists, she was rehabilitated in 1983 as a heroic martyr and subsequently memorialized in Chinese novels and films.

p. 151 "Happy Valley Prison"—There were two prisons on Gele Mountain (歌乐山): Bai Mansion (白公馆) and, behind it, the so-called Refuse Pit (渣滓洞). I visited both, the former the site of the concentration camp made famous in the novel *Red Crag (Hong Yan*, 红岩), and now a museum with a display of torture instruments and a wall of photos of Communist martyrs (including Zhang Luping, see note for p. 151). The latter a former coal pit turned into torture cells, the entrance bearing a banner with Dai Li's calligraphy: "Your youth will pass, never to return. Think of where you are and how much time you have." Nearby, a pit where 94 bodies were found bound with handcuffs bearing the inscription "Made in Springfield, Massachusetts." This was the site of the supposed massacre of 200 communists on November 27, 1949, an execution that allegedly took place with the help of the Americans (see notes for p. 203 and p. 211). This was NOT the site, however, of the execution of the seven Red Radio Spies, who died in yet another one of Dai Li's lock-ups in Guizhou.

p. 154 "Song of Everlasting Sorrow"—长恨歌, penned by the Tang poet, Bai Juyi (白居易) about the Han emperor, Xuanzong, and his tragic love affair with his concubine, the infamous Yang Guifei, variously portrayed in Chinese history as femme fatale or sacrificial martyr. A tribute to the utility of a woman.

p. 158 "Director of Telecommunications"— General Wei Daming, 魏大銘. "As majordomo of Dai Li's secret service communications, Wei Daming (whose wife was one of Dai Li's former mistresses) became known as the 'spirit of Dai Li' (Dai Li de ling hun). His importance to Juntong cannot be overemphasized" (Frederic Wakeman, Jr., *Spymaster: Dai Li and the Chinese Secret Service*, Berkeley: University of California Press, 2003, p. 274).

p. 162 "famous Tang poem"—See note for p. 154.

Normalization

p. 166 "the Premier"—of the PRC, Zhou Enlai, Chou En-Lai, 周恩来. Political survivor and skilled negotiator with the uncanny ability to win over foreign diplomats and journalists. "Chou was accessible, articulate, and charming, both in Hankow and later in Chungking," writes Stephen MacKinnon and Oris Friesen in their oral history of old-hand wartime China reporters. "One after another, these skeptical precursors of Henry Kissinger confessed their 'captivation.' Even when he told untruths or something less than the truth, he commanded their admiration. 'Why,' wondered Hank Lieberman, 'can only high-level communists have a sense of humor?'" (*China Reporting: An Oral History of American Journalism in the 1930s and 1940s*, Berkeley: University of California Press, 1987, p. 3).

p. 168 "the week that changed the world"—February 21-28, 1972, televised spectacle of the extraordinary meeting between anti-communist Richard Nixon and anti-imperialist Mao Zedong that took place behind the so-called Bamboo Curtain (see note for p. 93), an event so improbable that one composer even wrote an opera about it (see

John Adams, "Nixon in China"). Precursor to Normalization (see note for p. 43).

p. 178 "Spiritual Pollution"—精神污染, October to December 1983. Short-lived political campaign to eradicate so-called Western bourgeois culture, overlapping with my first year alone in China. A time when the Five Do's and the Four Beauties (五讲四美) were plastered on every billboard: Speak with Civility, Courtesy, Order, Hygiene, and Morality! Promote Beautiful Language, Environment, Spirit, and Behavior! How I learned to speak proletarian Chinese.

p. 179 "Zhongshan jackets"—A high-collar, tunic-style suit named after Sun Zhongshan, who, as the quintessential modern Chinese gentleman, wore it well. A patriotic yet classy cut somewhere between military uniform, Manchu gown, and Western suit, with Four Virtuous Pockets and Three People's Principles Buttons on each sleeve. Later re-tailored and re-named the "Mao suit," after which it was adopted by good Marxist revolutionaries everywhere.

p. 183 "Eight Big Things"—八大件. Mandatory gift list for Chinese Americans returning to China in the 1980s: (1) color television, (2) refrigerator, (3) washing machine, (4) stereo, (5) air conditioner, (6) camera, (7) camcorder, and (8) wristwatch. If necessary, you could swap out one of these for a motorcycle.

A Way Out

p. 189 "the 'tiger bench' and the 'acid bath'"—The former, a type of torture; the latter, a means of getting rid of the body.

p. 191 "International Settlement"—A geographic zone established in Shanghai as the result of a series of unequal treaties between China and England, France, and the U.S., where foreigners were granted extraterritorial rights to buy and lease property, conduct business and trade freely, and operate their own police, courts, and military. Existed from 1842-1941.

p. 197 "an American scholar whose obsession with the general rivals my own"—The late Frederic Wakeman, historian of modern China and author of *Spymaster: Dai Li and the Secret Service* (Berkeley: University of California Press, 2003). In his Afterword, Wakeman reflects on his experience of writing the book: "In the end, then, I fear I find myself one of Dai Li's unintended objects of prey. This safely distant conceit means also, of course, that by writing about Dai Li I can somehow imagine myself repulsing the daemon's indifferent glance. Thus do historians quell their remote nightmares and mute the horrors of the past. But do we sleep the better for it?" (p. 367).

Fedoras in Flight

p. 202 "Wei Daming"— See note for p. 158.

p. 203 "SACO"—Sino-American Cooperative Organization, 中美合作所, 1943-1946. Operated jointly with the Office of Strategic Services (forerunner of the CIA). Born after Pearl Harbor over a drink in a Washington hotel room between US Navy Admiral Milton Miles and Dai Li's special agent in DC. Initially proposed as a modest exchange of intelligence against a common enemy, it later became a much larger operation after Dai Li propositioned Admiral Miles (whom he named Winter Plum Blossom) for U.S. arms and personnel to train his Juntong guerilla troops. With the approval of President Roosevelt, SACO set up camp in Happy Valley, where they offered classes in combat, demolition, and radio communications—as well as, at Dai Li's request, special training for his secret police. As Miles later admitted, "...we were never able to separate the police activities from guerilla activities" (Frederic Wakeman, Jr., *Spymaster: Dai Li and the Chinese Secret Service*, Berkeley: University of California Press, 2003, p. 61). Even after the war, SACO veterans never knew for sure whether they had armed and trained soldiers to fight the Japanese or to kill the Communists.

p. 204 **"When the Americans entered the war"**—December 1941. The US dismissed warnings about the imminent attack on Pearl Harbor from the Fourth Department, which claimed to have deciphered Japanese air force codes. Afterwards, the Americans began to take Dai Li more seriously.

p. 204 **"Chinese ambassador to the U.S."**—Hu Shi, Hu Shih, 胡适, who held his position from 1938 to 1942. A student of John Dewey at Columbia University, he embraced pragmatism as the method for making China modern. Upon his return to China, he participated in the May Fourth Movement, but found that his pragmatic approach put him at odds with the ideologies of both left and right. "More study of problems, less study of ISMs!" he pleaded.

p. 208 **"Red Radio Incident"**—Infiltration of the Fourth Department by the Communist espionage ring led by Zhang Luping (see note for p. 151), "stabbing right into the heart of Tai Li's Bureau of Investigation and Statistics" (Maochun Yu, OSS in China: Prelude to Cold War, New Haven: Yale University Press, 1996, p. 44). Precursor to the dubious collaboration between Juntong (see note for p. 37) and SACO (see note for p. 203).

p. 209 "Four Virtues"—四种美德: 礼 (li), 义 (yi), 廉 (lian), 耻 (chi). What the Generalissimo, in a 1934 speech, called the essentials of the New Life Movement: propriety, righteousness, integrity, and a sense of shame.

p. 211 "the blog of a writer from Chongqing"—Xujun Eberlein, MIT PhD who quit algorithms for writing. Her website (http://www.xujuneberlein.com/index.html) mixes poetry with politics, history with fiction, memory with imagination. Her sister's drowning during the Cultural Revolution, as she tried to emulate Mao's swim across the Chiang Jiang, haunts her writing. In a five-part series for *The Atlantic*, she methodically interrogates the past and concludes that SACO was never involved in the mass murder of Communists in Dai Li's infamous prison on Gele Mountain on November 27, 1949—the Americans were long gone by then. "We are all products of our time, and we only have hindsight" (Xujun Eberlein, "Another Kind of American History in Chongqing," *The Atlantic*, January 31, 2011).

p. 211 "American guard dog houses"—According to a plaque at the Revolutionary Martyrs' Memorial on Gele Mountain, SACO offered Special Police Training Classes, including police dog pursuit. Special doghouses were built to board and train police dogs, with nearly 100 dogs in residence at one time.

p. 211 "Refuse Pit"—See note for p. 151.

p. 217 "a certain professor of Chinese literature"—Wen Yiduo, 闻一多, born November 24, 1899, assassinated July 15, 1946.

Perhaps he was a poet, perhaps a musician.
Perhaps he was a painter, perhaps a politician.
Perhaps he was a traitor, as the Nationalists maintained.
Perhaps he was a patriot, as the Communists proclaimed.

Perhaps, when he closed his eyes, he heard music
more beautiful than the noisy refrains of men.

(After Wen Yiduo's poem "Perhaps," 也许, an elegy for his
young daughter who died while he was studying in the US).

p. 218 "bai hua"—白话, vernacular Chinese. A conscious effort to
use daily speech in writing prose and poetry, as exempli-
fied in Hu Shi's *Experiments* (尝试集):

醉过才知酒浓.	Once intoxicated, one learns the strength of wine.
爱过才知情重.	Once smitten, one learns the power of love.
你不能做我的诗，	You cannot write my poems,
正如我不能做你的梦。	Just as I cannot dream your dreams.

(Hu Shi, "Dream and Poem," 梦与诗, translation by Kai-yu
Hsu, *Twentieth-Century Chinese Poetry: An Anthology*,
Ithaca: Cornell University Press, 1963, p. 2).

p. 219 "left-leaning trouble-making element"—左倾的捣乱分
子. What the right wing of the KMT called members of
the Chinese Democratic League (中国民主同盟), which
promoted a third way between the Nationalists and the
Communists.

p. 220 "the Old Gentleman"— Fei Gong, 费鞏, critic of the
KMT who disappeared on March 5, 1945 and was later
declared a Communist martyr. In Julie Mallozzi's *Once Removed* (First Run/Icarus Films, 1999), a documentary film
about her efforts to trace her family history and solve the
mystery of her great uncle's disappearance, the filmmaker
visits the supposed site of the nitric acid bath. "What's
important," she asks, "the thing that happened, or the
thing that's remembered?"

p. 221 "a funeral of another gentleman"— Li Gongpu, 李公朴, one of the Seven Gentlemen (七君子) who criticized the corruption and repression of the KMT regime.

The Utility of a Woman

p. 233 "U.S. Information Service"—USIS, 1942-1953, overseas arm of the Office of War Information under the State Department during WWII. Responsible for managing educational, cultural, and informational programs that supported American foreign policy objectives and mutual understanding between the U.S. and foreign countries. Precursor to the U.S. Information Agency (USIA). In a 1953-1983 retrospective in which my father's photograph appears with the caption "native assistant," the USIA describes its work as the dissemination of information—not propaganda—to foreign audiences.

p. 235 "Maybe the Americans would find a way to bring the two parties together?"—They didn't, split by their own ideological motives and unable to agree on the means or the ends. The failed Dixie Mission to Yan'an. The bungled brokered meeting in Chongqing. In photographs, the Generalissimo and the Chairman stand stiffly side by side in their matching Zhongshan jackets (the former's slightly more tailored than the latter's). The bombastic American ambassador grins broadly in his double-breasted suit and bow tie. In the end, the Americans were left pointing fingers at one another, haunted by the question: "Who lost China?"

p. 244 "People's Liberation Army"—PLA, the armed forces of the Chinese Communist Party, formed following the Generalissimo's 1927 purge of Communists in Shanghai that launched the civil war.

p. 246 "one egg or two?"—Reference to Chinese mooncakes, which vary in taste and value according to the number of salted egg yolks they contain, a detail overlooked by the American consumer.

Waiting

p. 260 "the Handover"—Transfer of sovereignty over Hong Kong (including Hong Kong Island, the Kowloon Peninsula, and the New Territories) from the United Kingdom to the People's Republic of China on July 1, 1997, based on the signing of the 1984 Sino-British Joint Declaration. While many cheered the end of empire, local protest erupted over PRC rule, and many Hong Kong citizens sought paths to migration.

p. 267 "New Territories"—Geographic border region between Hong Kong and mainland China, including outlying islands, which was leased to the British in 1898 for 99 years. As the expiration date approached, China refused to acknowledge the unequal treaties under which Hong Kong Island and the Kowloon Peninsula were acquired, and informed Britain of its intention to take back the whole of Hong Kong by 1997.

p. 273 "women from the South"—Women from the Philippines and other Southeast Asian countries who came to Hong Kong beginning in the mid-1970s to work as domestic servants for Chinese and expatriate families.

What Happened on the Train

p. 295 "Cultural Revolution"—文化大革命, 1966-1976. The cult of Mao. An attempt to speed up the revolution by purging the party of "revisionists," "reactionaries," and all who were disloyal to the Chairman. Indoctrination of youth into the Red Guard to achieve that end, turning students against teachers, children against parents, young against old—and eventually Red Guard against Red Guard. Destruction of the Four Olds: customs, culture, habits, ideas. Struggle against the Four Elements: landlords, rich peasants, counterrevolutionaries, bad characters. Use of struggle as a transitive verb, 斗, as in "I will struggle you." And not just you, but your whole extended family, sent down to the countryside to be re-educated. Decade of the dunce cap and the airplane position, arms akimbo, head bent, your crime hung around your neck or stuffed into your mouth. What my father would not have survived. An endlessly changing parade of bad characters in which you never knew if you were watching on the sidelines or marching in the line up.

p. 295 "China's lost generation"—a.k.a. "sent down youth" (知识青年). Urban students who were sent "down to the villages" and "up to the mountains" to be re-educated by poor peasants during the Cultural Revolution. For those like my brother who had just graduated from middle or high school when the revolution began and schools closed —i.e., the classes of 1966-1968 known as "lao san jie" (老三届)—education was severely disrupted for ten years.

Fare Forward

p. 311 "the Great Terror"—消灭, Xiao Mie. Mao's 1951 Movement to Suppress Counterrevolutionaries, based on a system of killing quotas for each city and province. Two weeks after initiating the campaign, Mao wrote: "On the question of executing counterrevolutionaries, in the rural areas the proportion has reached one out of every 1,000 individuals, while in the northwest and in the urban areas it is one for every 2,000, so mass executions should be halted immediately" (Li Changyu, "Mao's 'killing quotas,'" *China Rights Forum*, No. 4, 2005). (See also Frank Dikotter, *The Tragedy of Liberation: A History of the Chinese Revolution, 1945-57*, NY: Bloomsbury Press).

Where Memory Lies

p. 330 "His daughter needs to understand this novel"—红楼梦, variously translated as *The Dream of the Red Chamber*, *A Dream of Red Mansions*, and *The Story of the Stone*. Written by Cao Xueqin (曹雪芹). The novel follows a declining nobleman's youthful romances. Suspected of being a roman à clef with a thinly veiled critique of the Chinese aristocracy. Following Cao's untimely death, multiple versions of the manuscript circulated for three decades among family and friends, who added their own notes and commentaries. Finally published in 1792 with forty additional chapters that no one claimed. As more versions of the manuscript have surfaced, the mystery of authorship and the problem of how to read this book—as fiction, autobiography, or collective history—has only deepened.

p. 330 "Eight Eccentrics"—扬州八怪, Yangzhou Ba Guai, genre-bending artists of the Qing Dynasty who were notorious for their unorthodox mixing of image and text.

TEXT CREDITS

Epigraph 1: "You in your insistence on ferreting out facts..."
—Cao Xueqin. *The Story of the Stone, Volume 5: The Dreamer Wakes*, translated by John Minford, Bloomington: Indiana University Press, 1987, p. 375.

Epigraph 2: "These are only hints and guesses..."
p. 22 "The hint, half guessed. The gift, half understood."
p. 48 "Time past and time future"
"What might have been and what has been"
"Neither flesh nor fleshless"
"Neither from nor towards"
"In my beginning is my end"
"And the way up is the way down..."
"And what you do not know is the only thing you know"
p. 49 "And what you own is what you do not own..."
"I do not know much about gods..."
p. 70 "...watching the furrow..."
p. 206 "Time Present and Time Past"
p. 262 "Not fare well, but fare forward."
p. 264 "consider the future and the past with an equal mind"
p. 325 "Go, go, go... human kind cannot bear very much reality."
p. 334 "Between the hither and the farther shore."

—All excerpts and paraphrases from "Burnt Norton," "East Coker," and "The Dry Salvages" from *Four Quartets* by T.S. Eliot.

p. 107 "At the time I wanted to believe him..."
—John Hersey, *A Single Pebble*. NY: Knopf, 1956, pp. 13-14.

p. 113 "Among such as these I cannot hope for friends..."
—Bai Juyi, "On being removed from Hsun-yang and sent to Chung-chou," *A Hundred & Seventy Chinese Poems*, edited and translated by Arthur Waley, NY: Alfred A. Knopf, Inc., 1918, p. 219.

p. 220 "Let the dead water ferment..."
—Wen Yiduo, "Si Yu (Dead Water)," translated by Rachel Gao, *PoemHunter*, 20 August, 2009, poemhunter.com/poem/dead-water-27515-27700/ (accessed 1 October, 2016).

p. 316 "You ask when I am coming..."
—Li Shangyin, "Ye Yu Ji Bei (Night rain, a letter north)," translated by Francis Chin, *Bystander*, 7 July, 2002, bystander.homestead.com/bashan.html (accessed 1 October, 2016).

p. 338 "Truth becomes fiction when the fiction's true..."
—Cao Xueqin. *The Story of the Stone, Volume 1: The Golden Days*, translated by David Hawkes, Bloomington: Indiana University Press, 1973, p. 55.

IMAGE CREDITS

The 131 images reproduced in this book are drawn from an eclectic collection of sources, including photographs taken by mostly Western photojournalists, academics, and military personnel in China during the 1930s and '40s, U.S. and Chinese government maps of China during WWII, and photos and documents from my own family archive. When I discovered the existence of this trove of visual documentation of the times, places, and events that my father had lived through, these images began to infiltrate my writing. While the photographs failed to elicit my father's memory, they filled in holes in his stories and sparked my imagination, becoming accomplices to my own storytelling. Originally made for documentary purposes, the images function in this book as evidence of that which cannot be documented: memories, dreams and hallucinations, the forgotten and the repressed, the imagined and the invented. While some photographs are used in a more conventional biographical sense, others serve as pseudo-illustrations of a fictive story. The images thus work at a slant to the text, blurring the boundaries between fiction and nonfiction, memory and imagination, and calling into question the veracity of the stories told.

Every effort has been made to identify and credit the maker of each image, to trace copyright holders, and to obtain permission for the use of copyrighted material. I alone am responsible for any errors or omissions in the list below and would be grateful to be notified of any corrections that should be made in future reprints or editions of this book. Regrettably, the names of many Chinese photographers remain undeservedly unknown, as in the rich volume of wartime photographs edited by Qin Feng, *Kang zhan yi shun jian* (Guangxi shi fan da xue chu ban she, 2005).

COVER: "Ruins of a Confucian temple after the battle of Tai'erzhuang, Xuzhou front, China" (detail), April 1938. Photo by Robert Capa. © International Center of Photography/Magnum Photos. Reprinted by permission.

PAGE 3: "Refugees crowding the North bound train," Shanghai, November 1, 1949. Photo by Jack Birns/The LIFE Picture Collection/Getty Images. Reprinted by permission.

PAGE 13: "Second Sino-Japanese War" (detail #1), Shanghai, December 1, 1937. Photo by George Krainukov/adoc-photos/Corbis via Getty Images. Reprinted by permission.

PAGES 14-15: "Passengers find a precarious foothold on the locomotive of a southbound train," Shanghai, March 1949. Photo by Jack Birns/ The LIFE Picture Collection/Getty Images. Reprinted by permission.

PAGE 16: Still from *The Kid (My Son A-Chang)*. Directed by Feng Feng. Xingguang Film Company, Hong Kong, 1950.

PAGE 20: "Youth parade at political rally, Hankou, China" (detail), March 1938. Photo by Robert Capa. © International Center of Photography/Magnum Photos. Reprinted by permission.

PAGE 26: Raised ranch, Vestal, NY, circa 1970s. Photo by Ton-Shun Chang. Courtesy of the author.

PAGE 30: "USAT U.S. Grant," circa 1920s and 1930s. Photographer unknown. Courtesy of Donald M. McPherson, U.S. Naval History and Heritage Command, Catalog #: NH 67486, https://www.history.navy.mil/. Accessed 1 October 2016.

PAGE 32: "Scouting Marches On (On to Washington)." Painting by Norman Rockwell. *Boys' Life Magazine* (cover), Boy Scouts of America, July 1935.

PAGE 33: Two Chinese boy scouts, Yangzhou, circa 1935. Photographer unknown. Courtesy of the author.

PAGE 36: "Scouts of Orient welcomed to city," New York City, August 24, 1935. Photographer unknown. Reprinted by permission of Times Wide World/The New York Times/Redux.

PAGE 38: "Chinese scout raises Chinese flag," Washington DC, 1937. Photographer unknown. *The National and World Jamborees in Pictures*, Boy Scouts of America, New York, 1937.

PAGE 40: "Bicentennial goatee." Image created by author, 2016.

PAGE 47: Class of 1946, Department of Foreign Languages and Literature, National Central University, Chongqing, 1946. Photographer unknown. Courtesy of the author.

PAGE 50: The Dry Salvages, Cape Ann, Massachusetts, n.d. Photographer unknown.

PAGE 51: "12-point star series." Image created by author, 2016.

PAGE 56: "Chiang Kai-shek at Nanjing," January 1, 1931. Photo by Culture Club/Getty Images. Reprinted by permission.

PAGE 58: "Chinese upper river steamer carrying a packed mass of troops," n.d. Photographer unknown. *Yangtze Patrol: The U.S. Navy in China*, by Kemp Tolley, Naval Institute Press, Annapolis, MD, 1971.

PAGE 60: Hu Shi and Lucile Swan (detail), Beijing, circa 1930s. Photographer unknown. Chinese Academy of Social Sciences, Beijing.

PAGE 63: "Bodies piled on the shore of the Yangtze River, Nanjing Massacre," December 1937. Photo by Moriyasa Murase.

PAGE 67: "SS Kiangking," circa 1930s. Photo by Donald Brotchie. H.M.S. Falcon, Photograph Gallery Ten, © 2005 Donella Grimsdale, Internet Archive https://web.archive.org/web/20101031022757/http://hmsfalcon.com/Gallery/Gallery10/low/wrecks1/wrecks1.htm.

PAGE 70: "The SS Robert Dollar, of the Dollar Steamship Lines, arrives at Chungking in the early twenties." Photographer unknown. *Yangtze Patrol: The U.S. Navy in China*, by Kemp Tolley, Naval Institute Press, Annapolis, MD, 1971.

PAGE 72: "The river dragon catches up with the SS Robert Dollar, spring of 1924." Photographer unknown. *Yangtze Patrol: The U.S. Navy in China*, by Kemp Tolley, Naval Institute Press, Annapolis, MD, 1971.

PAGE 75: "The custom housing building and clock tower," Hankou, 1935. Photo by Stanley Till. Courtesy of the Till family.

PAGE 77: "Buildings of Wuhan University," circa 1937-1943. Photographer unknown. Courtesy of the Library of Congress, LC-USZ62-121748.

PAGE 78: "March in support of League of Nations covenant condemning Japan," Hankou, Spring 1938. Photographer unknown. *Kang zhan yi shun jian*, edited by Qin Feng, Guangxi shi fan da xue chu ban she, Guilin, 2005.

PAGE 81: "Crowds watching the air battle between Japanese and Chinese planes over Hankou, China" (detail), April 29, 1938. Photo by Robert Capa. © International Center of Photography/Magnum Photos. Reprinted by permission.

PAGE 81: "Second Sino-Japanese War" (detail #2), Shanghai, December 1, 1937. Photo by George Krainukov/adoc-photos/Corbis via Getty Images. Reprinted by permission.

PAGE 82: "People surrounding train bearing huge German flag on top of car, Hankou, China," July 5, 1938. Photo by Robert Capa. © International Center of Photography/Magnum Photos. Reprinted by permission.

PAGE 83: "The Chiangs," Hankou, 1938. Photo by W.H. Auden. Copyright © 1939 by W.H. Auden, renewed. Reprinted by permission of Curtis Brown, Ltd.

PAGE 84: "Children playing in the snow, Hankou, China," March 1938. Photo by Robert Capa. © International Center of Photography/Magnum Photos. Reprinted by permission.

PAGE 84: "Young women being trained as Nationalist soldiers, Hankou, China" (detail), March 1938. Photo by Robert Capa. © International Center of Photography/Magnum Photos. Reprinted by permission.

PAGE 87: "First school assembly" (detail), Yuanling, 1938. Photo by Edward Gulick. Reprinted with permission from *Teaching in Wartime China: A Photo-Memoir, 1937-1939*, by Edward Gulick. Copyright © 1995 by the University of Massachusetts Press.

PAGE 88: "The general's eyes." Image created by author, 2016.

PAGE 89: "Dwight leading the choir" (detail), Yuanling, 1938. Photo by Edward Gulick. Reprinted with permission from *Teaching in Wartime China: A Photo-Memoir, 1937-1939*, by Edward Gulick. Copyright © 1995 by the University of Massachusetts Press.

PAGE 90: "Curly's eyes." Image created by author, 2016.

PAGE 94: "Don't let them get deeper." Photographer unknown. *Country Expressions*, Sweet Valley, PA, March 13, 1974.

PAGE 95: "Confucius Say: Happy New Year!" Photographer unknown. *The Vestal News*, Vestal, NY, Feb. 4, 1965.

PAGE 96: "Vestal High School's Language Clubs Demonstrate Many Yule Customs." Photographer unknown. *Your Vestal Schools*, Vestal, NY, December 1965.

PAGE 103: "On our craft right down the middle of the mighty Yangtze," 1938. Photo by Edward Gulick. Reprinted with permission from *Teaching in Wartime China: A Photo-Memoir, 1937-1939*, by Edward Gulick. Copyright © 1995 by the University of Massachusetts Press.

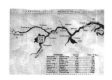

PAGE 105: Shanghai to Chungking map, 1937. Cartographer unknown.

PAGE 107: "Scenes along the Yangtse," circa 1930s. Photo by Donald Brotchie. H.M.S. Falcon, Photograph Gallery Ten, © 2005 Donella Grimsdale, Internet Archive https://web.archive.org/web/20101030235447/http://hmsfalcon.com/Gallery/Gallery10/low/pandp/pandp.htm.

PAGE 108: "Kung Lin Tan (rapid), Yangtze River," n.d. Photographer unknown. *Yangtze Patrol: The U.S. Navy in China*, by Kemp Tolley, Naval Institute Press, Annapolis, MD, 1971.

PAGE 111: "Chungking," 1938. Map by Edward Gulick. Reprinted with permission from *Teaching in Wartime China: A Photo-Memoir, 1937-1939*, by Edward Gulick. Copyright © 1995 by the University of Massachusetts Press.

PAGE 113: "Standing on a hill beside a building of the Shanghai Medical College" (detail), Geleshan, Sichuan, April 1943. Photo by Joseph Needham. Courtesy of the Needham Research Institute.

PAGE 114: "A Chinese woman holding a flat umbrella," Chongqing, January 1, 1941. Photo by Carl Mydans/The LIFE Picture Collection/ Getty Images. Reprinted by permission.

PAGE 116: "Casualties of a Mass Panic, Chungking, China, June 5, 1941" (detail). Photo by Carl Mydans. National Archives and Records Administration, National Archives Identifier 553338.

PAGE 118: "六五大隧道惨案现场 （June 5th Great Tunnel Tragedy)," Chongqing, 1941. Photographer unknown. Xinhua News Agency.

PAGE 119: "A student sitting on an air raid shelter looking down at the Jialing River at the National Central University," Shapingba, Chongqing, April 1943. Photo by Joseph Needham. Courtesy of the Needham Research Institute.

PAGE 123: Chongqing city map (detail), circa Qing Dynasty. Cartographer unknown. Three Gorges Museum, Chongqing.

PAGES 124-25: Chongqing city map (detail #1), 1948. Cartography by Chongqing City Government. *Sichuan Sheng Chongqing Shi di ming lu,* Chongqing Shi di ming ling dao xiao zu, Chongqing, 1986.

PAGES 126-27: "Chungking" (detail), 1938. Map by Edward Gulick. Reprinted with permission from *Teaching in Wartime China: A Photo-Memoir, 1937-1939,* by Edward Gulick. Copyright © 1995 by the University of Massachusetts Press.

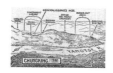

PAGES 128-29: "Chungking, 1940." Drawing by Graham Peck. *Two Kinds of Time,* by Graham Peck, Houghton Mifflin Company, Boston, 1950.

PAGES 130-31: "Map of Chungking City," 1943. Drafted and reproduced by 653rd Engr. Bn. under direction of chief engineer, China Theater. Beinecke Rare Book & Manuscript Library, Yale University.

PAGES 132-33: "A view showing the Yangtze River," Chongqing, December 1, 1945. Photo by Jack Wilkes/The LIFE Picture Collection/Getty Images. Reprinted by permission.

PAGES 134-35: Bombing of Chongqing, May 4, 1939. Photographer unknown. Three Gorges Museum, Chongqing.

PAGE 139: "USIS Public Affairs Officer and native assistant," Nanjing, 1949. Photographer unknown. *United States Information Agency: A Retrospective*, 1953-83.

PAGE 145: "People watching the bombing of Chungking from the Standard Oil dugout entrance," January 1, 1941. Photo by Carl Mydans/The LIFE Picture Collection/Getty Images. Reprinted by permission.

PAGE 149: "U.S. intelligence officer teaching Chinese personnel how to use a radio," Chong-qing, circa 1942-1946. Photographer unknown. Geleshan Revolutionary Martyrs' Memorial, Chongqing.

PAGE 153: "Members of staff of the Sino-British Cooperation Office, walking through the woods near Chungking" (version #1), February-March 1946. Photo by Joseph Needham. Courtesy of the Needham Research Institute.

PAGE 154: "Members of staff of the Sino-British Cooperation Office, walking through the woods near Chungking" (version #2), February-March 1946. Photo by Joseph Needham. Courtesy of the Needham Research Institute.

PAGE 156: Zhang Luping, n.d.. Photographer unknown. *Dai Li he jun tong*, by Jiang Shaozhen, Tuan jie chu ban she, Beijing, 2007.

PAGE 157: Chongqing city map (detail #2), 1948. Cartography by Chongqing City Government. *Sichuan Sheng Chongqing Shi di ming lu*, Chongqing Shi di ming ling dao xiao zu, Chongqing, 1986.

PAGE 160: "U.S. intelligence officer teaching Chinese personnel how to use a radio" (detail), Chongqing, circa 1942-1946. Photographer unknown. Geleshan Revolutionary Martyrs' Memorial, Chongqing.

PAGE 162: 長恨歌 (Song of Everlasting Sorrow). Calligraphy by Ton-Shun Chang, circa 2005. Courtesy of the author.

PAGE 164: "Nixon and Mao." Painting by René Milot, commissioned by the Cincinnati Opera for "Nixon in China," 2007. Reprinted by permission.

PAGE 167: "Photograph of President Richard Nixon and Premier Chou En-lai" (detail), Beijing, February 21, 1972. Photo by Oliver F. Atkins. U.S. National Archives and Records Administration.

PAGE 172: Family outing at Slender West Lake, Yangzhou, 1982. Photo by Robert Laubach. Courtesy of the author.

PAGE 176: "Study hard to gain strength to contribute to socialist modernization," February 1980. Poster designed by Xu Wenhua, Shanghai Renmin Meishu Chubanshe. Courtesy of the Stefan R. Landsberger Collections, International Institute of Social History, Amsterdam.

PAGE 179: Advertisement for Double Happiness Brand Cigarettes, n.d. Shanghai Tobacco Company.

PAGE 186: Tong Yuan Gate, Chongqing, July 2012. Photo by the author.

PAGE 189: "Dai Li's Bao An mansion," n.d. Photo by Frederick Wakeman Jr. *Spymaster: Dai Li and the Chinese Secret Service*, by Frederick Wakeman Jr., University of California Press. © 2003 by the Regents of the University of California. Reprinted by permission.

PAGE 195: "One of the most moved methods of moving about in Chungking is by the ancient chair car," December 1, 1945. Photo by Jack Wilkes/The LIFE Picture Collection/Getty Images. Reprinted by permission.

PAGE 197: "The general's eyes." Image created by author, 2016.

PAGE 199: "Beijing woman's eyes." Image created by author, 2016.

PAGE 199: "Nanjing woman's eyes." Image created by author, 2016.

PAGE 199: "Hong Kong woman's eyes." Image created by author, 2016.

PAGE 201: "Cap worn by Yang Hucheng when he was killed," n.d. Photographer unknown. Geleshan Revolutionary Martyrs' Memorial, Chongqing.

PAGE 203: "Chinese people overcrowding the buses," Chongqing, December 1, 1945. Photo by Jack Wilkes/The LIFE Picture Collection/ Getty Images. Reprinted by permission.

PAGE 206: Transcript of National Central University, Chongqing, 1942-1946 (detail). Courtesy of the author.

PAGE 214: Radio Station Martyrs' Memorial (detail), Geleshan, circa 1990s. Photographer unknown. Courtesy of Sun Dannian.

PAGE 215: "The administration building of one of the most influential schools of China," Chongqing, December 1, 1945. Photo by Jack Wilkes/The LIFE Picture Collection/Getty Images. Reprinted by permission.

PAGE 223: "Professor Chang Teh-ch'ang," Kunming, 1939. Photo by Edward V. Gulick. Reprinted with permission from *Teaching in Wartime China: A Photo-Memoir, 1937-1939*, by Edward Gulick. Copyright © 1995 by the University of Massachusetts Press.

PAGE 224: "Les fils du maréchal Chang Tsu Liang" (detail), Manchuria, July 4, 1931. Photographer unknown. Reprinted by permission of *L'Illustration*.

PAGE 225: "Dr. P.S. Chang and Dr. H.C. Chang," Changsha, 1938. Photo by Edward V. Gulick. Reprinted with permission from *Teaching in Wartime China: A Photo-Memoir, 1937-1939*, by Edward Gulick. Copyright © 1995 by the University of Massachusetts Press.

PAGE 226: Drawing by Graham Peck. *Two Kinds of Time*, by Graham Peck, Houghton Mifflin Company, Boston, MA, 1950.

PAGE 227: "Fleeing Refugees." Woodcut print by Li Hwa. *Woodcuts of War-Time China: 1937-1945*, by Chinese Woodcutters' Association, Kaiming Book Company, Shanghai, 1946.

PAGE 228: "These were the lucky ones," Changte to Yuanling, 1938. Photo by Edward V. Gulick. Reprinted with permission from *Teaching in Wartime China: A Photo-Memoir, 1937-1939*, by Edward Gulick. Copyright © 1995 by the University of Massachusetts Press.

PAGE 229: "Old sewing amahs outside hat shop," Shanghai, 1949. Photo by Sam Tata. Reprinted by permission of Antonia Tata and the National Gallery of Canada.

PAGE 232: "Eine Fähre wird durch die Schlammbänke des Wie-ho gezogen," Koko-Nor, China, 1933. Photo by Walter Bosshard. Copyright © Swiss Foundation for Photography/Archives of Contemporary History. Reprinted by permission.

PAGE 234: "Woman's neck." Image created by author, 2016.

PAGE 236: "US Marine standing guard at gate to US Embassy," Nanjing, February 1, 1949. Photo by Carl Mydans/The LIFE Picture Collection/Getty Images. Reprinted by permission.

PAGE 239: "Passport cover." Image created by author, 2016.

PAGE 240: "Passport binding." Image created by author, 2016.

PAGE 243: "Passport photo." Image created by author, 2016.

PAGE 247: "Hong Kong woman," circa 1950. Photo by Ton-Shun Chang. Courtesy of the author.

PAGE 250: "Xiao Bao (Little Treasure)." Image created by author, 2016.

PAGE 257: "Hong Kong from the summit of Victoria Peak, China," n.d. Photographer unknown. The Keystone View Company.

PAGE 259: Aerials of Kowloon, Hong Kong, circa 1950. Photos by Ton-Shun Chang. Courtesy of the author.

PAGE 263: "Government worker Tan Chuen-yu, receiving help from his wife with his packing," Chongqing, December 1, 1945. Photo by Jack Wilkes/The LIFE Picture Collection/Getty Images. Reprinted by permission.

PAGE 265: "The Nanking retreat," April 1, 1949. Photo by Jack Birns/The LIFE Picture Collection/Getty Images. Reprinted by permission.

PAGE 268: Hong Kong street scenes, circa 1950. Photos by Ton-Shun Chang. Courtesy of the author

PAGE 270: "Master plan for development of Kai Tak Airport, June 16, 1954." Photographer unknown. Courtesy of Charles Eather, *Airport of the Nine Dragons, Kai Tak, Kowloon*, Chingchic Publishers, Australia, 1997.

PAGE 275: "Huei Sheh," Shanghai, September 1, 1947. Photo by Mark Kauffman/The LIFE Picture Collection/Getty Images. Reprinted by permission.

PAGE 276: "North Station, Kuomintang officers with refugees leaving Shanghai for Hangchow" (detail), Shanghai, 1949. Photo by Sam Tata. Reprinted by permission of Antonia Tata and the National Gallery of Canada.

PAGE 279: Ton-Shun Chang on beach, n.d. Photographer unknown. Courtesy of the author.

PAGE 280: Ton-Shun Chang on road, n.d. Photographer unknown. Courtesy of the author.

PAGE 281: Ton-Shun Chang at Tao Fong Shan Christian Centre, Shatin, Hong Kong, circa 1950. Photographer unknown. Courtesy of the author.

PAGE 282: Man in boat, Hong Kong, circa 1950. Photo by Ton-Shun Chang. Courtesy of the author.

PAGE 283: Ton-Shun Chang in boat, Hong Kong, circa 1950. Photographer unknown. Courtesy of the author.

PAGE 284: Women on outing, Silvermine Bay, Hong Kong, circa 1950. Photo by Ton-Shun Chang. Courtesy of the author.

PAGE 285: Man on outing, Silvermine Bay, Hong Kong, circa 1950. Photo by Ton-Shun Chang. Courtesy of the author.

PAGE 287: Ton-Shun Chang on bed, Hong Kong, circa 1950. Photographer unknown. Courtesy of the author.

PAGE 288: Man with camera, Hong Kong, circa 1950. Photo by Ton-Shun Chang. Courtesy of the author.

PAGE 288: Ton-Shun Chang's baptism, Hong Kong, circa 1950. Photographer unknown. Courtesy of the author.

PAGE 291: "Sketch Map of Chinese Railways" (detail), 1951-53. Cartographer unknown. "Railway Construction in China," by Li Chang, *Far Eastern Survey*, Vol. 22, No. 4, March 25, 1953.

PAGE 292: Ton-Shun Chang with train in field, circa 1950. Photographer unknown. Courtesy of the author.

PAGE 293: "Locomotive view from another train," Republic of China, n.d. Photo by Fu Bing-chang. © 2007 C.H. Foo and Y.W. Foo. Courtesy of Yee Wah Foo and Historical Photographs of China, University of Bristol.

PAGE 295: Nanjing Da Qiao, Nanjing, n.d. Photographer unknown.

PAGE 298: "Four bads (based on Li Zhensheng)." Image created by author, 2016.

PAGE 301: "North Station, Kuomintang officers with refugees leaving Shanghai for Hangchow," Shanghai, 1949. Photo by Sam Tata. Reprinted by permission of Antonia Tata and the National Gallery of Canada.

PAGE 302: "A woman climbing into the train window," Shanghai, November 1, 1949. Photo by Jack Birns/The LIFE Picture Collection/Getty Images. Reprinted by permission.

PAGE 307: "Love letter." Image created by author, 2016.

PAGE 312: "China Execution, Fukang," January 1, 1953. Photographer unknown. Reprinted by permission of AP Images.

PAGE 313: "Guard aiming rifle at Chinese landlord farmer, Fukang," January 17, 1953. Photographer unknown. Reprinted by permission of AP Images.

PAGE 320: "Passport visa." Image created by author, 2016.

PAGE 323: Ling Liang Church series, Kowloon, Hong Kong, September 9, 1951. Photos by Ton-Shun Chang. Courtesy of the author.

PAGE 323: Ling Liang Church, Kowloon, Hong Kong, September 9, 1951. Photo by Ton-Shun Chang. Courtesy of the author.

PAGE 324: Hong Kong airport, September 10, 1951. Photographer unknown. Courtesy of the author.

PAGE 325: "Passport stamp." Image created by author, 2016.

PAGE 327: Painting of Jia Yuanchun renaming the harbor, by Sun Wen, from the series *Hong Lou Meng*. Lushun Museum, Dalian.

PAGE 343: Ton-Shun Chang swimming, n.d. Photographer unknown. Courtesy of the author.

ACKNOWLEDGEMENTS

With gratitude to the many people who conspired with me in the making of this book:

At Kaya Press, Sunyoung Lee, Neela Bannerjee, and Kaya's able staff of interns and volunteers picked up the manuscript and never put it down, shaping it with designer Chez Bryan Ong into the beautiful hybrid text that you now hold in your hands.

At Hampshire College, generous support was provided by the Dean of Faculty, the School of Critical Social Inquiry, and the Office for Diversity and Multicultural Education for the licensing and repro-duction of images. Special thanks to Jean Sepanski for help with image permissions.

Across the Five Colleges, the Asian/Pacific/American Studies Pro-gram and the Mellon Mutual Mentoring Grant enabled the sharing of writing and food during the initial stages of this project. At Mount Holyoke College, Jonathan Lipman was a bountiful source of books on wartime Republican China. *The Massachusetts Review* published an early excerpt from the book under the same title in its Autumn 2010 issue.

Librarians at the colleges and beyond were an unwavering source of information and support. At Hampshire, Alana Kumbier, Rachel Beckworth, and Asha Kinney were my go-to team for research and technical help. At the Harvard-Yenching Library, Ma Xiao-He pointed me to maps and other visual materials on wartime Chongqing. At UMass Amherst, self-described militant librarian Laura Quilter introduced me to the judicious world of copyright law and the audacious idea of "transformative use."

Over the decade-long gestation of this book, I benefitted from participation in several writing residencies. At the UMass Juniper Summer Writing Institute, I had the privilege to workshop with the late Grace Paley, Noy Holland, and Paul Lisicky. As a resident writer at the Vermont Studio Center, I was fortunate to consult with Christine Schutt. I am grateful to Noy for showing me structures of my own making, to Paul for the gift of proprioception, and to Christine for the promise of deliverance. And I returned again and again to Wellspring House in Ashfield, MA, where I never failed to find exactly what I needed in order keep writing.

Before there was a book, there was an idea turned into an obsession, encouraged and sustained by a few dear friends and fellow writers. Among these, Rachel Conrad, Floyd Cheung, and Miliann Kang have been my steadfast reading and writing companions and co-conspirators in creative form. Floyd and Miliann were among the very few who generously read and commented on full drafts of the manuscript, along with Arthur Kleinman, Noy Holland, Sally Segall, Deb Gorlin, Bob Rakoff, and Beverly Chang.

Before there was even an idea, there was the late great Nina Payne, who emboldened me to write about the reversals I live with.

In Hong Kong, my former student and now friend/colleague, Ho Wai Yip, accompanied me in retracing my father's footsteps during that year of interminable waiting.

In Chongqing, Sun Dannian showed me her mountain along with her dogged commitment to truth telling. Thanks to Xujun Eberlein for being on the same path and introducing me to Sun. And to the late Larry Young and his family for helping me find the old Chongqing in the new.

For help with Chinese language and translations, thanks to Liu Liming and Fang Yunyun.

For generous assistance in finding and using photographs, thanks to Susan Carlson, Charles Eather, Yee Wah Foo, Susan Gulick, Ken Light, Stephen MacKinnon, John Moffett, Daniel Nerlich, Antonia Tata, and Michael Till. Special thanks to the International Center of Photography for making accessible Robert Capa's collection of photographs of wartime China.

I am especially grateful to…

…my father, for the gift of the half-told truth. This book became our shared obsession as we both felt the press of time and the urgency of the project. Although he did not live to see its completion, he was in the end my collaborator in writing the past and I, his accomplice to memory.

…my mother, for her unending capacity for forgiveness for the transgressions of family.

…my brother, Xiangling, for sharing his mother's story. Thanks to our father, we share a propensity for storytelling.

To Tanmu, the unseen eyes behind every image in this book, all my love.

To the next generation, Kylie and Jessie, may you discover for yourselves the crucial distinction between fact and truth.

ABOUT THE AUTHOR

Q.M. Zhang grew up in upstate New York, lived in China and Hong Kong, and now makes her home in Western Massachusetts. She is a writer of hybrid non/fiction stories and forms, with a focus on "Chinese" and "American" identities and communities across the Pacific. She currently teaches at Hampshire College in Amherst, MA.